TAKERS

Also by Ann Swann

Yeah, But I Didn't

TAKERS

APOCALYPSE IN EDEN BOOK 1

ANN SWANN

WordCrafts Press

Takers
Copyright © 2016
Ann Swann

ISBN: 978-1-957344-24-9

Published by WordCrafts Press
Cody, Wyoming 82414
www.wordcrafts.net

Yes, believe it or not, hagfish slime is real.

CHAPTER ONE

Not A Care In The World

Dee Powell attached crinkly strands of blue and yellow crepe paper to the basketball goal in the Eden, Texas middle school gymnasium. She and three of her friends from the Art Department were decorating for the upcoming ninth grade graduation dance.

My buddy, Cade Johnson, had gone down to the basement and brought up the ladder on which Dee stood. We had brought up pretty much everything the girls were using.

"Well, don't just stand there staring, Jack Lewis," Dee called. "Go on down and find that last box of crepe paper."

I ducked my head; mortified she'd caught me ogling her. I'd been downright mesmerized by the glimmer of the fluorescents bouncing off the rhinestone headband in her dark hair.

In less than three months we would all be in high school. My dad had already started grilling me about colleges and career choices. My stomach knotted up at the thought. The idea scared me almost as much as the idea of asking Dee to dance with me tomorrow night.

"Well?" Dee smiled to take the sting out of her words. "Are you going to the basement, or do I have to climb down off this ladder and do it myself?"

"Go ahead, buddy," Cade said. "I'm pretty sure I saw that box just past the stairs." He nudged me and whispered, "Besides, I left you something. Know what I mean?" He winked and made an up and down motion in front of his groin with his closed fist.

I rolled my eyes. Cade might be my best friend, but he could be a real ass. I shoved his arm down. His attitude really irked me. I didn't want all of my dreams and desires to be nothing more than teenage *horn-mones* (Cade's word). I wanted these feelings to be something more, something *real*.

Something like ...

Derencia Powell.

Dee.

"Dude." Cade bellowed even though he stood right beside me. "I think Dee really *needs* that crepe paper."

Dee looked at me, and for a moment we shared something across that wide-open space that was almost as bright as the burnished floor. Her gentle smile said she knew how he was, but she didn't hold it against me.

I could've stood there, looking at her, for the rest of time, but one of the other girls called her name, and she turned to catch a new roll of tape in midair. Directly past her head, tree branches clawed at the narrow gym windows. The West Texas wind had been howling all day.

Hurrying out of the gym before my "best friend" could say or do anything else to embarrass me, I had to ask myself why I put up with him. I had a pretty good idea of what he had left me in the basement. Today he'd given his PowerPoint presentation in Biology. That meant he'd brought his laptop to school. Not only did he delight in looking at his dad's porn, he also delighted in sharing it with me—whether I wanted it or not.

I think he copied the dirtiest pictures just to shock me, to test me somehow. As if we both knew that if I gave in to the desire to demand more ugly pictures—which I really wanted to do sometimes—then I might end up tossing away all the tiny good things I haven't even experienced yet. Like dancing in the gym beneath a twisted canopy of crepe paper, or sharing a special glance that might lead to a first kiss.

Feeling like a fool, I yanked open the heavy basement doors. The stairwell and storage area were both lit by the usual flickery fluorescents. I hurried down the stairs and located the box of paper.

Cade's laptop sat on top of an overturned five-gallon pickle bucket. Setting the box aside, I pulled over a second empty bucket to sit on, and then I opened the computer. Instead of the pictures Cade had bookmarked, I pulled up one of my own nerdy websites. It was a science site run by a university professor who did his best to use physics to explain the unexplainable. I just didn't want to look at *Dirty Sluts of the South* and then go up and face Dee in the gym. On the other hand, if I went back up immediately, Cade would know I didn't look at all. I'd never hear the end of it.

My website sprang to life.

The lights went out.

For a moment, my skin tightened up around me like an old leather glove, but then I remembered the wind. It sometimes messed with the power in our little town. I took a deep breath and tried to relax. It was either that or run screaming for the stairs. Dee would really be impressed if I burst out into the hall screaming like a two-year-old. Thankfully I still had the laptop's screen light. I figured the power would come back on in a few minutes like it always did.

I glanced back down at *Dr. D's Adventures in Dimensions*. The credits claimed he was an astrophysicist. Today he didn't sound very academic. In fact, his voice was downright shrill.

"Listen," he demanded. "Our universe and the one paralleling it have been expanding at different rates. The fabric between them is growing *too thin*. The dimensions are colliding. The fabric is *shredding—*"

He removed his glasses, his eyes growing wider and wilder as he spoke. He glanced over his shoulder as if he heard someone approaching. Then he leaned closer to the camera and whispered. "One of the dimensions paralleling ours is called *Purgatory*. It's been said corrupted spirits go there to await cleansing." His voice dropped into an even lower register. "I don't believe in religion, but my colleague insists it's true. She says some of them have been waiting for *eons*. Get underground. You might be safe *underground!*"

It had to be a practical joke. The doc was trying to prank us into calling in and saying something stupid. Or doing something stupid like that *War of the Worlds* radio stunt my Granny told me about. She said the radio announcer had made it sound like a real alien invasion—until everyone started to panic. I decided that must be what Dr. D was trying to do. It would probably be trending before the webcast was even over.

As I watched the doctor stalk about, tugging at his Einstein hair, the LOW BATTERY message appeared, and the computer winked off.

I sat perfectly still, a rectangular after-image of the screen hanging in front of my face. Fear overtook me, and I was suddenly five years old waking from a nightmare in the dark. I closed the laptop and placed it on the floor beside me.

Rising to my feet, I took a tentative step forward.

My toes immediately encountered the empty pickle bucket and scooted it across the concrete floor. It threw me off balance.

I stuck my hands out in front of myself like a B-movie zombie. The absence of light gave the darkness a texture that made it hard to breathe. I shuffled forward, pushing the pickle bucket with my toes.

The professor said the inhabitants of Purgatory need new souls. What does that mean? What is Purgatory, exactly?

Don't think about it. It's just a prank like that War of the Worlds thing or those reality shows on TV that are supposed to be real but are really so fake. And why can't I find the stairs? Maybe the basement expanded right along with the universe.

I swept my arms from side to side, trying to locate the stair rail. They met only air.

The panic I'd been keeping at bay suddenly crawled into my gut and made itself a home.

A bead of sweat itched its way down my back like a pesky mosquito. I swatted at it and shoved the pickle bucket aside, heading for the place where the stairs should be.

Relief washed over me when my toes found the first step and I stumbled upward certain something would reach out before I could—

Scritch scritch scritch

My head rotated toward the sound as if pulled by a puppeteer's string.

The noise seemed distant, yet right on top of me.

I lunged forward, scalp tingling, certain that at any moment a hand would latch onto my ankle, or the empty pickle bucket would come flying at me through the darkness.

The next thing I knew a deep, throbbing vibration engulfed me. It was so intense I thought it might stop my heart. I fell to my knees, arms wrapped protectively around my head. It felt like a million tubas all blowing the same note in unison.

Unable to move, I curled myself into a ball, hands pressing against my ears, eyes squeezed shut so my eyeballs wouldn't pop out of their sockets. The steps vibrated beneath me as if a freight train might burst through the floor. I expected the building to crash down around me.

Then the sound swelled even more.

The panic in my gut exploded, and I jerked myself to my feet and scrambled up the rest of the stairs on my hands and knees.

Earthquake? Tornado? Bomb?

I didn't realize I'd reached the landing until I whammed into the unexpected push bar with my shoulder. I thought the doors would be blocked by debris from whatever disaster had befallen us.

But they weren't.

They flew open, and I fell out into a dimness that was somewhat brighter than the basement, but not nearly as bright as it should be.

The power was off in the rest of the building, too.

CHAPTER TWO

Where Is Everyone?

I raced down the hallway toward the gym. The powerful hum had lessened, but it was still so loud I could hardly focus. I wiped a trickle of blood from below one ear. A whistling sound echoed deep inside my head. *Did my eardrum burst?*

A muffled scream yanked my attention toward the front of the school. At least I thought it was a scream. With the vibrations threatening to rattle the flesh off my bones, I couldn't be certain.

Heart pounding in rhythm with the hum, I came to a halt, trying to decide what to do. *Shelter in place. Hide until the police or rescue units come.* That was our school policy. It had been drilled into us every time a tornado or another nut with a gun made the national headlines. *But where is everyone hiding?*

I looked for an open door. The floor continued to shake beneath me. I knew I should hide, but my feet began to move toward the empty foyer. Soon I found myself running. I had to find someone—anyone.

Slowing to a trot, I held my breath, listening. The hum had been replaced by something else, something much, much worse.

Not one scream, but many.

I stopped in front of the cracked glass entrance doors.

My mouth fell open in disbelief.

The sky appeared as tattered as a paper snowflake.

"The fabric between our dimensions is shredding—"

Dr. D's words echoed in my head as I stared through the window.

Many of the sky holes were little more than slits. Others were huge, ragged, gaping. Through each opening elongated globules of matter oozed down like strings of cloudy rain. The matter fell harder and faster until the ground was covered with slick, writhing puddles.

From those puddles strange humanoid creatures arose, hissing. When they left their pools of muck, it sounded like leeches being pulled from wet skin.

As they emerged from the glassy soup, the whole area became flooded with watery-gray, garnet-eyed creatures. Everything in sight dripped; even their black-slashed mouths and jagged silver teeth oozed with slime.

Dr. D said stay inside. Get underground. I had to get back to the basement.

I wanted to run, but my feet were glued to the floor. The syrupy downpour coated power lines and broke branches from the syc-amores as surely as if they'd been covered with ice. I saw people crumpled on the pavement, dead. Others hung from stalled car windows, moaning. As I watched, one of the gray creatures picked up a man and dragged him, screaming, across the street.

That decided me. I forced my feet to move, backing away as quietly as possible.

I wanted to turn and run, but I was terrified, afraid to turn my back on the huge, naked creatures now headed toward the school. The sound of their bare feet sliding across the wet ground matched the shushing sound of the rain. The throbbing lessened when the creatures arose.

As they came closer, I could see strange blue-black tattoos pulsing beneath their glistening skin.

My paralysis broke. I spun around and sprinted down the hallway toward the basement. Yanking open the double doors, I tripped back down the stairs into the darkness.

Inside my brain, a question flashed like a neon sign: *What if one of those monsters is down here?*

The door closed behind me a second time.

My breath was a blowtorch in my throat.

I can't just stand here, waiting for something to come up those stairs, or through the door behind me. The humming noise could have been the fabric of the universe ripping open the way Dr. D said.

I shook my head. The sky can't tear; it's only atmosphere. *Could there be a fabric between the dimensions, a skin we know nothing about? Dark matter?*

My mind wanted to shut down. It wanted me to hunker down into a tiny ball on the stairs like before. It wanted me to shelter in place. Wait for help, wait for rescue.

I took a deep breath. But I couldn't force myself back down into the unknown.

Shaking, head pounding, ears aching, I stumbled back up the stairs toward the door I had just come through. I couldn't wait in the darkness. I couldn't wait at all.

My fingertips pushed the door open a tiny crack. A sliver of dim light leaked inside. It lay across the landing like a sword. Shelter in place? I don't think so. Not in the basement with no way out.

I pressed my face to the narrow opening praying nothing would stab my eyeball through the gap.

There was no movement at all.

Rubbing my ears, I tried to think where I could find a phone. Call my folks. *If only Mrs. Stoddard hadn't taken my cell phone. It had only been one little text.*

Pushing the door open a little wider, I made up my mind to go back to the front office. That's where all the phones were located. I slipped through and allowed the door to close behind me. Creeping down the hall toward the foyer, I stuck as close to the wall as possible.

This time the hallway felt a mile long, the building now as quiet as a mortuary. I could see the secretary's overturned swivel chair through the chocked-open office door. I hadn't noticed it before. But I didn't have time to go in and investigate. Movement outside the cracked front glass caught my eye.

The slimy, red-eyed creatures were *everywhere.*

They were so close I could read their internal tattoos. Letters spelling out murder, torture, lust, and greed pulsed beneath their translucent gray skin. The words rose and fell like the fortune answers floating inside a Magic 8 Ball.

Great special effects, my brain insisted. But I knew this wasn't fake. I'd seen the things rise from their glassy puddles. Their skin was so moist and smooth the muted sunlight bounced off it in all directions. They resembled humans, but they didn't move like humans. They hardly turned their heads at all. They moved as if to the sound of a silent master, leaning forward slightly, as though pushing through invisible molasses.

I couldn't see their faces, but their profiles were flat. Their bald heads and naked bodies glistened. Their inside-out word-tattoos wiggled and swam beneath their skin. The tiny holes where their noses should be looked alien, unfinished.

Once again, I became paralyzed except for the knocking of my knees.

As they marched past the window, one of the monsters leaned down and scooped something off the ground, and then flung it away.

Another one broke away from the group—in slow motion—and grabbed a moaning woman right through the window of her stalled car. It dragged her out and slung her over its shoulder. It didn't seem to notice the kicks and blows from her hands and feet. It didn't seem to feel anything at all.

From out of nowhere, Coach Beatty rushed around the corner of the building brandishing an aluminum baseball bat. He swung at the nearest creature's head, punctuating it with a rebel yell. The sound of the bat connecting with the thing's shiny skull was like a cantaloupe slammed on tile.

The creature went down.

I sent up a silent cheer. *Thank God! I'm not alone.* I started to call out to Coach, but before I could, the thing rolled over, pushed itself up, and wrested the bat away. Hands over my mouth, I watched in horror as the monster bashed him senseless, then dragged the twitching, bleeding coach to the ancient tree on the edge of the yard. It stabbed him onto one of the broken branches like a chef sticking a chunk of meat onto a rough, wooden skewer.

I threw up in the secretary's peace lily beside the front door. When I looked up, the creature was ripping the flesh from the coach's bones, stuffing the meat into its toothy maw as fast as it could swallow. Even above the sound of the still falling rain I could hear the horrific gurgling noise it made.

Then I realized the other monster—the one that had pulled the lady from her car—was doing the same thing to her.

Only she was still conscious.

Her screams pierced the rain and echoed in my aching ears like a cruel disease.

Suddenly all the monsters were dragging people out of cars and snatching them up from the street and sidewalks. The coach and the lady seemed to be the keys that unlocked the reign of horror. It was like watching a deadly humanoid hive. What one did, they all did.

I became aware of someone gasping for air.

One of the monsters had crammed its mouth so full it could barely breathe.

Up and down the tree-lined street, shrieks filled the air. Within minutes, the loose squad had decimated every suffering, moaning human in its path.

I slumped to my knees. Why didn't the people run away? Most of them seemed helpless, writhing on the ground holding their ears or hanging from their cars or trucks. The only one able to move, besides me, had been Coach Beatty, and they got him anyway.

This is real. It's real.

I crouched beneath the window, my mind a blank slate except for the undercurrent of an old rock song my dad always played on his turntable. I thought when the apocalypse came, I'd be prepared. I had cheerfully shot, stabbed, sliced, diced, and blown up every shambling creature that had ever crossed my computer crosshairs.

But this was not that.

These things were not zombies.

They were not vampires or werewolves, or games or movies or books. These things, these *creatures*, were here—and they were real. They were close enough to reach out and touch.

I watched another one shuffle by dragging yet another body. It looked like Mrs. Flanagan, the secretary of the over-turned chair, but there was too much blood, and the wispy red curls were too clumpy with gore to be certain. As I considered my options, the thing reached down to get a better grip.

That's when I noticed the purple knit pants she was so fond of wearing. She wore them at least once a week. The kids called her Fat Ass Flanagan because the fabric stretched so dangerously every time she bent over to get a new stack of tardy slips.

Surprising tears sprang to my eyes as a tuft of curly red hair floated to the ground. Some of the strands stuck to the bloody purple pants.

I had to turn away.

Oh, Mrs. Flanagan. If I'd known what was coming, I never would have said those things ...

Through the cracked glass, I heard sirens warbling through the thinning rain. I'd never heard anything so sweet in my entire life.

I rose from my crouch, trying to spot the cavalry.

Slatted rays of weak sunlight penetrated the rain clouds, nailing my silhouette to the opposite wall. I shook so hard even my shadow trembled.

CHAPTER THREE

First Responders

Two police cruisers and one sheriff's car—lights blazing and sirens wailing—skidded up to the edge of the melee.

I wondered why they hadn't sent the entire force, then I realized that they were probably battling the things elsewhere. I was surprised their vehicles still worked. All the ones on the street seemed to have come to a complete and sudden standstill under the onslaught of the slimy rain. I saw a few shapes still slumped over steering wheels or hanging from open windows—as if looking up at the broken sky.

Why didn't the monsters pull everyone out? So far, I'd only seen them take people who were still alive. The ones who weren't moving were ignored.

I didn't have time to think about it because the cops were out of their cars and firing.

Creatures fell like bowling pins.

They were no match for the automatic weapons. Hope flooded my chest. I wanted to run out in the street and join the cavalry, but I knew that would be suicide.

I hunkered down to watch. As long as the fighting was in the middle of the street, I felt safe. And then something happened that changed everything.

One of the weapons jammed and the nearest monster grabbed the gun and flung it away. Then it took the officer by the head and draped him over its shoulder as if the man weighed no more than a toddler.

I could see a cloudy liquid leaking from the injured creature's torso, but there was no blood. Not until it stabbed the officer onto a broken branch. Then the human blood flowed, and the screams reverberated down the street, audible even over the continuing gunfire.

The creatures that were shot started to rise. The only ones not getting up were those whose heads were completely blown away. From them, the cloudy liquid gushed and was washed away by the lightly-falling rain.

The officers began to run out of ammunition. One by one they fell prey to the advancing cannibals. One officer made it safely back inside his car but before he could reverse out of the fight, the nearest creature simply punched through the glass and crawled inside with him. Then it crawled back out, in slow motion, dragging the screaming man by the head.

After that, the entire scene was overrun. The police cars disappeared beneath the crush of monsters. I slid back away from the windows but couldn't resist looking over my shoulder. Mutilated bodies hung from every available branch. And then from one of the larger sky-rips, new rain began to fall.

It was black.

The dark drops plopped to the ground and slithered across the surface of the earth toward the injured cannibals. The living drops squirmed around the monsters' feet, buzzed up their legs and joined together, spreading across their shiny flesh like a fever. The black rain devoured them even quicker than the monsters had devoured the wounded people.

Once the injured creatures were covered and consumed, the living black rain exploded into a buzzing swarm of dark locusts that winged themselves back into the largest sky-hole, sealing it shut behind themselves.

The hum of their wings fit right in with the horrific sound that had brought the monsters here in the first place. Not only had the buzzing drowned out the song in my head, but it had also vibrated the air and caused a huge triangle of cracked glass to shiver and fall from a high hallway window.

I threw up my hands as the glass shattered into a dozen fragments.

Moist air filled the gap, and I inhaled a taste of what was once sweet spring air but was now rank with the dark, coppery, shitty smell of death.

The foul air also brought in even more screams of people dying. Why did the monsters impale them on tree branches? And why haven't they come after me?

Thank God they haven't come after me.

I closed my eyes but that made me dizzy.

Where was everyone? Dee? Cade? Mrs. Jane, the principal?

For that matter, what about the library where Mom works—were they safe? They have an immense basement. Maybe she was in there, hiding. Or how about the bank, or the grocery store down the street? Was this happening all over town? If the things were *that* hungry, why didn't they just go to the grocery stores? They're full of raw meat.

Forcing my mind away from the horrific scene out front, I crept back along the wall. Dad might be in the basement of the high school where he taught music. He promised to take me to Universal Studios in Orlando this summer. I couldn't wait to see how they did the special effects for *Iron Man*, *The Hulk*, and all *The Avengers*.

I knew my mind was trying to skate away from what was going on right in front of my nose. It kept trying to convince me this mess was nothing more than special effects.

The only thing grounding me to reality was the feel of the rough brick beneath my palms as I made my way along the hallway toward the gym.

Stealth was the key. I tried to channel Harry Potter and his cloak of invisibility. I couldn't wait to experience *The Wizarding World of Harry Potter* at Universal. Cade called me a dork for wanting to go there. Dad said, *ignore him, he's just jealous.* We talked about taking Cade with us, but I was on the fence. Maybe he would ruin it. Maybe he would ruin it on purpose.

"Carry On Wayward Son," swelled in my head from background music to main-stage attraction. Sung by the band, Kansas, it was the song from my dad's old vinyl collection.

My hands stopped shaking. I welcomed the loud song. This

sometimes happened when I had to make a major decision, but it usually occurred after I'd struggled with something overnight. I would wake with a song in my head as if in answer to the problem. It was just part of me, a subconscious kind of thing.

Now, with my hands steady and Dad's song in my head, I knew what I had to do—I had to set a goal. I had to carry on. Get home and find my folks.

My mind kept asking why they hadn't come yet. They must know what happened. The cops came—even though it ended badly—so it must be all over the news. Why hadn't my parents come yet?

The song volume went up again, blotting out all questions.

"Carry on, Jack. Carry on."

I looked out the tinted windows. Slime dripped from every tree, light pole, and roofline. The TV towers might also be slimed. Cell towers, too.

The song played on the turntable in my mind. "Carry on wayward son. Just *carry on*." The voice of the singer had somehow morphed into that of my dad.

Indecision gripped me. I shook my head and rubbed my face with my palms. Anything to make myself move. I'd already set my goal, to get home; but first I had to find out about Dee and Cade. Finally, my feet took me deeper into the building. I couldn't leave without knowing. Then I would follow my plan. *Then* I would carry on.

The hallway hadn't grown any shorter. I stayed low as I scurried down it. Every now and then I peeked out a window to make sure nothing was sneaking up on me. The trees behind the school were loaded with ripe people-fruit. Thick pools of blood blackened the earth beneath them.

When the humming and tearing started, everyone who was inside must have run outside to see what was going on. Maybe some of the things were already on the ground. Maybe it was an ambush. Many of the humans were little more than skeletons with strips of flesh and clothing hanging down, as if the diner had been interrupted, or become engorged. I recalled the awful gurgle and gasp of the creatures stuffing their black maws. And what was that dark rain? Had it really changed into locusts as I watched? What if I hadn't been in the basement—would I have run outside, too?

Even as I made my way back to safety, I wondered why the cannibals ignored the dead bodies on the ground. *What is the difference between the living and the dead other than the spirit? Does the spirit leave the body at the moment of death, or is that the soul? Are they the same thing?*

Dr. D's warning flashed into my memory. "Get below ground," he'd said. "They're coming from Purgatory. They need new souls."

The Kansas song swelled again and brought me back to the present.

I peeked out and saw hundreds of creatures moving sluggishly away through the streets. They were all going the same direction. I couldn't believe it had taken them only an hour to wipe out the entire block and the first—and only—responders.

Just as I was about to glance away, I noticed something extremely odd. A couple of the gore-streaked creatures had pulled on pieces of clothing. One had on a yellowish shirt, unbuttoned, the other had draped a brown scarf across one shoulder. The clothing must have come from their victims.

I tore my eyes away. *It's ridiculous. Now they're clothing themselves? Am I asleep? Is it a nightmare?* I pinched the end of my nose and tears of pain pricked my eyes. *Nope, this feels real. Maybe I'm insane.*

The song blared into my consciousness. *Carry on, dammit. Carry on.*

My feet continued toward the gym, and then a sound caught my ear.

Snick.

I stood at the T-intersection connecting the many-windowed hall with the rest of the building. In the late, after-rain light, the tile floor was decorated with alternating squares of gold and blue—the school colors—that had been painted on the long row of windows.

This had been my favorite place in the whole school, this hallway. Every morning I had walked through the front door and entered this hallway almost reverently. With the sunrise shining through the gold paint, the start of each day had always seemed like some sort of *promise*. But I never mentioned it to anyone. I figured I was the only one who noticed.

Now I simply stood, peering around, waiting for that tiny sound to come again. Maybe it was the sound of another person hiding in the blue part of the patterned hallway, hiding in the shadows.

This light wasn't the promise-light of early morning. It was the apocalypse-light, and it was shining through cracked and broken glass.

My throat closed around a lump the size of a Gobstopper jawbreaker. The kind I used to get out of the quarter machine at the grocery store. I was suddenly gripped with the awful certainty I would never see the sun coming through the gold and blue glass in that early-morning way, ever again. There would be no more school, no more teachers, no more books—just like that old Alice Cooper song—"School's Out," another moldy-oldie from Dad's vinyl collection.

I should've told Dee about that golden morning light. She would have understood. I was going to ask her to dance. I was going to get up my nerve and ask her to dance. Or at least offer to get her a Coke.

But where was she now? I'd left her in the gym, laughing and giggling with Cara and Cade. She told me to go down and look for more crepe paper. When I hesitated, Cade insisted. The two of them probably saved my life. *I have to go look for them.*

Snick.

My head rotated back toward the front of the school as if in a dream—or a horror movie.

The sound came from the office. Where Mrs. Flanagan's chair was overturned. But I didn't want to think of her. The image of those purple pants and bloody red curls was etched on the insides of my eyelids like a permanent tattoo.

I crept toward the sound making certain to keep my head below the level of the cracked windows. The floor was like a cloud. I could hardly feel it at all.

Go ahead, my mind whispered. *Go to the office first, but you know you'll have to return to the gym eventually. But go on to the office right now and kill a little more time. Put it off as long as you possibly can.*

I heard the voice in my head, it seemed to live under Dad's songs, but I ignored it. I didn't *want* to go to the office, and I didn't *want* to go to the gym. But that sound needed investigating. What if it was Dee, hiding, waiting on someone to come and save her?

I stopped just inside the chocked-open doorway.

Mrs. Flanagan's swivel chair still lay on its side, wheels up. Nothing moved. The air left a strange flavor on the back of my tongue from that awful odor wafting in from outside. It made me want to hawk and spit, but it was way too quiet to do anything like that.

No AC. That's why it was so quiet, and so stale. I looked around for the source of the sound, but I saw nothing.

Am I the only one left?

Is this really the apocalypse?

CHAPTER FOUR

Snick

I held my breath. I wasn't too worried about the creatures being in here. So far, I hadn't seen any indoors. Besides, I'd watched the whole bunch of them shuffling down the street in the same direction. They seemed to have an agenda. *Probably dessert,* my morbid imagination thought.

So, what *was* that sound?

Carry on son . . .

I know, I know. Time to jet. Nothing's here—

Snick.

Was it a doorknob being turned, or a file cabinet drawer being pulled open? Was it someone in Mrs. Jane's inner office?

Snick.

My knees began to tremble. I had to move one way or the other—toward the office or toward the gym—*Carry on dammit. Carry on.*

Snick.

I passed through the outer office, Mrs. Flanagan's domain. I looked under her desk. No one was there.

The only other place someone could be hiding was behind Mrs. Jane's closed door.

I gathered my courage and reached for the knob. It felt smooth and cool in my palm—not cold, not warm—just cool to the touch because they usually kept it like an icebox in here. I braced myself. *I'm going to open this door and see something, and I don't know what*

*it is but it might be Dee or it might be Cade but no matter what it is
I have to open it I can't just not know and—*

Snick.

I turned the knob and pushed. The room appeared to be empty.
My breath *whooshed* out of my chest. The principal's high-backed
swivel chair was turned around, facing the window. I knew in my
gut that when I reached over and turned that chair to face me, Mrs.
Jane would be sitting there, flayed to the bone, sightless eye sockets
glaring, jaw hanging down on her collarbones because once the
muscle is removed there is nothing to hold it closed. *At least old
Jacob Marley's ghost had a bandage to hold his jaw up.*

Sucking in a huge breath of courage, I took two strides forward,
reached across the desk—I had to lean over a bit—and grasped the
top of the high-backed leather chair. I knew whatever was sitting
in that chair was responsible for that *snick* sound.

With a slight pull-push, the chair swiveled around and banged
into the desk with a padded arm.

*Now I will see a real skeleton up close and personal even though I
didn't think any of the monsters came inside.*

But I was wrong. Mrs. Jane wasn't there. The chair was blessedly
empty.

Snick.

I almost peed myself.

And then I saw it.

It was just a *branch.* Just an old tree branch *snicking* against the
window behind the desk. If the air-conditioner had been on, I
never would have heard it.

Carry on, son, just get a grip and carry on.

I congratulated myself on my bravery and turned back toward
the door to carry on.

Snick.

Like an idiot, I glanced over my shoulder at the window. I knew
Mrs. Jane would never have allowed a branch to scratch her precious
tinted window. The school was her pride and joy. She told us that
every morning on the PA and in the entryway when she greeted
us and patted our shoulders and shook our hands to check and

make sure we were all on the same page: "Are you going to take care of my pride and joy today?" she always asked. And we knew, every single one of us; that the correct answer was, "Yes ma'am."

Once she received the correct answer, she would smile and pat and send us on our way and God help the new kid who didn't know the correct answer or couldn't figure out what she was talking about, because Mrs. Jane's philosophy was that if the students took pride in *her* school, it would soon become *their* school and then, and only then, would they take pride in *it* and in themselves.

No, Mrs. Jane would never have allowed a stray branch to scrape across the dark surface of her window. She would have had Mrs. Beel—the custodian—out there with the ladder, clipping that branch. And fixing that cracked glass, too.

But Mrs. Jane didn't care about that stuff now.

Mrs. Jane was the *reason* the branch hung so low that it scraped the glass.

Snick.

I couldn't look away.

Mrs. Jane's thin body was impaled upon that branch. The tip of it, the one that scratched at the glass like a phantom, had gone clean through her middle. What little meat she had left on her body was completely naked.

That broke my trance. I was finally able to look away, because seeing my principal dead with her eyeballs on her cheeks and a tree branch protruding from her chest was bad enough. But seeing her naked just added insult to injury. I'd heard Mom say that one time—*to add insult to injury*—but I hadn't understood it.

Now I did, but I wished I didn't. I backed away, averting my eyes. So, what if she was naked? She was way more than just naked without clothes; she was naked without *flesh*. On impulse, I reached down and picked up the receiver on the old-fashioned desk phone and pressed it to my ear.

Nothing but dead air.

I replaced it gently, wondering if Mrs. Jane had been the last one to press her ear to it before me. Then I continued moonwalking toward the door, leery of turning my back on the skeletal corpse, afraid, in some dark little-boy corner of my mind, that the next *snick* I heard might be her nails scratching at the glass, trying to get a grip on the slippery surface, attempting to force the tree branch back out of her chest, wanting to come inside, back to her office where she belonged, not me.

So much for my plan of finding a phone.

When my rear hit the edge of the door, I drew in a jittery breath and backed through without taking my eyes off the window. I didn't look at her directly, but I kept her in my peripheral, so I would know if I needed to run.

And then I was out, stopping only long enough to pull the door completely closed. I halted just past Mrs. Flanagan's desk. I wanted a phone. I *needed* a phone. A phone to call home just like *ET, The Extraterrestrial.*

Everyone was gone.

Everyone was dead.

There was no one left but me and the shadows that yawned in the corners and stretched halfway across the floor all the way down the long, beautiful, windowed, hall.

But what about the gym? I still hadn't checked the gym.

I squared my shoulders. *Enough of this running scared crap. Carry on, dammit, carry on. Where's my cell phone?* Even if I couldn't call, maybe I could text. Sometimes that worked. It was probably in the file cabinet. It had already been two weeks since I'd had it confiscated. Either of my parents could've retrieved it from Mrs. Flanagan, who kept them locked up, but my dad had said, *No, you knew the rule and you chose to break it.* If I'd had no more infractions, my phone would've been returned to me on the last day of school.

But there won't be any more infractions. Not unless you count becoming dinner for a bunch of faceless creatures with tattoos crawling beneath their skin.

I shook myself like a wet dog. It was the only way to control the shivers creeping up my legs, threatening to bring me down. The file cabinet was right there, on the opposite wall. My phone had to be in there. Could I break the lock? Or dig through her desk to find the key? Would it still be charged, after two weeks? No way. But even if mine wasn't, maybe another one would be.

I pulled open the top desk drawer and gazed down at the hefty key ring. I'd known it would be there. I'd seen her put it there many times. I also knew what the file cabinet key looked like. Small and silver, it had a tiny barrel that fit into the hole near the cabinet's handle. The fat key ring held several, but one of the keys was separated from the others by two tiny beads.

That's it, that's the one. She's in and out of that drawer umpteen times a day. Of course, she'd want to be able to lay her hands on the most used key right away.

Moving as if in a dream, I made my way across the office. I thought I would fit the key right in, but it chattered around the hole like a chipmunk. My hand shook so hard I couldn't even get near it. I clenched my jaw and took a grip on my right wrist with my left hand.

Finally, it went in.

I turned the key, heard the lock disengage—very loud in the creeping silence—and then slowly pulled the drawer open. For some reason, I expected it to screech or moan, but it slid out soundlessly.

When the drawer hit the stop, the phones inside shifted and slid. There were several phones, mostly older models like mine, but also a couple of expensive smart phones that no one had been given the chance to come back and pick up. I even spied a sparkly pink iPod with ear buds still attached. I thought they had stopped making those.

No one's coming back for them. Or the phones.

I reached in and scooped up all the phones and shoved them down in my pockets. Surely there would be an undamaged cell tower somewhere. But right now, I had to go. I'd put it off long enough—it was time to face the music. To get going. To carry on.

Darkness was encroaching the way it always did when the sun straddled the horizon. One moment the sky would be soft gray and yellow-pink, and the next it would be blue-black with stars winking.

I left the drawer gaping and turned to go. I had six phones in all, two in each front pocket, and one in each back pocket—one of them my very own Galaxy—Mom's old castoff. But something pulled me back and I reached down inside the drawer and grabbed the iPod and ear buds and shoved those in a back pocket, too. It made quite a bulge in there with my smooth, nylon wallet.

Now, I *had* to go. A slight breeze tickled the back of my neck, and I turned toward the main entrance.

I'd waited too long.

A word-pulsing creature pushed against the door, opening it an inch or two each time before it sprang back almost comically. It was trying to push its way inside when the sign clearly said PULL.

I took off like a shot, barreling down the hallway toward the gymnasium where I knew there was another outside door.

Suddenly, I heard the door glass shatter like the window had done before. The thing must've seen me.

It was coming, but it sounded draggy, as if it might be limping, injured. Maybe that's why it didn't go with the others.

I could hear it breathing. Could hear its oddly shuffling footsteps behind me.

When I glanced back, I could make out the blue-black words moving beneath its gleaming skin. But the words were in a language I couldn't understand—Latin, perhaps.

The creatures rained down through holes in the sky like a flood of infected souls. I'd thought it was a joke. Down in the basement, I'd thought the lack of light was a Cade-prank.

I took the shortcut through the cafeteria.

Big mistake.

Most of the kitchen staff were hanging on hooks above the long silver counters—hooks that usually held nothing more than huge cook pots. *The monsters had been in the building after all. So much for being safer inside.*

I recognized two of the lunchroom ladies. They had been flayed with their own butcher knives and meat cleavers. What was left of Mrs. Beel dangled from a large stock-pot hook, her knees bent, feet useless upon the silvery counter.

Blood from the three bodies had cascaded down the stainless-steel counters and splashed onto the linoleum floor. It created a dark ocean of gore that stuck to my shoes as I dashed through the room. In one particularly wet puddle I nearly went down.

I could hear the thing slipping through the mess behind me—

Somehow, I managed to stay upright.

It was gaining ground.

Its feet had grown sticky, its footsteps smacking and uneven.

I turned the corner and yanked open the gym door, an image of the three ladies—tendons and veins hanging down like strands of bloody yarn—spurring me on.

Dee Powell hung from the basketball goal.

Her narrow body had been shoved right through the hoop so that her arms hung down over the rim. Her face, and most of her flesh, had been scraped and torn away. There was no mistaking it was Dee, though. Her shiny black hair was still mostly attached to her skull, the blue headband tangled in the strands by all those sparkly rhinestones.

That headband.

I thought it might be my undoing.

The ladder overturned beneath the hoop was decorated with blood. I slid to a halt. Cara hung from the heavy punching bag in the far corner. The chain had been wrapped around her throat, almost decapitating her. Her feet dragged the ground. One of her Skechers was still on, but the other foot was a mass of twisted bone and gristle.

Behind me, the creature pulled open the gym door.

I didn't stop to look back. It finally hit home. No one was going to save me. There was no one left but me.

The door leading to the parking lot was tucked into the far corner of the gym, near the pullout bleachers. I shot toward it like a human arrow. I could see a blue-jean clad leg sticking out from beneath the bleachers. I thought it was Cade. He had those shoes.

The murky light from the high gym windows urged me on across the blood-smeared floor. In some tiny, self-preserving lock-box in my mind, I was thankful everyone was dead. If I'd heard moaning, if any of my friends had still been screaming or crying out for help, I probably wouldn't have made it across that wide expanse.

I crashed into the door leading outside just as I had crashed into the double doors at the top of the basement stairs, shoulder leading, body stiff, elbows bent. The door flew open and at the last nano-second before my feet left the gym floor and met Mother Earth, I remembered that in this world ruled by terrorists, and mass murderers, no one gets into a school except through the front door. If you exit by any other door, you're locked out. *Too late to worry about that now.*

I glanced over my shoulder.

Just before the heavy door clicked shut, I saw something else. The black rain-swarm had also got inside. It had caught up to the injured monster. I watched as it flowed up the thing's legs, spreading out just like before, covering the creature from head to toe in an inky, undulating blanket.

Risking four broken fingers, I made a wild grab for the edge of the door so I could see more.

Stunned, I peered through the gap as the creature disappeared. The black mess that had resembled a blanket now covered it like a new skin. Thanks to my grandma's cat and her penchant for pregnancy, I knew what a birth sac looked like, and this looked like birth in reverse, as if a dark womb was devouring the monster.

Like an idiot, I continued to stand with my fingers in the door, gaping at my unlikely savior. When the creature had been ninety percent absorbed, I noticed its multi-faceted, maroon eyes staring right at me.

There was nothing recognizable in those garnet orbs. They appeared to be nothing more than chips of red glass, the eyes of a video game villain. Then the blackness slurped across them, thick, crawly, and *fluid.*

Then it flowed toward me.

For a moment, I was certain the gym floor had tilted and poured the stuff in my direction, but maybe it just sensed the fresh air coming through the door gap.

I let the door slam and took off across the back parking lot at a dead run. The pavement crackled beneath my feet. The sky-slime had dried to a thin glaze. It crunched but it wasn't slippery.

I felt as if I could run all the way home, as if a heavy load had fallen from my shoulders. Then my toe caught the edge of a cement parking barrier and down I went, skidding across the pavement on my palms and chin.

"Sonofa*bitch*!" I wasn't sure how many of the stars were in the darkening sky, and how many were exploding inside my head.

I lay perfectly still for a few seconds, willing the stars to stop flashing, then I held my grated palms up in front of my face and marveled at the parking lot gravel embedded there. Tears rolled down my cheeks. I instantly recalled how Cade had wailed the time he'd broken his arm playing paratroopers off our roof onto an old mattress. I hoped that wasn't him in the gym. But then the burning agony of my chin blocked out everything except the pain.

Carry on, son. Don't be a crybaby! You fell over a stop bar. You didn't jump off a roof or get stabbed onto a tree or hung up in a basketball goal.

I swept those thoughts from my mind and listened to the music from Kansas. My jaw felt broken, or at least dislocated. I hadn't seen the ankle-high barrier at all. Went over it and down as if hurled from a slingshot.

Now I need that freakin' jaw bandage like Jacob Marley.

I wiggled my chin back and forth gently. The taste of blood salted my tongue. Behind me, the gym door began to open outward.

Pulling myself to my feet, eyes glued to the door, I waited for the nightmare to seep out. But it didn't seep, it pushed open the heavy door and flew out in a black and buzzing swarm so huge it momentarily blotted out the sky.

There was no where to hide from a bunch of bugs. The door had already closed; they would be on me in nothing flat. *Carry on, son,* my music-Dad sang. *Carry on!*

I took off running again, skirting the parking barriers, shuffling somewhat, watching the ground carefully for any more booby traps. I needed shelter; I needed to be back indoors. There was no protection out here, not against *that*. I felt completely exposed.

But then I realized the humming buzz had lessened. It didn't seem to be coming after me at all. The entire swarm entered one of the raggedy sky holes. The edges closed behind it, and I was so thankful I pumped my fist and shouted, "Yes!"

Continuing across the crackly lot, slower now, I wondered when another monster would appear, but none came. A few seconds later, my feet left the paved lot as I came to the grassy practice field. The grass was glazed, too, but it didn't make much sound beneath my feet. The near-silence was beyond eerie. It reminded me of the interval after a storm before the birds come back out and pick up their songs.

Once more, I glanced back to make sure nothing was sneaking up on me.

At first all appeared to be clear, and then I spied another dark shape in the sky. It looked like a cloud of helicopters, but they were so far away, I couldn't hear anything. Were they really there? In the twilight, I couldn't be certain. It could be another swarm of black insects, farther away.

I hated to get my hopes up, but of course I did.

It had to be helicopters. It had to be.

CHAPTER FIVE

Snake

I stared at the *helicopters*. They didn't seem to be getting any closer. They seemed to be moving farther away. I wanted to jump up and down, wave my arms and yell, "Here I am, come back!" But I didn't do that. If I couldn't hear them, there's no way they could hear me. Besides, what if they weren't helicopters at all?

I resumed walking. At least I no longer felt as if I were the only one left alive. Just the possibility of helicopters meant the possibility of military.

It's going to be okay. The Army will come and clean the monsters out. They will figure out what happened. It will get better—I just have to stay alive—and find my folks.

I glanced back once more. A few of the larger sky holes fluttered at the edges. With night coming on, it became more difficult to see them. In the places where the sky had been torn, the areas were deep black but starless.

Beam them back up, Scotty. Please, beam them all the hell back up.

Serious tears finally came. They were hot and heavy, running down my face, stinging my abraded chin and cleansing away some of the pain.

Dee. That was Dee in the gym, and she had suffered. She had suffered so horribly while I was downstairs, oblivious.

I kept walking. My house was only a few blocks away. Dead things were everywhere. I picked up speed, my heart a wild sparrow trapped in my chest.

A white poodle lay stretched out in the middle of the sidewalk. Its eyeballs protruded from their sockets. Something dark stained the fur around its ears. *That looks like Snowball.* I didn't know the names of all the neighbors, but I did know all their pets. Snowball lived in the last house on the left. What was she doing way down here?

I leaned a little closer. Sure enough, there was her pink collar, but a blade of grass was stuck to one bulging eyeball. I looked away. It might've been the hum that killed her. Blew out her eardrums and eyeballs the way too much electricity can blow out a light bulb. One of my own ears had bled, and I'd felt as if my eyes were going to pop out of their sockets down there in the basement. Imagine if I'd been topside when it came. This probably would've been the result.

For a moment I allowed my eyes to scan the area, looking for Snowball's owner, but I didn't see her anywhere. Up ahead another row of sycamores lined the street. *Is she there, hanging from a branch like Mrs. Jane?* It was hard to tell from here. But the trees did look fat. Or at least too wide.

I hurried on. If Snowball's owner was in a tree, I didn't want to know.

Here and there other pets lay dead in yards or at the ends of leashes once held by now-missing owners. Black and gray spots in the grass, especially beneath the trees, had to be birds—sparrows and grackles, mockingbirds, and mourning doves. Some adorned the crackly streets and sidewalks, too.

I tried to give the birds and pets a wide berth, but they were everywhere, like debris after a tornado. Only this was no tornado, just the opposite. This time, the buildings were all intact, but the people and animals had been destroyed.

The song swelled again. *Carry on, son, carry on.*

Thank you, Dad. I knew it had to be him, or at least my subconscious channeling him, and at the four-way stop, I came upon my first real wreck since leaving school. Two cars and a pickup had collided in the intersection. The gold car appeared to be empty. It was the one with the least amount of damage. It seemed to have been hit and knocked away, but the other two, a pickup and a Camry, were locked together in a grotesque flesh and metal sculpture.

There were no streetlights, but twilight had quickly given way to moonrise, and I could see a dead man behind the steering wheel of the pickup.

I stuck to the sidewalk wondering again why the monsters didn't eat the dead. The new moonlight glinted off the twisted chrome of the vehicles, and the music in my head urged me on. I wondered where the cannibal-monsters had gone, but mostly I was just glad they were.

Oddly enough, I didn't even worry about the dead man. I knew he wasn't going to pull himself free of the wreckage like a zombie. I knew he wouldn't call out for me in a gravelly voice asking me to come back and help him—

My scalp prickled.

Call.

I slapped my pockets in search of the cell phones.

Most were gone, including mine. Lying somewhere near the evil parking barrier in the school parking lot no doubt, but I still had two others. I pulled them out and tried them one at a time. They were toast.

My spirits fell. Before losing my phone for texting in class, I'd never been without any means of communication. *Never.* I cocked my arm back and flung the useless things away. One hit the sidewalk, a small but distinct sound of metal and plastic connecting with concrete in the distance. But I didn't hear the other one. *Must've landed on grass.*

I felt like an idiot.

Better to have hope. Better to just carry on.

I was almost home. I still had the iPod. I told myself I would try it later. I couldn't take another disappointment right then.

My feet picked up speed even at the risk of falling over something again. In the early darkness, the bodies hanging from the branches were not as obvious. But the breeze lifted their odor my way as if to spur me on.

I couldn't wait to get home. At the same time, I couldn't help but wonder what I should do if no one was there. My only remaining set of grandparents lived in Colorado; I had an aunt in Abilene, and an uncle in the military somewhere. That was all. We didn't have a large family. I sent up a silent prayer for their safety, but I couldn't *feel* the prayer. Not the way I did when Mom said grace at the dinner table on Thanksgiving, insisting we all join hands.

A new song entered my head, *Amazing Grace, how sweet the sound.*

A random thought occurred on the heels of the song. Coach Beatty had come running up out of nowhere when he attacked the monster with the baseball bat. Could he have been in the basement with me? Could it have been *him* shoving things across the floor, trying to find *his* way to the stairs, making that odd scritching sound? I'd once heard a rumor that Coach kept a bottle down there somewhere.

If it were true, that might explain why both of us survived when all the others were dead, or dying, in the street. We'd been underground, just like Dr. D had said.

I thought of Cade's laptop still down in the basement, and that reminded me of my own laptop sitting on my bed where I'd left it while getting ready for school this morning.

This morning? Could that be right? It felt like another lifetime. Ideas began to swirl through my mind. *Are the things really from Purgatory? Are those sins tattooed on their faces—no, in their faces? In their whole bodies? Are they eating people to get new souls? Are there really holes between the dimensions?* The strange ideas whistled around and around in my mind without slowing. *Beings from Purgatory? How ridiculous. But if it were true, why would they want our souls? What IS Purgatory? And that black stuff, the locusts, what could that be?*

It was all too much. If only I could Google it.

If only I could do that now.

I stumbled along through the encroaching night thinking of all the things I would do if my parents were there when I arrived. But if they were not there, I needed to come up with a plan.

A plan to what? Survive?

The very idea sounded ludicrous. Survival is some state of being reserved for storm victims, or victims of mass shootings. Survivors are people in disaster movies—they're not me—not kids whose greatest fear so far has been asking a girl to a dance.

A vision of Dee stuffed through the basketball goal leapt into my head followed closely by my new buffer song.

Amazing grace, how sweet the sound,
    That saved a wretch like me,
  I once was lost, but now I'm found,
    'Twas blind, but now I see.

What's that all about, I wondered. *Carry on wayward son* sort of made sense. After all, it was one of my dad's favorite songs and well, it made me get up and go when all I wanted to do was find some place to hide. It made me literally carry on. But "Amazing Grace?" Why that song? *I was lost but now I'm found?*

Hey, maybe I'm about to be found, maybe that's it. It wasn't the first time I'd *found* myself motivated by music. Just like the musical phrases sometimes stuck in my head when I first woke up in the morning, those snippets of song that often helped me make decisions.

I thought everyone did that, until I mentioned it to Cade one day. He'd laughed and called me dork as usual. It was obvious he didn't believe me, so I had never mentioned it again.

Saved a wretch like me? I hoped so. My first goal was just to get home and find my folks. I figured to save my wretched self. I might need another goal—

A strange sound, part moan, part something else, arose from the bushes. Chillbumps rashed the backs of my arms. The sound was almost human, could it be a person hiding, someone injured? *But what if that someone is hanging up with their flesh hanging down? I don't want to see that. There's nothing I can do to help that.*

I tried to tiptoe past; it made no sense to go backward. Carry on, that's what the song said, and that's what I intended to do. Carry on and hope for amazing grace.

The sound came again, louder. This time it was followed by a sound I recognized—the rattle of a dog chain. I glanced at the nearest house, recognizing the beige brick right away. It belonged to Mr. Granger, the neighborhood grouch. The dog chain was most likely attached to the old man's pit bull, Snake. Actually, I recalled, he was only half pit.

When I told my dad one day how cruel I thought it was to chain the dog up that way, Dad had told me the dog was half pit, half boxer, and all deaf. He'd said the chain was for the dog's own good because if he ever got out of the yard, he wouldn't be able to hear cars coming or his master calling him back.

I remember thinking that sounded like a crock—just an excuse for being too lazy to make sure the fence was secure. Even after my dad's speech I'd silently cursed the old man every time I passed by the house and observed the big brown dog sitting placidly at the end of his chain. I still thought chaining a dog was a horrible torture. I also thought it probably made them vicious.

My gut said, *hurry on, carry on, wayward son*, but I'd always heard running would trigger the chase instinct in a dog. What if Snake was off the chain somehow? Or what if that wasn't even the dog dragging that chain? I thought of all the dead animals I'd seen already, like poor Snowball. What if it was a ragged dog with one eyeball on its cheek—a bulging eyeball with grass stuck to it? What if it was all that but somehow still upright, still dragging that chain?

I walked faster. The low moon paved my way on the gray concrete sidewalk. My shadow freaked me out. It reminded me of the blackness that flowed over the creature in the gym.

Nnn-hnn-hnnnnn

That sounded like a dog whining. *Could it be Snake?* I thought of the way he stared at me every time I passed his house.

I was almost too far away, but I hesitated, waiting for the sound of the chain.

It did not disappoint. It wasn't a big sound. It seemed more like the chain was being moved back and forth, a little at a time rather than dragged across a wide expanse. I recalled the dog's deep brown eyes, round as marbles.

I stopped walking. I didn't want to go on without knowing if it could be him. The only thing that scared me was that possibility that it might not even be a dog anymore. That it might be nothing more than a flayed mass of meat and bone like the people in the trees, or like Dee.

Without thinking I rubbed my rough palm across my sore chin.

The fierce pain stopped the spiral of fear, and I looked for a place where I could see into the yard without going into the yard.

'Twas blind, but now I see.

Yeah, yeah, I thought. *Something like that.* I told myself I would just check. If the dog *was* too mangled, I would heed the song and carry on. But either way, I had to know. It was the only living animal so far—if you didn't count the plague of locusts, and I certainly didn't. I didn't even want to think about that black rain.

As quietly as possible, I crept toward the house. The front yard wore a mantle of moonlight. Obviously, the dog wasn't there. But the side yard was dressed in deep shadow.

That's where he is.

I approached the chain link fence.

Hnn-hnn-hnnnn

It was coming from the side yard. The chain link separated Mr. Granger's house from the one next door. But on the corner side there was no house.

I circled the yard, the whine leading me on. *Maybe he saw me walking by, or maybe he smelled me, whatever, it doesn't matter. He's in the fence and on the chain, there's no reason to be afraid.*

I forced my feet to keep moving. The night breeze stilled, waiting.

I have to know, have to see—

The toes of my high-tops fit into the diamonds of the chain link just the way I knew they would. I climbed the five-foot fence and hopped lightly down on the other side, Snake's side. I stayed close to the fence in case I had to hop back out.

Am I stupid? I could imagine the headlines: Kid survives cannibals only to be eaten by an injured pit bull. Film at Eleven.

Except there's no more film at eleven. No more news at eleven. No more—

Kansas blared into my skull. *Carry on, dammit, carry on!*

Another whine cut through the song.

I took a tentative step forward, and there he was. From behind a tall clump of pampas grass, I observed the large dog. He appeared to be lying half in and half out of a dugout space beneath the house. Near the hole stood a large Igloo brand doghouse. The Igloo glowed whitely from the shadows. The dog was harder to see. His fawn coat was lighter than the grass, but the shadows blurred the outlines so much that I could only discern shapes, not details.

Then he raised his head and stared directly at me.

I couldn't see his eyes, but I could sense the intensity of the stare as surely as if he had charged the fence, barking. Somehow, this silent plea was even worse.

Without giving myself a chance to wimp out, I approached the animal at a slow, steady pace. "It's okay," I murmured, forgetting the dog was deaf. "Hey, Snake. It's me, Jack. I pass by here almost every day. Hey boy, it's all right, it's just me."

Still ten feet away, I held out my injured hands, palms up, the way I'd seen the Dog Whisperer do on TV. And then I heard the growl.

Oh, shit.

I stopped in my tracks. Maybe what I'd thought was a psychic connection was only on my part—not his.

The growl turned into a chest-deep rumble.

I took a step backward. It took every ounce of willpower not to turn around and run, but I knew how long that chain was, I'd seen Snake drag it all over the huge yard.

The rumble grew louder as the dog attempted to gain his feet. His big head wobbled as if his equilibrium had gone offline.

I stopped. He couldn't seem to get up.

That saved a wretch like me.

Nnn-hnn-hnnnn

"Snake?" I kept my hands out. "C'mon buddy. You know me."

The dog struggled to stand. The rumble halted, then started up again.

I stepped forward instead of backward, and the dog's rear collapsed back into the dugout hole, pulling the rest of its body down, too.

Probably dying.

Two more tentative steps forward, and I could see that Snake was definitely still chained, but the chain wasn't holding him back. It lay slackly across the grass.

Snake raised his head slightly, whining and rumbling at the same time.

I gave in to the Kansas push and crossed the remaining space to kneel beside the broad flat head. A small amount of dark stickiness stained the fur below his ears, too.

"Hey, boy. Hey old Snake. How ya doin' buddy?" I offered my palm, and the dog's long pink tongue swiped my ragged wounds. I exhaled, and the song lyrics alternating through my head backed off. I sat quietly beside the big dog, wondering if I could save him.

I let my hands caress his tawny coat, feeling the muscular body for injuries all the way down his back into the cool damp hidey-hole.

Nothing seemed to be wrong with his legs or spine. "So, what's the problem?" I stood, hoping he would follow. If he didn't, I had no backup plan.

After a second, he attempted to pull himself up and out from under the house. It was apparent something wasn't working correctly. His front half came up but collapsed again before he could get his back half to cooperate.

The breeze picked up, and I heard the creaking of branches as the sickening smell of death wafted over us like a ghastly perfume. This seemed to spur Snake on the same way Kansas spurred me on. He struggled to his feet again, the rumbling whine emanating from his chest making him sound as if he'd swallowed a small train.

"That's it, c'mon boy. You can do it." I picked up his chain. It was surprisingly light. "Let's get the hell out of here," I mumbled. "Let's blow this pop stand as Granddad would say." I unclipped the chain from the stake beside the doghouse. In the back of my mind, I had the idea that I would need to keep him on the chain to ensure that he followed, but as I walked away, the big dog dragged himself after me.

He must have been staggering along like that when I heard him. Or maybe he'd just been dragging himself out from under the house. Maybe that's why he survived—he was underground like me.

The chain clinked and clanked. It was ridiculously long and unwieldy. I unclipped it from the dog's collar and let it fall to the ground. Snake peered up at me with those brown marble eyes. "You're welcome," I said. Simply having another creature alive, walking along beside me—okay, staggering—gave me a burst of hope.

That saved a wretch like me. Hmm. Maybe I had that saving part backward.

I wondered if I should check the house for Mr. Granger, but every window was pitch black. If the old man was alive, wouldn't he have found a candle or a flashlight by now?

I felt like a coward, but my *Carry On* song didn't make an audio appearance, so I skipped it. I just couldn't make myself go into that dark, confined space. It did give me something to add to my list of goals, though: get home, find my folks, *and* get a flashlight. And if possible, get some Tylenol for my chin.

I pictured the flashlight. Was it in the house or in the garage?

What if the car is in the garage? Can I drive it if it's there? Yes, of course I can. I will. But if either of the cars are there, then Mom or Dad will be there, too.

I set off with renewed purpose.

Snake staggered along beside me like a TV drunk, heading first one direction then the other, neither very straight. His back end seemed disconnected from his front end. I assumed it was that equilibrium problem.

A couple of times, I found myself chuckling when he headed off on a drunken tangent, but that made me feel bad. I reached down to pat him on the head, and that seemed to bring him back in line, so I made it a point to touch him every now and then, whether he needed it or not.

After a couple of minutes, I realized we were both doing better. I decided I liked travelling at night. Seeing all the pets lying dead in the yards like forgotten stuffed toys had been almost as bad as the people in the trees—no, that wasn't right. It wasn't nearly as bad as that. But I seemed to be getting used to the bodies in the trees—as long as I kept my eyes trained straight ahead or on the ground so I couldn't really see them.

CHAPTER SIX

Home Again, Home Again

Home.

Every bit as dark as all the other houses we passed.

All the air whooshed out of me, and I had to sit down on the front walk. I wanted to run up on the porch, stick my key in the lock, open the door, and yell, "I'm ho-o-me!" like I always did. But not this time. The entire block was silent except for the panting of Snake who flopped down beside me.

"What now?" I asked. "I can't go in. Not in the dark." I heard what I was saying, but then my music started up again, drowning it out. *Carry on. 'Twas grace that taught my heart to fear—*

"And grace my fears relieved." I spoke the words aloud to make the music stop. I could picture the small emergency Dynamo flashlight in the kitchen junk drawer. The large yellow one was probably in the garage in Dad's toolbox. *Which should I get? Better get both.*

I looked up at the house. *What if they're in there, dead? What if that's the reason they didn't come for me?* I closed my eyes and pictured the inside of the house. *To the right of the front door is the hall table that holds the mail tray.* Everything that comes in the mail goes there so Mom can go through it later. Not much comes in the snail mail anymore, mostly junk mail, catalogs, and flyers.

I continued to picture myself moving through the living room— careful not to trip on the corner of the rug Mom bought when she had all the wall-to-wall replaced with hardwood—then on into the dining room which is just an extension of the living room, and then, finally, the kitchen.

Snake whined, and I patted his head. I was ready to try it. I'd pictured the layout of the house, and now I felt more comfortable. I no longer thought my parents were in there waiting for me. That wasn't logical. They wouldn't simply sit and wait for their only child to find his way home when the whole town had been invaded. But now that I was here, I still had to go in. It was my home.

I stood and heard the old familiar creak of the second porch step. Then I heard another sound, some sort of stealthy movement.

My head spun toward it. Snake couldn't hear it—*that's about right, I finally get that dog Mom would never let me have, and he's as deaf as a post*—but the purple sage bushes hugging the side of the house seemed to be rustling. It's one of *them*, I thought. Except *they* aren't stealthy. They don't hide at all. Could it be Mom, or Dad? Could they be injured and hiding?

Someone exhaled and my entire body turned to stone. I made myself move, touching Snake on the head to try and get him to stay put, but when I stepped down, the dog pulled himself up, ready for action.

I peered toward the sage. The bushes were thick, one of my mom's favorite plants. I couldn't see anything, but the voice that came out of the darkness was a soft, sandpapery whisper. "Are you alone?" It sounded like a woman's voice.

My heart thundered. "Mom! Is that you? What are you doing outside?"

The person moved away from me through the bushes.

"Wait!" I yelled. "Where are you going?"

The figure stopped. "Who *are* you?"

My hopes sank. That wasn't Mom. The voice was rough, young.

"My name is Jack." I waited for a response. "This is my house. Who are you?"

The rough voice bordered on hysteria. "Do you know what happened?"

I shook my head and then realized this person, whoever she

was, probably couldn't see me in the darkness. "I think we've been invaded. I've seen these horrible creatures—"

"No," the woman shrieked. "Don't say that!" She took off running along the side of the house, the shaking bushes mapping her journey.

"Wait, don't go!" I started to chase her, but I didn't want to go backwards. Not when my home was right here. *She must be terrified. Maybe she'll come back. At least I know there are still other people.* In a moment, the bushes stilled. As if she hadn't been there at all.

I looked down at Snake. He hadn't even tried to chase the woman. "Lotta help you're going to be." I smoothed my thumb across his amazingly soft head. "Good company, though." I stepped back up on the porch, walked up to the door, stuck my key in the lock, and let myself inside. I didn't yell out, I'm ho-o-me, or anything else. It was way too weird, standing there in my open-door rectangle of moonlight, feeling the nighttime house surround me.

Snake hesitated. His balance was better, but he didn't seem to want to cross the threshold.

"It's okay," I whispered, appalled at the flat silence that swallowed my words. "You can come in." I turned back and touched his head, then tugged on his collar to let him know he should come inside. The big dog rumbled softly, then stepped gingerly into the room.

It took a few seconds to get my bearings. The picture window let more moonlight into the living room once I pulled open the drapes. And once my vision adapted to the gloom, it felt a lot better.

Just as I thought, Mom and Dad were not there. The house was achingly empty. The question was *had they been there?* I headed to the kitchen to look for the Dynamo, but when I saw the fridge, my mouth watered. I opened it, momentarily surprised when the light didn't come on, and felt for the milk jug. It still felt cold, so I turned the gallon up and chugged deeply. I started to put it back and then decided it might last longer in the freezer with the ice.

How long before the ice melts?

Carry on, my song whispered. Just carry on.

I pulled open the junk drawer to the right of the fridge. The Dynamo flashlight was there, just like always. I squeezed the handle-crank a few times and thumbed the switch. The beam shot across the kitchen; no batteries needed.

Just the heft of the flashlight in my palm gave me a feeling of power. I knew my hand would get tired of squeezing the handle, and I knew the light wouldn't last long unless I was constantly squeezing, but it was okay. Finally, I'd found something I could control.

I slipped the light into my front jeans pocket and my pants almost hit the ground. Another goal: Get a belt or a backpack to carry stuff in. I knew we couldn't stay here very long. In the back of my mind, I was certain I would have to venture back out tomorrow to search for Mom and Dad. And I would have to carry things with me. Things like food and water in case the monsters had taken over the whole town.

In case they'd taken everything and everyone. Takers. That's what they were. Taking everything in search of the one thing they really wanted.

That made me think of the monster I saw that stopped and picked up some kid's backpack as the bunch of them moved away from the school. It had also been one of those that had pulled on a guy's jacket. I wished I could fire up the computer and ask Dr. D what was going on. If you tweeted him a question, he'd put it in the queue. He'd always said if you wanted to know the truth, just ask. I had never sent him a question, but it had been cool just knowing I could.

My hand paused as I closed the drawer. My backpack was still at school, probably in the gymnasium where I dropped it when we started decorating. The thought of it there amidst the blood and horror of the gym made my legs feel like rubber—*and Dee, don't forget Dee, not that I ever could forget seeing her in the basketball goal with her sparkly headband and*—suddenly, a big head nudged the back of my knee. *Sixth sense? He may not be able to hear, but he sure seems able to feel.*

I swiped the back of my hand across my face and let it fall to my side. Snake licked away the salty moisture. I leaned down and hugged his stout neck, astonished at how docile he was. Without thinking, I pressed my face to the side of his square snout and that made all the difference. My tears disappeared, and my belly rumbled, surprising us both.

In the meat tray of the fridge, Mom kept packages of cold cuts. I grabbed bread from the box beside the microwave, slapped a wad of honey ham between two slices, and pigged out standing in a soft shaft of moonlight from the window over the sink. After the things I'd seen, I couldn't believe I had any appetite, but the thin-sliced meat was sweet and delicious.

Snake sat at my feet.

I slapped a second sandwich together but gagged on the first bite when I unexpectedly flashed-back on the horrific gurgling sound the Takers made as they fed. I tossed that sandwich to Snake, and he caught it easily. He had absolutely no qualms about gulping it down and hoping for more.

I made another and gave that one to him, too. *Might as well eat it all. Won't keep with the power off.*

In the lining of my mind, the music started up again. *Carry on, Jack. You know what you have to do. You have to look in the garage, look for the car.*

Right now, I had to give Snake a bowl of water. But the voice—and the music—would not be ignored. Kansas grew louder and louder.

"Okay," I said. "Okay. I'm carrying on. Time to see what we're made of." The dog continued lapping at the bowl of water until I left the kitchen. He followed automatically.

I squeezed the Dynamo and pointed the beam at the floor. I knew I was procrastinating, putting off looking in the garage, but I was certain I already knew what I would find there. As a result, I convinced myself I should check the rest of the house first. "If no one has been here, we'll spend the night. Then when daylight comes, we'll head to the library and then to the high school."

I can't be the only one of the family left. Maybe Mom and Dad are holed up in the basement at the school or the library. Maybe they are afraid to come out. Or maybe they're on their way here right now.

I glanced at the desktop computer in the corner of the living room. The blank screen watched me like an eye. The wall-mounted flat screen TV over the fireplace seemed to watch me, too. Everything in the house was strange without the juice of electricity. All except my Dynamo. It's the only thing that worked the way it should. And maybe the iPod. I still had the pink one from the school's office.

I pulled it out and examined it. Pink, sparkly cover—probably belonged to a girl. For a moment, I wondered if it could've belonged to Dee, she was *very* girly. *Was*, my mind whispered. *Was very girly. Now she's just . . .* but I couldn't go there. Wouldn't go there. Besides, it couldn't have been hers. She never would have gotten it taken away and locked in the file cabinet. She was a good girl. *Had been.* I shook my head and thought of all the girls it could have belonged to. *Where were they now?*

The ear buds were wrapped securely around the iPod. I started unwrapping them, but then Kansas blared in my head. *Carry on, Jack!*

I got the message and walked straight to the garage door. I knew if the cars were not there, they never made it home. If by some chance the cars were there, then it would be time for me to go out and look in the trees for their bodies. I could hear myself breathing. It reminded me of the woman in the bushes.

Snake pressed against the back of my knees. It gave me strength. I twisted the knob and pulled the door open.

The thick odor of oil and grease leached out through the gap. The empty garage sported the shadow of an old oil stain in the center of the right-hand side. No cars. Mom and Dad never came home. Of course, they didn't. If they'd gotten this close to my school, they would have come for me.

My beam of light stretched across the empty space and hit Dad's toolbox. Aside from electronics, the old red toolbox was his pride and joy. It had belonged to *his* father who had been a carpenter.

The big flashlight's in there—but does it still work? All I had to do was walk across the garage and get it. I should also get the hammer or some other type of weapon. So far, I'd been just hiding, but if I did wind up on my own, completely alone, maybe I'd better start thinking about other means of surviving.

My folks were strictly anti-gun, but if I intended to go in search of them tomorrow, I'd need something. Maybe something more than just a hammer. I didn't know how to get a gun, though. And if

I did manage to walk all the way to the library and the high school, I would still have to come back here tomor—

I couldn't finish that thought. The idea of having to come back to this empty house tomorrow was too much. I sank to the floor, my back against the doorjamb, tiny Dynamo in my hand. They weren't here. They haven't been here. *Where are they, where could they be?*

Snake pushed up against me, and I pulled him onto my lap and buried my face in his wrinkly neck. He didn't move a muscle except to lick my cheek.

Carry on, son. Carry on.

I unraveled the ear buds of the pink iPod and smashed them into my ears. For a moment, I heard sound, and then I realized it was just my head music on repeat. Kansas played through, and then "Amazing Grace" began a new verse:

Through many dangers, toils, and snares,
    I have already come,
'Tis grace hath brought me safe thus far,
    And grace shall lead me home.

I thumbed the on/off switch, but my music played on. *I must be crazy.* The music had never been like this before. Until now it had been only a snippet here or a melody there. Like the day my great-gran dropped dead in her garden. I had awakened that morning with the first line of the old hymn, "In the Garden," going through my head. *I come to the garden alone, while the dew is still on the roses . . .*

The fact that my Mom and Dad were not churchgoers was one reason I thought it so odd. I remember telling Mom about it as soon as I woke up. "That's your great-gran's favorite song," she'd said. "I haven't heard it in years."

That's when the phone rang. It was my great-gramps telling us the sad news. "She died in her rose garden," he'd said. "She didn't suffer."

The look on Mom's face had been classic. "How'd you know?" she asked.

"I didn't," I told her. "I just heard the song." Later I decided Great-Gran had sent me the song as a way of saying goodbye.

But that had been years ago.

Now this.

I felt completely drained. My hands smoothed Snake's coat over and over, soothing me as much as it did him. I jerked awake when my head fell forward onto my chest. The flashlight lay on the floor with its weak beam pointed across the garage. For a moment, I thought I must still be asleep.

My music had gone silent, but there were shadows of feet moving along the narrow gap at the bottom of the overhead door. My heart crashed against my rib cage. Snake must have felt it. His big head came up off my lap and a rumble emanated from his chest.

"Shhh." I curled my fingers under his collar. I had no idea who might be walking past the garage, but they had to be close if I could see their shadows, and stealthy, too. I couldn't hear them at all.

I grabbed the flashlight and pushed the switch to kill it. My head turned toward the front door. Had I locked it when I came in? I didn't recall doing so.

I cupped my hand around Snake's square muzzle and mouthed the words, "No barking." He cocked his head sideways and stared into my face. I removed my hand and crawled toward the front door so I wouldn't be visible through the living room windows. I yanked the ear buds from my ears and threw them aside. *No wonder I couldn't hear anything!*

Snake looked at me once more before trailing along beside me, toenails clicking across the floor.

CHAPTER SEVEN

Survivors

I'd left the living room door standing wide open. The storm door was closed, but it was only aluminum and cracked glass. Not much of a barrier to anything.

In the yard, shadows mixed and mingled. I was pretty sure the shadows belonged to people, not monsters. They moved like people, stopping and starting, looking and searching. They were so quiet though. Eventually I heard whispers. I couldn't make out the words, but I had a feeling they knew I was there.

Mom and Dad?

My gut said no. They wouldn't stand out in the yard; they would open the door and come inside. Besides, wouldn't they have their cars?

I crouched beside the sofa on my hands and knees. Looking through the cracked glass, I watched the shapes poking around in the sage. I counted three people, two women and one man. Each appeared to be carrying some sort of tool or weapon. One woman had a rifle, and the man had what I thought was a shovel. The other woman had something that looked like a metal pole. I wondered if they were searching for the girl I'd spoken to earlier. I inched closer to the door to observe them as they moved on down the street, and then a hand yanked open the storm door.

"What're you doing kid?" The voice was deep, coarse.

While I was watching the searchers, the guy had simply walked up from the other side of the porch and opened the door.

"This is my house," I blurted. *They must have seen my light under the garage door.*

The man was tall. His wave of gray hair added another inch or two. He continued to hold the door open. In his other hand, he held a handgun pointed casually at the ground.

Snake rumbled. I placed a calming hand on his quivering back.

"Watch him," the man said. "I don't want to have to shoot him. He's the first live animal I've seen."

I moved my hand down Snake's coat the way I'd done earlier. "We were underground," I said. "He won't hurt you." I tucked all four fingers inside Snake's collar to make sure, although if the stout canine wanted to charge, I doubted I'd be able to stop him.

"What do you mean, underground?" Behind the man, moonlight illuminated the silhouettes of the other people. They must have heard us talking. They were all headed back toward the house.

I stood slowly, one hand still holding Snake's collar. "I was in the basement at my school. When I came up, I saw those *things* killing people." I shook my head to clear the memories. "I waited until dark to come home, but no one is here." *Damn, why did I let him know I'm alone?*

The guy looked at Snake. "He at school with you?" He sounded suspicious.

"Of course not. I found him chained up in a yard down the block. He'd just crawled out from under a house." I looked the man in the eye. "Guess that's what saved us both."

The man hesitated. "Guess it did." He turned toward the three people crowding around the porch.

I didn't recognize any of them. Until today, I would have said I knew everyone in my small town. "How come y'all are still alive?" I didn't mean to sound so challenging. It just came out that way. Snake trembled against my leg, ready to fight.

"We were having our weekly info session in the basement of the office," said the woman on the edge of the group. "We all work for Thad here." She indicated the big man. "He's an attorney, that's why he sounds so la-de-dah all the time." She frowned. "We're his staff, well, all except for Kevin."

The man holding the shovel nodded. "I'm just the resident snitch." He snickered a bit. "Technically, I guess you could say I'm on the staff, too." He peered past us, attempting to see into the living room.

Snake's rumble became a growl. The man named Kevin glanced at him nervously. "We were tracking Marla, my girlfriend. She freaked out and took off on me. It was her day in court. She in there with you?"

I shook my head again. "There was a woman hiding in the bushes, but she ran off when I tried to talk to her."

"Oh, man!" Kevin stabbed the ground with his shovel. "She's probably wasted. I've been trying to get her off that shit." He glanced at Thad, the attorney. "Mr. Stewart's been helping." He ran a thin hand through his even thinner hair. "I can only *imagine* what she thinks is going on. She was in the basement, too. But she freaked out when we went up top."

Another woman, a bit older, spoke up. "Do you have water? Can we just get some water out of your hose or something?" She sat down on the porch. "It's a long way from the office."

"Help yourself." I pointed toward the faucet near the porch. "But why are y'all walking? Why not drive?"

The man named Thad peered at me closely, as if I should know this. "When *they* came, it did something to the vehicles. We didn't find a single vehicle that would start." He smacked his lips together. "I'm no mechanic, but I looked under the hood of my Lexus, and everything was coated with a cloudy film, like a glaze of some sort."

I remembered the slime that dripped from the highline wires. *Wonder if they did that on purpose so no one could escape, or if it was just a happy side-effect for them?* I wanted to ask the attorney's opinion, but when I opened my mouth, what came out was, "Bikes."

They all turned their eyes toward me.

I began to stammer. "Well, I mean. I have a bike, and I guess I'll take it to town tomorrow to look for my folks."

The big man looked me up and down. "Kid, I like the way you think. Here we are, four adults, and not one of us thought to look for a damn bicycle." He stuck out his hand. "Thad Stewart." His tone was formal. "Pleased to make your acquaintance."

I felt my insides loosen up. "Jack Lewis." I shook his huge hand brusquely, wincing at the pressure on my scrapes. No way would I allow this man to see me flinch. "This is Snake." I indicated the dog whose collar I still grasped.

The attorney leaned down and extended his hand to the dog. To my surprise, Snake placed his paw in the man's palm.

He squeezed the paw once and released it. "Pleased to make your acquaintance, too."

I was so relieved I wanted to jump up and down. "Where y'all headed?" I stepped out onto the porch. For some reason, I still wasn't ready to let them in the house. On one hand, I wanted to go with the little boy inside me and just fall in with them and let them make all the decisions. But on the other hand, I wasn't a little boy. I had to think for myself now.

Besides, these folks were already a group, a clique. I wasn't sure where Snake and I would fit in—I needed to find my own group, my folks.

The attorney tucked the handgun into the waistband of his pants and placed one hand on his hip. "Truthfully. We thought we would've caught up to Marla by now." He smoothed his wave of white hair with his other hand. "Until you said you'd seen her, I was beginning to wonder if we were chasing a shadow."

I tried to process everything the man was saying. He seemed like sort of a showboat, but at least he was human. And he seemed to like Snake. That made him a good guy in my book.

He continued, "I've known those two kids a long time. I'm the one who helped Kevin get straight. That's why he came to me when his girl got in trouble." He lowered his voice. "Didn't know they'd both got back on the stuff, though." He gazed across the yard at Kevin who had gone back to poking through the bushes with the shovel. The older woman was checking out the faucet, the other trailed Kevin. "Now we just need a place to crash for the night."

I didn't know what to say. With everything that had happened, I couldn't imagine having a drug problem, too. "That's really tough," I said. But I didn't offer them my house.

Thad looked at me oddly. "Right you are, Jack Lewis. Right you are."

The more he talked, the more I liked him. "Have you seen them in action?"

His mouth turned down. "You mean the aliens? Hell yes, I saw them in action. Pretty much wiped out all of downtown." He touched his wavy hair again.

I clenched my teeth together. "My mom was at the library downtown. That's where she works. Maybe she was in the basement, too. They have meeting rooms down there, you know." I took a breath. "Guess that's where I'm going tomorrow."

"Yes. They have a huge basement," he said. His voice was kind. He could've told me not to get my hopes up.

We stood on the front porch in the mild spring evening. On any other night, there would have been crickets chirping, mosquitoes buzzing, and cars ferrying neighbors home from work. Garage doors would have been groaning open and porch lights would've been flicked on. But tonight, there was nothing other than the sound of our breathing, and the creaking of tree branches down the block. I was very thankful my yard had only the sage bushes and a flowerbed full of petunias.

"Did you see any other survivors on your way here?" The new word slipped off my tongue like an accident. *Survivors.* I guess that's what we were.

Thad wagged his head. "All we saw were the ones who *didn't* survive." He tucked his thumbs in the front pockets of his jeans and rocked back on his heels. "On the other hand, we didn't see any more monsters."

"Takers, you mean." The word popped out.

Thad stopped rocking and shrugged. "That fits. They've pretty well taken everything, haven't they? The last time I saw them, they had all joined up and were headed south in some kind of platoon, or herd or something."

"That's what I saw, too. I hope they keep going, all the way to Mexico." I meant it, but after I said it, I had to stop and consider the idea that maybe they already were in Mexico.

Just then, the older woman came back. "They can't find her

anywhere," she said. "And I'm done searching for tonight." She looked directly at me.

The attorney said, "This is Maureen. She's my best secretary." The introduction was obviously tongue in cheek, as if the man was known for saying the same thing about each of his secretaries.

I held out my hand, and she took it briefly. "Pleased to meet you." I felt stupid acting so normal, as if our manners were like that brown strip of paper holding bundles of cafeteria napkins together. If that strip of paper gets torn, all the napkins spill out in a big mess. If our manners were to get torn, there's no telling what might spill out.

I briefly recalled having to restock the napkin dispensers in the cafeteria last year after a food fight I didn't even start.

I'll never forget how much fun it was to smash cold potatoes in Perry Armbruster's hair. I hadn't been defending anyone's honor. Hadn't been taking up for anyone. I just flat didn't like Perry. Never had liked him. He was the football star and yeah, maybe I was a little green with envy, but he was also the one who started the fight by shoving the new kid's tray in his face.

Cade had kept me from getting my butt kicked by throwing a pint of chocolate milk across the table, splattering us both. Thankfully, Perry had been too dumb to realize we were in cahoots, and then Mrs. Jane had arrived with Mr. Porter, the assistant principal.

Every kid in the cafeteria had been made to sit exactly where he (or she) had been standing while parents were called to come and see what their offspring had wrought.

I got grounded and had to clean the garage and wash both my parents' cars. Worse yet, Mom said I'd done such a good job on hers; the job was now mine, permanently. She'd been very disappointed in me.

Cade had gotten off easy with just a couple weeks grounding from his dad. We both—along with most of the other kids—had a month of cafeteria D-hall. That's where we learned the intricacies of filling napkin holders and helping Mrs. Beel and the other custodians clean up and then take down the cafeteria tables every day. Mrs. Jane said let the punishment fit the crime.

It worked for me. After that, I gained a whole new respect for how much hard work was involved in their jobs. Of course, Cade made light of the whole thing. "Never would've happened if we didn't have a closed campus," he'd complained.

When I'd finally taken the bait and asked what he meant, he said, "Because then King Perry and his court would've been over at the Taco Bell instead of stuck in cafeteria-hell with the rest of us dorks."

I wondered if that was Cade's leg behind the bleachers. I hoped not. I hoped he survived somehow. I wouldn't have been surprised if he did. His nickname should have been Teflon because nothing serious ever stuck to him. But then I remembered my last sight of Mrs. Jane. And Coach, and Mrs. Flanagan. And Dee and Cara. Even Mrs. Beel. I knew all too well what had become of them. Very doubtful Cade could have avoided that fate.

So why did I? Just luck?

Glancing at the dark tree-silhouettes to the north, I felt the woman named Maureen staring at me. Her eyes were dark. In the moonlight, I couldn't make out their true color. She had her brown hair pulled back into a low ponytail, and every now and then the moon would light up the silver threads that ran through it. She wore a pair of reading glasses on a cord around her neck. I was sort of amazed the glasses were still there, considering all that had happened.

"Pleased to meet you, too," Maureen said as I stood, woolgathering. "Call me Mo, everyone does." She glanced away when she said that, as if the word *everyone* might not apply anymore.

I wondered if she'd lost her family, too.

She gazed at Snake. "My Tippy was dead in the yard when we went to my house." A tear plopped onto the glasses hanging down on her chest. "My husband, Bill, was in a tree." Her voice disintegrated.

I suspected it was the first time she'd said those things out loud. I stood aside and allowed Thad Stewart to take her elbow and usher her inside. Snake also let them pass.

"I don't understand why they came." Her voice trembled. "I mean what are we? The McDonald's of the solar system?" She gratefully accepted the cold water I brought her from the fridge. "I also don't understand how they were able to kill everyone so quickly." She sounded on the verge of collapse.

"I didn't know what was happening when I came up from the basement at school." I spoke slowly, trying to make sense of it myself. "The power went off, and I stayed down there a while longer thinking the wind had caused it—you know how it does sometimes—"

They both nodded and turned off their flashlights after explaining to me how lucky they'd been to find them in the dark basement. "Batteries were unopened beside them," Mo said. "Right there alongside the reams of copy paper." She chuckled self-consciously. "I really stocked up on survival stuff after 9/11. And then I restocked after the virus, you know?"

"Guess we don't need to stock up anymore," Thad said. "Every store in town is having a going out of business sale."

His black humor shocked me, but it also sounded like something Cade might have said. It made me like him even more.

Mo ignored her boss. "Go on, Jack. What happened next, after you got up top?" Her eyes were bright with tears and curiosity.

"Well, when I came up and realized the power had gone out, I figured all the people had rushed outside to see about that awful noise."

"I think that's when the sky ripped open when that humming began. I think it killed the people and the animals." Mo looked at Snake. "I mean, those that were outside."

Thad Stewart nodded his agreement. "That's what we were discussing on our long walk over here." He sat on the sofa and pulled off one of his cowboy boots. "These boots were *not* made for walking." He peeled his black sock away from his heel revealing a crop of broken blisters. A bit of skin came off with the sock.

"Why, Thad," Mo said. "Why didn't you tell us? We could have stopped at Walgreen's or CVS."

That statement struck me as oddly comical, but I stifled the laugh.

"I kept thinking one of you *ladies* would need to stop for Band-Aids and I would just casually borrow one." He raised his eyebrows at me. "I didn't want to be the wuss."

I couldn't help grinning at the notion that a man of his age still worried about his image—especially in the middle of all this. "You sound like my dad. Mom calls him Macho Man when he does stuff like that." My voice fell off, and I realized I might never see them again.

No matter what I said or did, the reality of our situation kept jumping out at me, reminding me that everything was wrong, and nothing was right. No matter how we minded our manners and acted normal, everything had gone to hell.

"Are there any more people, anywhere?" I tried to sound manly when I asked. I didn't want to be a wuss, either.

No one replied. That answered my question.

But I couldn't believe it. There were plenty of other basements and cellars in town. *We can't be the only ones left.* "Hey, did you guys see any helicopters? They were a long way off, but I'm pretty sure I saw them."

They shook their heads. "Haven't seen 'em. Thought I heard 'em once or twice," Thad said. "Damn glad to know we've got some military somewhere."

I felt the same way, but I still thought they should all be a little more concerned. "I just can't believe our whole town is destroyed."

They regarded me as if he I'd spoken out of turn. "Well, I mean, you know . . . there have to be more of us. Right?"

My guests remained silent.

I hoped they were just too tired to think about it. They were much older than me, after all. *Maybe when you get old, it's easier to simply accept things.*

"I'm going to the library tomorrow," I blurted. "And the high school where my dad teaches music. Maybe I'll try the hospital and the police department, too."

"That's a great plan, Jack," Mo agreed. "Just because we didn't see anyone, that doesn't mean they aren't hiding out somewhere."

"Right. That's exactly what I think." I watched Thad Stewart pick at the burst blisters on his heel. "My dad has plenty of socks in his top drawer." I pointed my Dynamo down the hall toward my parents' bedroom. "I think there are Band-Aids in the medicine cabinet, too." I visualized the economy size bottle of Tylenol in that same medicine cabinet. My chin still hurt, but somehow, I no longer cared. The pain didn't even bother me anymore, not since the other people had arrived.

"You don't think your dad will mind?"

"No, I don't think he would mind at all." I appreciated him asking, though, as if he expected my dad to walk in the door at any moment.

CHAPTER EIGHT

Thieves

After Thad returned to the living room, Mo said, "If no one minds, I think I'll just lie back here and close my eyes."

She does look tired. "Go right ahead," I said. "There's some lunch meat in the fridge and cereal and stuff in the pantry. I don't think the electricity is coming back on anytime soon."

And that's how it happened that they all ended up settling in at my house.

Thad crossed to the kitchen. "I sure hope your dad was a drinking man. I could use a cold beer." He stopped, a comical look crossing his face. "Or at least a cool one."

"There should be one or two." I examined my gravel-embedded palms with my flashlight. "Dad always has to have a beer when he grills steaks out back." *Something we'll probably never do again.*

Mo sat upright on the sofa. "Let me see those hands."

I hesitated and then held them out. It seemed like a minor thing, now. "Fell in the parking lot at school."

She clicked her tongue against her teeth in the *tsk tsk tsk* sound my own Gran would have made. "We need to clean them with soap and a little peroxide." She took them in her hands, palms up. "Looks like you've got quite a bit of dirt and debris under the skin." She stared into my eyes. "Wouldn't pay to get an infection."

No, I think. *I definitely want to be healthy when they stick me in a tree and fillet me like a giant fish.* But I knew what she really meant. If I got an infection, who would treat it? One more thing to check out when I go to town tomorrow. Not just the hospital, but also the regular clinics. Drugs may become very valuable. Doctors, too."

"I think there's some peroxide in the bathroom." I started down the hall to search for it. Then I noticed movement outside the storm door.

Kevin marched up the walk, flanked by two women. One appeared to be the younger woman who worked for Thad Stewart. The other was a thin blonde wearing a tank top and tight jeans. Kevin had his arm wrapped firmly around her waist. She looked as if she might bolt at any moment. I opened the door, but in the pit of my stomach, a feeling of doubt clenched into a fist.

"Hey," Kevin said. "This is Marla."

The blonde did not acknowledge me. I assumed she was the girl from the sage bushes.

The younger woman smiled tiredly. "Are Mo and Thad still here?"

"Sure." All my instincts screamed don't let them in, but my good manners—those tenuous things holding everything together—took hold, and I stepped aside. In my head a repeating snippet of song resurfaced: *'Tis grace hath brought me safe thus far, and grace will lead me home . . .* Did that mean I was supposed to share my home?

Dad? Should I?

Carry on, son. Carry on.

Kevin passed in front of me; arm still hooked around his girl's waist. "Thanks."

Marla's gaze darted from shadow to shadow in the dark house. "Nooo," she began to wail. "Nooo, they might be hiding."

"S'all right," Kevin murmured. "C'mon." He led her to Mom's recliner and plopped down, pulling her onto his lap.

She buried her head in his neck and sobbed.

I didn't know what to do about that. I didn't want them in my house. And I didn't want them in Mom's chair. At first, I felt sorry for them, knowing how terrified the girl must be, but seeing them up close, I just wanted to be rid of them. *Bad vibes.* Like the difference between giving the homeless guy on the corner a few bucks or inviting him home to spend the night in your room. I knew that wasn't a very Christian way to act, or to feel. It wasn't even very humane, but I couldn't help it. The music played softly behind my thoughts. *And grace will lead me home . . .*

What does that mean? This *is* my home.

Snake stayed at my heel. He didn't growl, but I could still feel the tension in his muscles.

"My name is Lara," the other woman said, holding out her hand. "I don't think we actually met earlier."

I shook her hand gently.

If she noticed my weak grip, she didn't comment.

"I was just going to get some peroxide," I told her. "Mr. Stewart is in the kitchen."

Snake followed me. I had my little flashlight. Since Kevin and Lara also had theirs, I knew I wasn't leaving them in the dark.

The hallway was full of black pockets. Each pocket opened onto a room. I could easily find my way about the house in the dark; I'd done it enough times hoping to catch a glimpse of Santa on Christmas Eve.

But that was then. Now, the house feels completely different. As if the old familiar bedroom doors might open onto other rooms, in other universes, perhaps, just like Dr. D had said.

I stopped at the hall bathroom, but the peroxide wasn't there. It must be in Mom and Dad's bathroom, along with the Band-Aids. I crept on down the hall to my parents' room. Thad Stewart had not accepted the earlier offer of socks.

"I'll look for a pair of walking shoes tomorrow," he'd said. Then he'd gone in search of another beer. I didn't care. I thought about drinking one myself, but I was afraid of what a beer might do to my senses. I'd only tasted Dad's from time to time when he was grilling. I certainly didn't want to be drunk if we had to run again.

I hoped the peroxide would be in this medicine cabinet. I could picture the brown plastic bottle easily; I just couldn't picture where I'd last seen it. Mo said to wash my wounds first. Come to think of it, that's what Mom would've said, too. I stopped in the doorway and took in my folks' bedroom. I'd glanced in earlier, to make certain they weren't home, but this time, it really hit me. Everything was just the way they'd left it when they got ready for work this morning.

There were Mom's pink slippers peeking out from under the edge of the bed where she'd exchanged them for her loafers—what she called her library shoes.

Over the closet door hung an empty hanger that had probably held one of Dad's good blue shirts. He always wore a light blue shirt and tan slacks in the classroom. He called it his own personal uniform.

It stunned me to think that this morning had started out like any other day. When we left the house, we'd all assumed we'd be coming home to pick things up after work and after school. We probably would've had pizza for supper since it was Friday.

Dad's pajama bottoms were draped across the foot of the bed. He never wore the shirt, just the bottoms. I moved across the room in slow motion. A pair of Mom's turquoise earrings shone softly when I played my light across her dresser. I picked them up—one had a back on it, but the other didn't—and slipped them into my shirt pocket without thinking.

I stepped into the simple bathroom and shined my light all around to make sure nothing was hiding in the shadows. Marla's words had reminded me just how close the Taker in the school gym had come to catching me. If not for the black rain, it might have got me when I fell. But now, back here, in my home, all of that seemed as unreal as a bad dream the morning after.

Were there really people hanging in trees, dripping blood? I let the images loose in my mind for a moment. Of course, there were. I figured I would see a lot more tomorrow when I left my little street and went into town. Probably see more monsters, too. Unless they've turned on each other or something. Wouldn't that be something to come across, the Takers all eating each other . . .

I placed the flashlight on the counter and opened the medicine cabinet, its familiar squeaky hinge amazingly loud in the new silence of no electricity.

The brown bottle of peroxide was right there where I hoped it would be. I took it out and set it on the counter, then squirted liquid soap into my palms. The fiery sting was immediate.

I gritted my teeth and dabbed some of the soap on my chin. The stinging there wasn't nearly as bad. Gazing into the mirror I was glad to see that my chin was hardly even swollen. I couldn't look at myself for very long, though. In the reflected glow of the flashlight, my face was almost as alien as one of the creatures.

If Mom were here, she would pinch the tip off an Aloe Vera leaf and smear the clear gel on my chin. She always kept an Aloe on the kitchen windowsill in case of burns or cuts. It was one of her Native American grandmother's remedies. I made a mental note to try the old cure on my cuts for good measure.

I twisted the faucet handle with my fingertips. Cold water rushed out. I scooped some into my hands to rinse my chin. *How long will the city water continue working if no one is at the treatment plant?* I pushed the worry to the back of my mind, took the peroxide and poured it over my palms. I also splashed a little on the point of my chin. It bubbled merrily in all the right places. Should have thought of this myself.

I glanced down at Snake. *We have to look after each other now, don't we? Look out for number one, that'll be my new motto, look out for number one and carry on like Kansas and my dad keep telling me to do. That's what we'll do, Snake. That's what we'll both do.*

Snake turned his head in that sideways you-do-know-I'm-deaf-look-right? that I now recognized.

I replaced the peroxide and closed the medicine cabinet. The squeak wasn't as loud this time. I held my palms over the sink for another second, letting them air dry—I'd actually washed a few grains of gravel out of my skin—and then I picked up the flashlight and walked through the bathroom doorway into the hall.

But I didn't want to go back in there where Kevin and Marla sat cuddling in Mom's chair so I went the other way, to my own bedroom instead. Snake surprised me when he hopped onto the bed, turned around in a circle two or three times, then tucked himself into a doggy fetal position.

I laughed when he began to snore. I couldn't keep from smiling as I dug my old backpack out of my closet and dumped out my baseball glove and cleats. I shoved some underwear and t-shirts into it, and then added a pair of socks. Thinking of Thad's blistered feet, I added several more pairs of socks.

In the back of my mind, a plan had started to form. First light, I intended to head to town to check out the high school and the library. Probably should have kept going tonight when I discovered they weren't here. But I won't let myself get sidetracked with that kind of thinking. Carry on, man, just carry on.

I'd already decided if I couldn't find my folks at their jobs, I'd try the hospitals, clinics, and the police department. *Wait, maybe I should go there first. They have weapons. But I don't know anything about guns. I just have to hope someone else is there.* And last, but not least—if I don't find my parents or probably even if I do—I plan to head off to Colorado where my grandparents live.

I once saw a Travel Channel documentary about a government compound beneath the Denver airport. If people—survivors—are congregating, that might be one of the places.

Then there was Cheyenne Mountain Complex. It was famous from movies and TV, and it had been reactivated during the pandemic. Maybe after I found everyone, we would go there.

Having a backup plan, another goal, made me feel better. But something about the word *underground* kept nagging me.

Then it hit me. Underground. My dad's sister, Aunt Edna, owned a hundred acres of land near Abilene, Texas, and right smack in the middle of it was an abandoned Cold War missile silo. The man who sold her the land said he'd always planned to make it into a bachelor pad, but he'd frittered away his inheritance and wound up having to sell the land to pay his taxes.

Edna had also entertained the thought of making the silo habitable—her word—but she had never had the time to tackle such an over-the-top project. Instead, it had become something of a familial legend. Anytime we went to visit Aunt Edna, we all begged to go and check out the missile silo.

I recalled how hidden it was. The only thing visible above ground was an old Quonset hut surrounded by tall chain-link fencing and a funny-looking door set in concrete. Unless you knew what you were looking for, there was nothing to indicate the place once housed an Intercontinental Ballistic Missile—an ICBM. On the outside a set of massive iron doors were set flush into the ground, the doors welded shut. Those doors covered the opening to the vertical shaft from which the missile would've launched.

Fifty or sixty yards away the upright door was built into the side of a small concrete shelter. That door had simply been padlocked. It led down into what had been the operation center for the silo.

I had only been down to the first two levels, the 6,000-pound blast door at the third level had been welded shut so no one had ventured down there, but on the first two levels there was evidence of offices and bathrooms. It would make a *perfect* safe place until the world got back to normal.

The original owner had told Aunt Edna there were once twelve of the silos in that part of Texas, all of them armed with nuclear warhead missiles and all aimed at the USSR during the Cold War of the 1960s.

After further research, Aunt Edna learned that while most of the silos had been dismantled, one had been flooded and turned into a scuba diving location. Another had been sold to a zillionaire from New York who created an out-of-this-world vacation home.

When I thought of those 6,000 lb. blast doors protecting each level of my aunt's old silo—I knew I would have to go there. After I located my parents, of course. Should I take these new *friends*? And what about Colorado? It was in the opposite direction.

"I have to go to Abilene," I whispered to Snake. He snored on, unconcerned. "It's only an hour away by car—"

That stopped my planning.

An hour by car, but how far would that be on a bicycle? Approximately 75 miles—

A tiny metal squeak interrupted my thoughts. I recognized that sound. I'd just been in that medicine cabinet myself. I listened intently to see if it came again.

All was quiet. Probably just someone needing a Band-Aid. I went back to stuffing my backpack. I debated taking all the money I'd earned over the school year. I kept it tucked away in my sock drawer. But would there be any use for money now? I'd better take it. Maybe this had only happened here. Maybe everywhere else was still normal.

A loud clatter caused me to jump up and turn around. It was followed by a second loud rattle and a woman's voice. "Crap!"

I dashed down the hall and straight through Mom and Dad's bedroom to their bathroom where I encountered Marla. She was scooping medicine bottles out of the sink where they'd fallen from the mirrored cabinet. The problem was her jeans were so tight she couldn't fit all the bottles into her pockets.

As I watched, she dropped another bottle into the sink. Her hands shook so badly that every time she picked up the bottle, it slipped from her grasp and clattered back into the sink.

I walked in and took three bottles of pills from her.

She made a feeble grab at one of the bottles. "I need those."

I took her flashlight off the cabinet and turned it off. My Dynamo was in my other hand. "You should've asked." My voice was serrated with anger. "Those belong to my mom."

Marla began to cry. "I just feel so bad. I need those pills." She made another ineffectual grab at the ones in my hand.

I could see another bottle-shaped-bulge in her back pocket. "Give me all of them."

Eyes wide, she slapped her hand over her back pocket and ran from the room. In the bedroom, she pinballed off the corner of Mom and Dad's king-sized bed before recovering and running down the hall toward the living room.

By this time, the rest of the group had heard us. They were all standing, ready to come to her aid.

I marched in behind her. "I want the pills she took out of the medicine cabinet." I aimed my flashlight at her behind so every-one could see what I meant. But even as I said it, I wondered if I was overreacting. In light of all that had happened, I thought it very possible.

A new song convinced me otherwise. Bob Marley's *Get Up, Stand Up!* blasted into my head. Another of Dad's vinyl icons, the song insisted we should all stand up for our rights.

I took this as a sign that I should stand up for myself. What if I found my folks, and they were injured? They might need those pills, especially the pain pills. I stuffed the other two bottles into my own loose pockets. Later it would occur to me that this was my first test. My first test as a survivor.

As I stood there pointing my flashlight, the girl attempted to hide behind Kevin. He wrapped his arm around her. "C'mon, man. Chill out." He felt behind Marla and pulled the bottle from her pocket.

"Nooo…" she wailed.

Kevin held the bottle up to his own light and read the label. "Hydrocodone. Good for what ails you." He tried to make light of the situation.

"Those belong to my mom," I said. "She got them when she had dental work."

Kevin's voice turned ugly. "Well, dude. I don't think she's going to miss them." His lips sported a tiny, hard smile.

A rumble started somewhere around my right knee. Snake pressed his shoulder against my leg. "Give them to me and leave." My voice quivered. "I won't share my house with a thief."

The smile disappeared from Kevin's face. He tightened his grip on the bottle. "You know, you can get this shit in any pharmacy now." He looked around the group for support. "It's really not that big of a deal."

I didn't care. Without the buffer of my parents, I felt like I had to draw a line. I just couldn't seem to back down. Bob Marley agreed.

"Great," I said. "Then you and your friend go find yourselves a pharmacy and stock up." I stared into Kevin's eyes. "But you aren't taking those."

CHAPTER NINE

Tragedy

Snake took a stiff-legged step forward. His hackles stood straight up, and the rumble turned into a growl. I curled my fingers under his collar again. I didn't want him to get shot.

Thad Stewart stepped up, stripped the pill bottle out of Kevin's hand, and tossed it to me. "That's enough. We have plenty of problems without this crap." He stared straight at Kevin when he said it.

I also looked at Kevin and Marla. "I think maybe you should all just go." My voice sounded steadier than I felt. "I have no qualms with the rest of you, but I understand that you're together."

Mo shook her head. "You two should be ashamed. This young man brought us into his home and look how you repay him."

"Damn drugs," Lara said. "They always lead to no good." She glanced at me. "I agree. We should just go."

I felt like a heel. But Bob Marley sang on in my head. "Stand up," he said. "Get up, Stand Up." I had to follow the musical advice. I liked the other three people, but those two druggies couldn't be trusted. I was determined not to give in.

"We'll go," Kevin said. "But you'll regret it down the line, boy. We need to stick together now. Those things are still out there, you know. They might've got their fill for a while, but they're still out there—"

At that, Marla began to shake. Tears flowed like water.

"You happy now?" Kevin glared at me as he pulled Marla toward the door. "That make ya happy, cowboy?"

Snake took another stiff-legged step in their direction. I tightened my grip on his collar. Thad Stewart shrugged and smoothed his hair. "Guess we'll be heading out to the nearest Holiday Inn. Ladies?" He cocked his arms out and waited for each woman to slip her hand into the crooks of his elbows.

Snake rumbled and strained against my grip.

The storm door slammed open, and Kevin and the crying girl burst out into the night.

"Sorry," I muttered. "I just . . ." my voice trailed off. I couldn't finish the thought. I really was sorry. I didn't want to be left all alone, even though it was my home. I began to second-guess my decision, wondering if I'd been too hasty in condemning the thief.

"No harm, no foul," Thad Stewart said.

And that's when the screaming began.

The four of us looked at each other stupidly, and then we all rushed toward the door at once. Snake got there first, though I'm almost certain *he* didn't hear the screams. He hit the slightly open storm door with his shoulder—it hadn't had time to close properly—and launched himself off the porch.

Out in the street, a Taker had Marla by the hair.

Snake, a snarling mass of muscle and teeth, smashed into the monster from the side and latched onto its leg. I couldn't believe the transformation. Only an hour earlier, the dog had been staggering like a drunk.

"Shoot it!" Mo yelled. "Someone shoot that thing before it kills her!"

Kevin must've left his shovel in the house. He began punching the monster with one hand while holding onto Marla with the other.

The girl's high-pitched screams were as inhuman as the creature dragging her away.

I was immediately bathed in guilt. If only I hadn't forced them to go out.

"Stand aside," Thad screamed. "Stand aside, Kevin!"

He drew down on the monster with the handgun. But from where I stood, I could tell the bullet was more likely to hit Kevin than the Taker.

"Wait!" I leapt toward the gun as it went off. The report deafened me. I'd been only a step away from grabbing it, but I wasn't quick enough. I staggered backward; hands clapped over my ringing ears.

Thad's gun arm drooped as Kevin fell to the curb, blood gushing from his mangled shoulder. The unharmed Taker shambled away with its fist wrapped in Marla's stringy, blonde hair.

She stumbled along, still shrieking, doing her best to stay upright to keep the thing from ripping her hair out completely. Twice she fell forward, and I was certain I heard a sound like two strips of Velcro being pulled apart.

Snake had let go when the bullet tore into Kevin, but now he dashed back and forth between the Taker's legs biting and ripping at its calves and thighs, looking for a place to latch on with those pit bull jaws.

The monster didn't seem to notice the dog. It trudged on as if on autopilot, words appearing and disappearing under its bald scalp, the moonlight gleaming sullenly on the glazed skin. It appeared to be headed toward the only thing similar to a tree on this end of the block—the neighbor's ornate yard light three doors down. The light sported a wrought iron arm upon which hung a tasteful sign displaying the house number.

I knew the Taker intended to swing Marla up and stab her onto that black metal arm. I could already imagine how that piece of wrought iron would look protruding from her chest. I couldn't let that happen, not with Kevin lying in a heap on the curb, his shoulder torn and bleeding.

When the thing finally stopped to kick at Snake, I saw my chance. I grabbed the handgun from Thad's nerveless grip and dashed toward the surreal scene.

Still in his doggy frenzy, Snake tore swatches of skin and meat from the Taker's legs. Marla scratched and clawed at the monster's hands and forearms, but it was no use. Her attempts at escape were almost pathetic.

I couldn't help but wonder why the thing was out here alone. Why wasn't it with the rest of them? We'd all seen the platoon moving out, but this one had hung around. Where had it been—in someone's house? The thought made me shudder.

"Snake!" I screamed. "Get out of the *way*." Then I remembered the dog was deaf. I rushed past him, placed the barrel of the gun against the back of the monster's head, and squeezed the trigger.

Nothing happened.

I glared at the weapon in shock. I'd prepared myself for a huge *bang* followed by the splatter of fluid and brains—assuming the things had brains—but this gun was a big, single action revolver. And I hadn't cocked it.

Snake continued to tear chunks from the thing's legs. One of its knees began to buckle. I could see fluid running down its leg, then I heard another Velcro-like rip and Marla was free.

The Taker staggered and went down, a handful of blonde hair trailing from its fist. Snake kept tearing at the gray flesh, but now he was able to reach its neck and face.

I couldn't believe it. I pulled back on the hammer of the revolver with both my thumbs and waded back in for the kill.

The kneeling Taker swatted Snake away with one hand and pivoted toward me in slow motion. It slapped the gun away just as I pulled the trigger.

The bullet went wide, and the monster grabbed me and stood, bringing me up with it. In slow motion the thing pulled my head toward its black, tooth-rimmed, maw. The breath coming from that dark hole was as noxious as the school science lab on dissecting day. The twin holes of its flat nose were like tiny black eyes, staring down at me. Ugly, blue-black sin words pulsed beneath its shredded skin: *murder, murder, murder . . .*

In the moonlight I noticed some of the words had leaked out onto its gray skin, but I didn't have time to think about it. *Maybe this is my punishment for chasing Kevin and Marla out of the house.* I tried not to care. Mom and Dad were gone. What did I have to fight for? I resigned myself to a bloody, painful end.

But I forgot about Snake.

The big dog wasn't done.

When the Taker swished him away like a mosquito, Snake had

simply rolled onto his feet and came charging back. He ripped at the monster with renewed strength, leaping to get at the arms imprisoning me, his new master.

When I saw the dog's determination, I instinctively began to fight back, kicking at the shins and biting at the knuckles. I tried to get a knee up into the monster's private parts, but they had no private parts. They seemed to be little more than evil, unfinished, templates with internal tattoos.

The Taker lifted its monstrously strong arms, and I found myself dangling in midair. *This is it. I'm dead.* All the sounds went away, and I was reminded of the time our car got stuck at the apex of the Ferris wheel at the county fair. I could see Snake leaping and snarling, but I could no longer hear anything. Time seemed to have stopped.

C-R-A-A-C-K

The rifle cartridge tore through the Taker's head, and I hit the pavement, hard.

Snake raced for cover.

Rolling to my side, I looked up at Mo holding the rifle in her hands like Annie Oakley ready to shoot again.

The monster on the asphalt didn't make a sound, but all of a sudden, my eardrums felt flattened, as if they were about to implode.

A darker-than-normal spot in the sky fluttered open and black rain poured from the hole as if summoned. I knew that certain insects such as wasps and hornets emitted alarm pheromones when they were hurt or under attack. Maybe the Takers emitted something like that, something that said, *come and get me, I'm injured.*

Maybe they take them back to Purgatory and fix them up before sending them back down. Like a field hospital in the midst of battle.

That idea was so crazy I wanted to laugh.

But of course, I didn't. I was far too busy getting away from the slithering raindrops as they massed together into one solid flowing sheet.

Everyone headed back to my house on the run. Thad and Lara dragged Kevin between them. He moaned and muttered, and his head lolled about as if it might fall right off. Blood from his shoulder made a sticky wet trail across the pavement.

Marla led the way. She stumbled through the storm door as I regained my feet. *Hope she doesn't lock us out.* I grabbed Mo by the arm and together we hurried toward home.

Snake didn't have to be told. He sprinted back to the safety of the house just as the fluid blanket flowed across the remains of the head-shot Taker. The darkly writhing blanket absorbed the creature as easily as its inky color absorbed the moonlight. Then it broke apart into hundreds of buzzing black locusts, which took to the sky, obliterating the stars.

CHAPTER TEN

On Our Own

Lara stared at the bloody mess that had been Kevin's shoulder. "I don't think peroxide is going to fix that."

Marla flew at me biting, scratching, and kicking. Clumps of her hair fell to the carpet, bloodied tufts of flesh clinging to the roots. "You!" she shrieked. "It's all your fault. If you hadn't shoved us out, this wouldn't have happened."

I had no experience defending myself against a girl. I collapsed back onto the sofa as Snake rushed in between us, snarling and biting.

Marla fell to the floor holding her bloody calf. "You bastard, I'll shoot you. I'll shoot you both!"

Snake backed off when she stopped attacking me. But he didn't go far.

"Stop it!" Mo yelled. She stepped in front of Marla and slapped her across her upturned face. *Whap!* "If you hadn't stolen the *pills* none of this would have happened. Now, you shut your ugly face and help us get Kevin on the table so we can look at him."

A grayness stole across my vision. I'd never fainted before, but I recognized the sensation immediately.

"Jack!" Someone snapped his fingers under my nose.

I could feel the nubby weave of the sofa beneath my sore palms, but my vision remained dim.

"Dammit, boy, wake up. We *need* you." Thad Stewart stepped away when I opened my eyes. Everything rolled back into focus.

Everyone seemed to tread carefully around me now that they had seen the damage Snake could inflict.

Lara helped Marla to her feet, checking the deep puncture wounds on her calf. "Soap and water, then peroxide."

I only heard part of her sentence. It took a few beats for me to catch up to what had transpired. First Snake saved Marla from the Taker, and then Mo saved me from the same monster. Now Snake had saved me from Marla. What a mess.

"Where is it?" Lara demanded.

My face must have mirrored my confusion.

"The peroxide! Where is it?" Lara's face was speckled with blood, but I was almost certain none of it was her own.

In the dining room, Thad and Mo wrestled Kevin onto the table. Grandma Jean's antique lace tablecloth had gone from off-white to dripping red.

Dumbfounded, I started down the hall to get the peroxide.

"Bring towels," Thad yelled.

Snake shadowed me. The nightmare from which I couldn't seem to awaken grew worse and worse. A dark cloud of hopelessness hovered above my head. *Gotta get to town, find Mom and Dad. Then to Aunt Edna's.* My plan resurfaced in my mind like the sin words surfacing beneath the Takers' skin. *How many more are out there? Are they still coming through, or are they hiding, waiting? Is this our life now?*

Is it the apocalypse?

I gathered the towels and peroxide then threw all the remaining medicine bottles into the mix and carried it all to the dining room. Most of it was over-the-counter stuff.

Mo had cut away Kevin's shirt with my mom's kitchen scissors. Part of the fabric had been punched into the wound by the bullet. I could see tiny threads of frayed plaid sticking out.

"Hold this flashlight." Thad's fingers probed the bullet hole.

Kevin moaned.

"Turn him over, Mo. Let me see that exit wound."

I was impressed. The older man seemed to know what he was doing.

"Saw a lot of this in Vietnam," he said.

Lara grabbed the peroxide and poured it onto Marla's leg. The girl winced but didn't cry out. I took the bottle of Hydrocodone from my pocket and threw it at her feet. I hated her for causing this. But I still felt guilty. What if I were a Taker? What would *my* sin words be? *Selfish, self-centered, greedy?*

"Amazing Grace" began to play softly in my head. I sat down in a chair, and Snake laid his muzzle on my knee. The fur around his snout was stiff with gore. "Thanks, buddy," I murmured. "Thanks for saving me." I rubbed the top of his velvety head with my thumb.

"Jack!" Mo's voice broke my reverie. "We need those *pills*."

Marla held up the bottle.

I took it from her hand without looking at her face.

"Here." I handed them over.

"Crush two in some water, and we'll pour them into him." Thad continued to probe the wound. Kevin gurgled and began to twitch.

"He's convulsing," Mo cried.

Kevin's body jerked and jackknifed right off the table onto the hardwood floor. Marla screamed and started toward him, but Thad got there first.

"Kevin," he bellowed. "Stay with us, boy!" He tried to hold the flopping arms and legs, but it was too late. Kevin gagged and sputtered. Vomit spewed from his mouth and ran back down his throat. Horrific gargling noises came from his chest. It sounded just like the Takers when they stuffed their mouths too full.

"He's choking," Marla shouted. "Help him, someone, he's choking!"

Together, Thad and Mo rolled Kevin onto his side as I fell to the floor to help hold him still. And then we all saw it. In the short time he had been lying on the dining table, the blood had run off onto the floor creating a small red lake.

"Do *something*." Marla's voice trembled. "Please don't let him die." She crumpled to the floor near his head. "He's all I've got."

Kevin's body relaxed as the convulsions stopped. Vomitus ringed his mouth, and everyone could see how unnaturally pale his skin had become.

Mo turned her face away. "Bullet must have nicked an artery."

Thad sat back on his haunches. "I killed him." His hands were slick with blood. "I killed him."

Marla sobbed, one hand wrapped around her own wounded leg.

"You were trying to save Marla," Mo said gently. She, too, sat back on her heels. "You were only trying to help."

I didn't say anything at all. I didn't want anything else to do with these people. They had made everything so much worse. I gazed around at all the damage. The mangled body on the floor; the pool of blood beneath the table; the antique tablecloth that my great-grandmother had brought from her native Ireland; the ragtag group of people all smeared with gore. I walked down the hall on shaky legs. My backpack stood packed and ready in my bedroom. They had ruined my home, my shelter. It was no longer a safe house. No longer even my home.

Behind me, I heard Marla whisper, "I will kill him."

I kept walking, and then veered into my parent's bedroom where I scooped up a key from the wooden tray on Dad's dresser. The large silver Ford key was the extra that belonged to Dad's classic red Mustang. The one we'd restored together.

I slipped it into my pocket. *Something from Mom*—I felt of the earrings miraculously still nestled inside my pocket—*and now something from Dad*. In the back of my mind, a hopeful thought surfaced on the melody of *and grace shall lead me home*. Sometimes Mom parked her car in the underground parking garage at the library. She didn't really like it though, said it gave her the creeps. She only parked there if the weather was bad or some event was scheduled, and all the street parking was gone.

I thought back to the last few hours I had shared with her. Had she mentioned anything going on? A book club meeting? Story hour? Maybe even a puppet show?

Nothing came to mind. But if the car did happen to be underground—it was a big if, but not an impossible if—wouldn't it stand to reason that it had been protected from the initial blast of energy and slime the same way I had?

It was worth a try. I planned on going there anyway. And if I couldn't find her or her car, I still intended to go to Abilene. I figured I could make it on my bike, it would just take longer—several days, maybe even a week—but what else did I have to do? Besides,

I couldn't sit around in a town full of corpses. If the silo didn't pan out, I'd just make a hard left and head to Colorado. There should be grocery stores full of food for the journey.

But I hoped I'd find Mom, Dad, *and* a car. I was certain we could outrun any Taker in a car. On my bike, it might be a lot trickier; and if new sky holes opened up, with that killing noise, Snake and I would be nothing but toast.

At least I had a plan. No matter what the people in the other room were going to do, I had a plan. *Carry on, boy. Carry on. Grace will lead you home.*

I patted Snake's head. Mom and Dad, even Cade, would be surprised at how focused I'd become. *Especially* Cade. He'd always considered me little more than his wingman.

A moment of doubt washed over me. Could he still be alive? Wouldn't it be great if he were? But no, the carnage in the gym had been the worst. Best not to even go down that memory road. Thinking Cade might have escaped when all the others had not, that was just childish. Still, I should've stopped for two seconds to find out for certain if that leg belonged to him. But if I had, I probably wouldn't be here.

I tightened my jaw and carried on. My Dynamo flashlight and some matches went inside my backpack. The pain pills went there, too. I hadn't even had the chance to crush any for Kevin.

Snake watched as I quietly pushed the screen off my bedroom window and crawled through. His doggy toenails made tiny clicks on the sill when he followed me out.

Once again, we were on our own.

CHAPTER ELEVEN

On The Run

The night felt as soft and quiet as a roll of cotton batting, the kind Mom used when she made her artsy quilts. My footsteps were inaudible in the deep grass beneath my bedroom window. With Snake at my heel, I crept around the outside of the house, pausing only to pick up my old bike from the side yard. When I picked it up, flakes of clear glaze showered the ground. Thank goodness I hadn't put it in the garage yesterday like I should have. I hardly ever rode it anymore. But every now and then, I needed to get somewhere in a hurry. Like to Cade's house yester-day—*yesterday?*—to help him with his PowerPoint presentation.

Walking it through the yards, I stuck to the shadows, relying on Snake to tell me if anything lurked nearby. I wondered how long it would be before the others missed us. Leaving them there in my home was a very difficult thing to do. But I had no choice. Trust was gone. Rules were gone. A dead man lay in the dining room floor. I just wanted my folks.

Well away from the house, I threw my leg over the bike and began to pedal slowly. After the black swarm disappeared back into the sky, there had been little evidence of the battle that had killed Kevin. Maybe I should have brought one of the guns. The rifle had been completely effective against the Taker.

The Big Five Sporting Goods Store wasn't too far away. It wouldn't be difficult to veer over a couple of blocks and see what sort of weapon I could get. Or maybe I should just stick to my original plan to go to the police station and sheriff's office. Both were downtown near the courthouse. Not too far from the library.

They had weapons, and I was pretty sure they also had a huge basement. Maybe there were people alive there, and if there weren't any, then it wouldn't matter if I took a gun or two. Apparently, we were all going to be thieves now.

Snake trotted along silently. His natural gait made him appear to be walking on tiptoe. I wondered if it was a trait of the bulldog breeds, or if it was peculiar to Snake alone. Maybe that's why he was called Snake, because he was as silent as one.

We progressed slowly, examining each shadow to make sure it didn't move before riding into it. The moon was bright, but clouds scraped the edges of it now and then, and when one happened to cross its face completely, the night became as black as a cave. There were no working streetlights, no yard lights, no porch lights. Only two more blocks to Big Five. Wouldn't hurt to check it out. I'd feel safer with a gun of some sort. Downtown was quite a distance, yet.

I came to the end of my street. There had been only two more cars dead in the road, and both of them had been empty. I didn't ride over to investigate further, just stuck to the yards full of shadows.

We turned onto the busier street that led into town. Both sides of the wide avenue were lined with sycamores and live oaks. And just like the ones at school, every tree bristled with corpses.

The smell hit me as soon as we turned the corner. The breeze, even though it blew away from us, could not cleanse the night of the foul odors of death.

Snake stopped in his tracks. I stopped, too. I could not make myself ride beneath those trees, but the only other option seemed to be to ride down the middle of the street instead.

I glanced at the loaded branches. Many had broken under the strain. Many more had not; they held their treasures up to the sky, fleshless faces gaping at Heaven. *That could've been me,* I thought, remembering how the Taker had clasped me to its shiny chest; recalling how the sin words had pulsed within its flesh. "Carry On Wayward Son" streamed back into my brain, and I began to retch.

The rancid smell combined with the creaking, swaying branches, brought up everything I'd eaten. The partially digested sandwiches splattered the grass. Snake looked at the mess and looked away. I was impressed. Most dogs would have been there in the middle, lapping it up.

Should've brought some water. We had bottles and bottles of Dasani in the pantry, but I hadn't thought to grab them. *I'll have to stop at a convenience store. We will need water more than anything.*

Wiping my mouth with the back of my hand I was dismayed to find that my hands and arms were filthy with blood, and now with puke. I looked down at Snake. "I don't know any other way to get where we're going." Then I pushed down on the pedal and headed straight into the middle of the street.

As soon as my tires met the pavement, I halted. The street was littered with thousands of hard-shelled bugs. The sound of crunching beneath my tires grew so loud I couldn't go on. It had to be because of the trees. It stood to reason there would be more insects where there were more plants and trees.

I wondered if this could be the thing that would finally wipe out the cockroaches. My biology teacher had said they could withstand even a nuclear winter. They would probably survive this. Their natural habitat was under things. I guess there was something to be said for that after all.

It took only a few seconds to go the two blocks.

Nothing leapt out at us; nothing shambled into our path.

Big Five was in a strip mall where the avenue intersected Main, the street that would take us to the library. The high school stood a few miles the other side of town.

I sat on my bike at the edge of the store parking lot. The black asphalt was patchy in the moonlight. In places, the insect bodies were drifted deep like dark snow, especially beneath the small, decorative pear trees that dotted the mall's landscaping. Guess they're not the right kind of tree to hold a body.

Everything appeared normal, except for the lack of light and the handful of cars parked willy-nilly. I figured they must've been driving along when the world burst open and drove them off course.

Snake sat beside my bike's front tire. We'd been moving so slowly he was barely panting.

Suddenly I had reservations. We might be better off to get a gun at the PD or Sheriff's department. These would be locked up anyhow. *And where were the people who worked here?*

That thought nagged me most of all because the store should have been open when the world ended. *So where were all the people—over on Sycamore Avenue, decorating the trees?* It seemed possible. This whole area appeared quite clean compared to what I'd seen outside my school. For some reason, that fact gave me more pause than if the ground had been dusted with human corpses instead of insect corpses.

But we might need a tent and a camp stove if we're going to be traveling on the interstate. I sucked in my doubts and prepared myself to enter. I thought we should also pick up some other camping supplies, too, since we didn't even have a bottle of water or a sleeping bag. *Carry on, son, what are you waiting for?*

"Okay," I muttered. "Here we go."

I rode past an SUV with its tires pointed hard to the right. The driver's door was open but there was no driver. I spied an empty car seat in the back. It made my shoulders hunch up as if from a blow. I hurried on, avoiding the other vehicles completely.

Snake stayed right with me. His toenails did not click on the asphalt. It was odd all the things I noticed now that the world had gone silent. I thought of the pink iPod I'd left on the floor when I saw the shadows of Thad Stewart and the others crossing the driveway. I didn't even get a chance to see if it worked, though I'm certain it wouldn't since no other electronic device did. Nevertheless, the thought of it lying in the floor, discarded, made my scalp prickle. It had been at that very moment that my home had been invaded by the only living people I'd seen since the school.

I stopped in front of the big double doors of the store. I was not surprised when they didn't open automatically the way they usually did. I knew I could simply push them open. I'd been inside when the electricity went off back in the winter during an ice storm. The question was, did I really want to go in there now?

Snake gazed up at me, patiently awaiting direction. "You're no help with decision making." I laughed nervously. "But you're a big help when something needs biting." My little joke fell flat, even to my own ears.

Okay, time to carry on, Jack. Time to grow a pair and go in and get a tent and a canteen and whatever else we might need. Maybe they even have one of those collapsible dog bowls I saw advertised on TV.

I realized I had begun to hold entire conversations in my mind, and sometimes out loud as well. But it helped me think and goaded me into action.

Okay, that's enough. Here we go.

I pulled my Dynamo from my backpack and squeezed the handle to turn the wheel inside. Then I parked my bike and pushed open the automatic doors—they were heavy, and I had to push them in and then pull them apart—and voila! The two of us strolled right through.

The smell of death coated everything inside the closed-up store.

This is a bad idea.

My beam of light winked off a metal clothing rack. Breathing was near impossible. All around was nothing but bleak silence and poisoned air. The only sound came from my fist constantly squeezing the Dyno light. I peered around as my eyes adjusted to the gloom. The round metal racks had rods that radiated out from a center post like the arms of an octopus. Some of the posts held the half-eaten remains of citizens who hadn't been fortunate enough to die in the initial onslaught. The odor of blood mixed with feces was completely overwhelming.

I began to back away. I should have known better.

The doors were slowly closing back together from the sheer weight of the heavy glass, but from the corner of my eye, I caught the movement of clothing.

A Taker with garnet eyes and pulsing skin appeared to be trying to pull on a jacket that was still attached to the rack.

As I noticed it, the thing also noticed us.

One arm jammed inside a jacket sleeve, the Taker lunged forward. The jacket remained connected to the rack by a slim cable meant to prevent shoplifting.

My hand shook and the light wobbled.

I didn't see any more monsters, but the pools of darkness swallowed the width and breadth of the store. They could be anywhere. There could be dozens. Hundreds.

What was I thinking coming in here in the dark?

In my heart, I had been convinced that the things liked the outside, not the inside. Up until now, I'd only seen the one inside the school gym, and it had been injured. Now, here was one looking extremely healthy and trying on *clothes*.

The cable holding the Taker's jacket drew taut, and I prayed it would hold the thing like a leash. But no, it kept coming. It didn't even notice when the rack turned over with a crash. It never even acknowledged the ripping of the fabric. When the rack jerked to a halt after becoming entangled with the legs of other racks nearby, the monster didn't even slow.

I pushed and pulled at the doors. They opened sluggishly, their weight seeming even heavier than before.

The thing was coming. I heard the solid ripping of fabric. Snake and I slipped through the door gap just as the Taker lost the now-sleeveless garment. I grabbed my bike and pedaled madly.

The monster slammed into the almost closed doors.

Snake must not have seen it inside. Maybe the horrid smell prevented him from sensing it. I pedaled so fast the wind cooled my skin. Snake kept pace beside me. When we made it across the parking lot, I had to stop and look back.

The Taker continued to push at the doors almost comically. In its ignorant haste, it had pushed too hard and jammed them up. The trick was to push inward while pulling apart at the same time. I raised my face to the stars and mouthed a silent thank you. *No more buildings. No more buildings, they're nothing but traps.*

I glanced back once more. I could barely make out the glowing red eyes of the creature as it managed to pull the doors apart.

It seemed easy for them to learn—and to adapt. For some reason, that reminded me of cockroaches, too. I stuffed the flashlight back in my pack and clasped the black rubber handgrips of my old bike tightly. I didn't even notice my sore palms anymore.

Cockroaches. Just overgrown cockroaches that eat everything in their paths. I ignored the crackling of glazed bugs beneath my tires but swerved sharply to avoid the stiff body of a large gray dove. The clear glaze was much more prevalent in the moonlight. It gleamed just like a mirror.

CHAPTER TWELVE

Traps!

We rode straight down the middle of the street all the way to the library. I went so fast my feet kept slipping off the pedals.

After a few minutes, I realized I couldn't hear Snake panting along beside me anymore. "Snake!" I called out. "Where are you boy?" I waited expectantly, knowing full well the dog was deaf, needing to call out for him anyway.

Snake did not appear.

I halted in the middle of the road and checked out the surroundings. I'd become so adept at trying *not* to see everything, trying not to see the dead people hanging from every tree and lamppost, that I didn't even realize I'd ridden right into the library parking lot.

There were lots of cars. Most had broken windows, and many had bodies still inside. I rode slowly through the lot, searching for Mom's Ford Focus. It wasn't there. Either she'd made it away, or she'd parked in the underground garage.

I cruised past another row of cars. In the moonlight, I could see bodies, many of them children. If a cloud were to cover the moon, it would be pitch black without the streetlights. I gave a quick thanks for the bright moon. Then I dug out the old Dynamo and gave it a few squeezes. Why were there so many dead people here?

I hadn't seen this many corpses in one place unless they were hanging from things. Did it mean readers were more susceptible to the vibrations that had only stunned many others? Did that leave them open to the waves of Takers that preyed on the survivors?

That seemed like a silly idea, but I couldn't help it, my mind kept constantly searching for reasons where there were none. Why were some windows broken and not others, for example? Did it have to do with the thickness of the glass, or the window frame itself? Were some of the windows—like those at Big 5—Plexiglas instead of regular glass? Or maybe the energy released by the rip was more powerful in one spot than another. There was no way to answer these questions. But they still circulated in my head—I couldn't stop them.

I looked for Snake again and was relieved to see him getting a drink from a birdbath at the entrance to the adjoining pocket park. Relief washed over me the way the black rain washed over the injured Taker. There was no way I could make myself go in another building alone, but I had to look for my mom.

No more buildings, my subconscious said. *Traps, remember?* I did remember. I hadn't seen any more Takers, but I knew they were there. The leftovers just didn't seem to be sticking together since the big group had marched on.

I rode up to the front of the building and pressed my face to one of the tinted glass doors. It was cracked but not broken. I couldn't see any movement inside. But the tinted windows—meant to keep out the harsh Texas sun—also kept out the bright moonlight.

I tried shining my flashlight inside, but it reflected back at me. I decided it was not a good idea. Not unless I wanted to announce myself.

Stepping backward, I was pleased to feel Snake at my heel. "Yes, or no?" I asked. "Go in or stay out and wonder forever?" Of course, I already knew the answer. It's why I came. "I have to go in," I said. Then an idea hit me. "But it *doesn't* have to be tonight, in the dark." I touched Snake's smooth head. "We'll find a place to hole up until daylight. Then we'll go in and find Mom."

Snake looked at me as if he understood. Then he wagged his stubby tail in agreement. I snorted. "Maybe you have ESP to make up for your deafness. Or would that be DSP?" I'm not sure why

I suddenly felt so light. Maybe it was because we'd skirted death again—in Big 5—or maybe it was because we were outside the library, one of my original goals. Or maybe it was just hysteria creeping in. Whatever the reason, I couldn't help it. I felt giddy and alive. I touched Snake's head again, and we made our way back to the park.

My mom had worked at the library forever. I knew the little high-walled park next door like the inside of my own bedroom. Puppet shows were performed here during the summer. As I got older, I would sometimes help Mom set up the portable stage. The park might be a good place to curl up and catch a few winks. But there were dead people in the trees, at least in the ones out here.

Anything could be in there, behind that wall.

Even my mother.

I decided to try my luck with the cars instead. A couple of them had windows still intact. Some were empty. We could get inside one and lock all the doors. And if, by chance, there were keys in the ignition, we could try driving one. It wouldn't be stealing. Not now. I didn't let myself think of Marla and the pills. That was different.

What if one of the cars had keys? The thought of a car engine in the new silence was frightening to consider. I could imagine hordes of Takers flocking to the sound of a living person trying to start a car. Sitting in one right out in the middle of the parking lot seemed iffy, too. Like tempting fate.

So find one that isn't right out in the open.

I gazed down at Snake. "All we can do is try."

We located an SUV at the edge of the lot. The brick wall around the little park created a short blanket of shadow. I could hardly believe our luck. No one was inside the vehicle, and the doors were closed, but not locked. One of the benefits of living in a small town. I opened the passenger door as quietly as possible and shined my light all the way to the back. It was empty.

I clicked off the light to keep from having to squeeze the handle again. I wondered if the person who owned this vehicle had brought their lunch to the little park to eat. Lots of people did that when the weather was nice. I motioned for Snake to get in, and then debated a moment about my bike. I lifted the SUV's hatch, slid my bike inside, and closed it as quietly as possible. Then I coaxed Snake into the back seat, shut the door and crawled into the still open passenger side.

Once we were in, I locked all the doors and took off my backpack. My belly growled, but I'd never had the chance to load up any food.

There were no keys in the ignition. I flipped down both visors and felt under the seats, but there didn't seem to be a spare. Mom kept a spare key in a magnetic box in her wheel well. "But that's going to come to a halt when I get my new car," she always said. "Because it will be one of those fancy ones with the keypad on the door so I can never lock myself out!" It had been a running joke. Mom was the world's worst about locking herself out of things.

I attempted to swallow the lump in my throat. *She has to be okay. And Dad, too.* But I knew the odds of finding them both alive were extremely slim because if they were alive, they would have found a way to get to me either at school or at home. I knew that as well as I knew my own name. I just had to keep reminding myself from time to time.

Angrily, I yanked open the glovebox. A bottle of water rolled out into my waiting hands. I hugged the bottle to my chest. I hadn't realized how thirsty all the pedaling had made me.

There was nothing else in the glovebox, but it made me believe I'd been right about the owner having stopped for lunch. I pushed the release and opened the center console. There were only papers and what appeared to be a first aid kit in a small white box with a red cross on the lid. I picked it up and beneath it found a stash of energy bars.

A healthy snack. That was okay with me. I ripped open a honey-nut bar and shared it with Snake. The other two went into my backpack.

I unscrewed the cap on the water and sipped slowly, willing myself not to gulp. Then I poured some into the center drink holder for Snake.

He lapped it delicately.

When finished, I tossed the empty in the floorboard. Then I crawled into the back seat with Snake, examined all the nooks and crannies in the doors and in the fold-down rear console, but I could find nothing except some loose change and a couple of old napkins which I used to try and clean some of the gore from my face and hands. When my spit bath was done, I pulled a clean t-shirt from my pack and changed. The other one smelled like death.

Propping my feet on the console, I leaned back with my arm around my dog. Eventually, we both dozed, but only in short stages. It was just too quiet. At home I always went to sleep with my music on, or with the sound of my folks watching TV in the other room. The lack of noise was disconcerting. I jerked awake every few minutes in a panic, certain something was there. But the only thing I saw each time was my buddy, Snake, snoring softly on the seat beside me.

As I sat there, waiting to fall back asleep, I observed the sky, wondering what was going on out there. The moon rode high and mighty above the trees, and above the black scars where the monsters fell through. When I reclined just right, I could watch it. It looked the same as always, as if nothing at all had happened. It made me think that perhaps it *was* just Eden under attack. That maybe in the rest of the world, the apocalypse was still just a pos-sibility instead of a fact. It was a comforting thought. But it was a cold comfort. Just like the big old white moon.

Watching the sky as I struggled to sleep, I couldn't stop thinking about my school, and my friends, about my parents and the night-mare that seemed to have taken them from me, and then I thought about all the things I'd seen and done in the past few hours. I realized I could choose to accept it all as real so that I could try to protect myself—carry on—or I could choose to just give up and go crazy.

That's when I heard the strains of a new song going round and round in my head. I couldn't place the band at first, and that almost drove me crazy, but then it came to me, and I wasn't surprised to find it was another of Dad's favorites—The Eagles. And the song that kept playing was *Take it Easy*.

That did it, finally, especially with the help of a loudly snoring dog, but when I awoke the next time, I could still see the image of a mangled corpse lying beneath the dining room table in my bloody childhood home. *Take it Easy?* How?

Sunlight polished the hood of the silver SUV the last time I jerked myself awake. It winked off the chrome, and I was both thrilled and dismayed to find that we'd made it through to morning. Glad the night had ended, dismayed that the morning highlighted the same horrors that were there when we fell asleep.

My legs were cramped. Snake took up way more than his share of the back seat. I yawned and rubbed the dog's smooth head. "You're a hog, you know."

He stood on the seat and arched his back in a catlike stretch.

"Can't believe we slept." I sat up and examined the area. *Thank God the parking lot is empty. Maybe they all moved on.*

I opened the door and stood beside the SUV, ready to dive back inside at the slightest provocation. The cool morning air blessed my face, but I knew it would warm up quickly. By noon it could be in the nineties, or worse. The thought of all those bodies trapped indoors in the Texas heat made me nauseous.

I dragged my backpack out of the SUV and reached inside for one of the honey-nut bars. Then I remembered opening and eating them—sharing with my buddy of course—sometime during the night when I'd jerked awake certain I was back in the arms of the red-eyed monster.

Some of the other cars probably had snacks and water, but in the daylight, I could see, for certain, that a lot of them contained much more than that.

My eye strayed to a Chevy with a man slumped over the steering wheel. No way I could go searching through those tombs. I just couldn't do it.

The library doors beckoned.

"It's time," I said. Time to carry on, time to get up, stand up. *Through many dangers, toils, and snares, I have already come . . . and grace will lead me home.*

The music grew in my head. Kansas said to carry on. Or was it Dad? He was the Kansas fan. *Okay, now you're just putting it off.* I took a deep breath.

Time to find out about Mom, one way or the other.

CHAPTER THIRTEEN

In The Library

The library was totally old school. There were three tinted glass doors running across the front of the building. I pulled open the one in the middle. The stench of death coated my tongue and forced me back a step. Snake sneezed and shook his head. The door closed slowly. Snake sneezed again.

"Sorry, buddy," I said. "We have to go in. Even though it might be a trap. Even though I vowed not to go inside any more buildings. Even though I'm almost positive no one could be alive inside a place that smells that bad, we still have to go in." I reached for the door handle again.

The dog seemed to understand. He waited while I opened the door a second time, holding it wide in hopes that some of the odor would escape. After a moment, inspiration hit, and I pulled the heavy trashcan over and used it to prop open the door. Then I pulled the neck of my shirt up around my nose and breathed in and out a few times.

Better.

I settled my backpack a bit more comfortably across my shoulders and then took it off to dig out the flashlight.

Not waiting for Snake, thinking the dog would surely follow, I strode into the foyer and began squeezing the handle of my Dynamo. I'd been in the library hundreds of times. It had always been one of my favorite places, quiet, peaceful. But this was bad. This abnormal stillness coupled with the stench of death was alien to me now, a perverse mirror image of a place that had always been almost holy.

Carry on, Jack. Dad's voice.

My flashlight picked out shadows of tables, shadows of chairs, even the shadow of the huge ornamental fig tree in the corner, but there were no bodies visible. Nor were there any Takers.

Where would she be, Dad? Where? Kansas sent me another verse telling me to carry on. I heard the click of toenails on tile and turned my head just in time to see Snake tiptoeing across the threshold. I couldn't suppress a smile—I'd known he would come—even though it had to be so much worse for him with his sense of smell being a thousand times greater than mine. I turned back to the job of finding my mom and determining why there was such an atmosphere of death with no bodies visible.

After my eyes adjusted, I realized the flashlight wasn't necessary. The sun had climbed high enough to penetrate most of the first floor, slanting across the ancient mica-infused tile like a sundial.

I crept forward listening intently for any hint of movement. My flesh crinkled in anticipation each time I rounded another long bookshelf and gazed down its length. With every step, I grew more and more convinced that all the bodies must be in one area, and that when I found them, I would be terribly sorry. I could think of no other explanation for the horrific smell and empty rooms.

I moved through fiction, biographies, non-fiction, sports, and into mythology before I finally came upon a closed room. The door leading into the Comparative Religions room wasn't secure enough to contain the stench. This was the room that housed books so rare a docent with gloves was required to help you use it. This was the place I'd been dreading.

Every cell in my brain said *Don't Go There*. But I had to. I couldn't leave any place unsearched. After a brief hesitation, I cracked open the door.

The toxic odor made my eyes water. My hand refused to pull the door open any wider. I peered in through the narrow opening and there they were, a dozen Takers. They were moving around the crowded room, piling bodies into neat stacks like human cordwood.

I sucked in air so deeply and suddenly that a bit of t-shirt went in my mouth. This was the last thing I'd expected to see.

One of the monsters stopped its work and turned its red-eyed face toward the door. Its blue-black sin-words bobbed eerily beneath the translucent surface of its skin.

I stepped backward, losing my grip on the knob, almost tripping over Snake.

The monsters weren't the worst things in that room.

The worst thing was Mom's favorite sweater. The turquoise one. The same one she was wearing when she dropped me off at school yesterday morning. I thought of the turquoise earrings in my pocket. Maybe she'd meant to wear them but couldn't find the missing back. Without a thought for safety, I grabbed the doorknob and pulled.

I had to look again.

Her body was near the bottom of the stack beneath the window.

Her red-gold hair hung down across her face. I recognized both her hair and her sweater. She always said she'd got her red hair from her Irish ancestors, despite her Native American blood. Sobbing, I turned and ran, my backpack smacking my spine like a large tumor.

Without realizing where I was going, my intuition took me back through the main room toward the stairs that led to the basement and the parking garage.

Suddenly, I became aware of Snake's growling.

Shadows of Takers crawled across the wall toward us.

I made a U-turn back toward the front door. My breath felt as hard as diamonds. The things were impossibly silent. *They must be telepathic.*

Snake bumped my legs, almost tripping me, nudging me, making me veer to the right, away from the entryway.

That's when I realized I could no longer see light slanting across the tile floor. The Takers had converged on the front of the building—they were completely blocking the light.

I gave up and followed Snake. I had no choice. He seemed to know where to go. I knew every inch of the public areas of the library, as well as some of the private ones, so I was fairly certain he was leading us to the exit through the executive offices wing. *But how would he know that?*

The big dog never hesitated. He made one maze-like turn after another until I began to fear we were lost. Then I caught a whiff of fresh air and figured Snake had simply been leading us toward it, getting as far away from the smell of death and Takers as possible.

In two more turns, we came to the side door leading into the parking lot. The air smelled almost normal. I reached down and touched Snake's head in thanks. He rolled his eyes up at me, tongue lolling out the side of his mouth like a pink flag.

I pressed his head against the outside of my thigh in a modified hug. Then I pushed open the door and walked out into the sunshine.

The air was so still I could hear the shuffle of bare feet on asphalt around the corner. They were in the front parking lot, and we were in the back. If only we could have gotten to the garage. But we couldn't. And there was no way we could go back. No way. The garage entrance was covered, too.

The image of Mom in her turquoise sweater kept trying to invade my thoughts, but I wouldn't let it. I clamped down on that part of my mind. *I can't go there. Not yet. Maybe not ever.*

I touched Snake's head and we started around the opposite corner of the building where the high brick wall stood guard over the park. I had a vague notion we could enter the park from the rear, walk the length of it hidden behind the wall, and wind up even with the SUV where I'd left my bike. Then we could simply dash across the short space between the wall and the SUV. I didn't let myself wonder how I would get the SUV's hatch open without attracting the Takers' attention. We would cross that bridge when we came to it.

At the wall I took a deep breath and darted inside, right into a world of hanging skeletons. Every tree dripped with pieces of people. The shady spaces beneath the trees bloomed with body parts and bits of putrid flesh and entrails.

I pulled the neck of my shirt back up over my mouth and nose. The high brick walls trapped the odor almost as well a building. From the corner of my eye, I caught a sense of movement just like in the sporting goods store, just like in the Comparative Religions room.

Takers.

Everywhere.

But what were they doing?

I stared, unable to comprehend what was happening. Snake trembled beside me, confused, but set on go, ready to attack at the slightest provocation.

The monsters appeared to be gathering up the bits and pieces of bodies from beneath the trees. But they weren't eating the flesh; they were shoving it all into wheeled plastic trashcans, which they trundled along between them.

My jaw did the Jacob Marley thing again.

They were cleaning up.

On the far side of the park, I saw other Takers tugging remains down from the trees and stacking them up just like the ones inside the Comparative Religions room where my mom—

No! Don't go there!

I felt Snake's body quivering against my leg, and I laid my hand on his shoulder to calm him. Together we backed out of the park and took off in the opposite direction. I wondered why he didn't try to attack them. But I couldn't worry about that. I was just thankful I hadn't left my backpack in the SUV.

I can find another bike, somewhere.

In moments we were a block away from the library and the park. Then it was two blocks away, then three, until finally, we found ourselves deep in a residential section I'd never seen before.

At least there were no Takers here. They all seemed to be back at the library. Up and down the silent, tree-lined street, I could see broken branches with darker puddles of shadow beneath each tree. The air wasn't bad, but every now and then I inhaled a rancid trace.

There were no bodies, anywhere.

We slunk through the shadows on the side patio of a lovely well-manicured home.

"Mom would have loved this place," I told Snake. Then I scolded myself again. No matter how I tried, I couldn't keep her out of my thoughts. What I'd seen was real, but unreal. So unreal I might never believe it. Nonetheless, I knew I'd never ever un-see that turquoise sweater and her shiny hair hanging down.

I fell against the wall of the lovely house. Silent tears fell. I couldn't help it. I couldn't stop it. We stood there, Snake and me, and then a noise broke through my sorrow, and I forced myself to stop thinking about her and go on. Everything crashed into my brain as I walked. First the rip and the horrors at school, then the tragedy at my house, now Mom …

And just when I'd convinced myself the monsters were moving on, we came upon the crew in the park cleaning up to stay. What other reason could they have for clearing out all the carnage?

But what will they eat?

I remembered how I initially thought they should just go to the grocery store if they were that hungry—and that thought made my stomach growl.

"C'mon, buddy," I touched Snake's head. "Time for a Big Gulp." I scrubbed my shirttail across my wet face. "Then we head to the high school." Probably futile—I hated to get my hopes up again— but in for a penny, in for a pound as Gran used to say.

I completely forgot about going to the police department or sheriff's office. The sight of my mom had damaged more than just my delicate psyche. It had damaged my ability to make rational decisions. Now my only plan—my only thought—was to find my dad. No matter what.

CHAPTER FOURTEEN

Idiot . . .

The first store we came to was not a 7-Eleven with a Big Gulp machine, it was an Uncle's Convenience Store. The one I never went in because it was so far from my house.

I could see it from a couple blocks away. There were haphazard cars parked everywhere, and there had been several more pile ups, although they never appeared very violent. Instead, they just seemed to have occurred at intersections where people were looking away—looking up, perhaps, when the ripping noise began—and then they just sort of crashed into each other at slow speeds.

It suddenly occurred to me that I hadn't seen any more rips in the sky. I hoped that meant no more Takers would be coming through. Because if the Army ever did arrive, I felt certain *they* could deal with the one big group in Eden. But if more monsters arrived it might be a different story. In fact, this bunch had begun to seem almost docile.

But Dr. D said the fabric between the dimensions had stretched too thin. If that were true, then it was bound to keep happening. Was probably happening somewhere else at this very moment.

Guess I'll find out when I get to another place. If I get to another place.

I cut off that line of thinking. "Negativity serves no purpose." That was a Dad-quote. *Carry on, Jackie. Carry on.* That was a quote from Dad and *me*. And Kansas. That thought made me grin. The music was almost always in my head, sometimes loud; sometimes so soft I could barely feel it, much less hear it. It was comforting though, at least that much was true.

Snake trotted along beside me.

I found myself growing hungrier and hungrier the closer we got to the Uncle's Store.

There were two vehicles at the gas pumps. One was an old red Chevy pickup with spots of rust where rocks had dinged it over the years. The windshield had been blown out, and the side windows were also gone. A lanky man in a blue chambray work shirt and faded jeans sprawled on the ground between the truck and the pump island.

I eyed the truck. "We could sure get across town a lot faster if we had wheels."

Snake cocked his head. He seemed to know I was talking if my mouth was moving. Maybe he hadn't always been deaf.

Rounding the fuel island, giving distance to the dead man in the blue work shirt, I stood off to the side of the cracked store-length plate glass and peered in. I could see a couple of bodies near the counter, but no movement of any kind.

Without giving myself a chance to back out, I carefully pulled open the glass door and waited. If anything was in there, I figured it would head to the fresh air the way Snake had done in the library.

When nothing appeared, I scooted the trash receptacle over and propped the door open just like at the library. I waited a few more seconds. Still no movement. "Of course, the drinks are on the opposite side. Can never be easy, can it?"

Squaring my shoulders, I touched the big dog's head, pulled my t-shirt up like a bandit, and in we went, straight to the tall coolers that held everything from Sprite and Mountain Dew to Budweiser and Dasani. I glanced at the beer sadly. Now that I could have it, I didn't want it. I picked up a Mountain Dew and an eight pack of water instead.

From the snack aisle I grabbed packets of nuts, crackers, beef jerky, and chips. Then I spied a bag of powdered donuts and snatched them up for good measure. Force of habit made me turn toward the counter to pay, but there were two customers already there. No matter how long I stood in line behind them, they were not going anywhere. I wondered if they had died in here or ran in from outside to get away from the noise. I also wondered why they hadn't been eaten.

From the condition of the trees near the parking lot, it appeared bodies *had* been hung up along the streets. *So why not these two, and the man at the fuel island? Why do the monsters only take the living and not the dead—and why not any animals? What do living people have that animals and dead people do not?*

Souls, of course. I looked down at Snake. "Sorry buddy, but that's what I've always been taught. Animals don't have souls. And when a person dies, his or her soul is immediately released." A vision of my mom's soul leaving her body in the library entered my brain. *Is* that *why they eat only living people, in an attempt to capture the victim's soul at the moment of death? Does it* work? *Have they got new souls now, and that's why they're cleaning up?*

The questions and ideas nearly overpowered me as I stood there in that reeking store. And then a new thought occurred. *Is that why some are still killing and eating survivors—like the one at my house that tried to kill Marla and me—because not all of them have got their new souls, their second chances, yet?*

The ideas were flowing so fast and thick I was reminded of the Native American custom of going off in the wilderness and fasting in order to have visions—to seek answers to life's questions. I'd read that some eastern religions did it, too. Maybe my involuntary fasting has led to these ideas—

A new song flowed into my head along with the ideas.

> *Whatever my lot,*
> > *thou hast taught me to know,*
> *it is well, it is well,*
> > *with my soul.*

Gran. That was another of Gran's old hymns. "It Is Well with My Soul." Great hymn. But what does it mean?

I stepped away from the counter, anxious to be away from the dead people lying nearby. "Guess I don't need to pay. C'mon." I touched Snake—to make sure he followed—in what had fast become a brand-new habit. As we exited, I saw the dog food aisle and rushed back to grab a small bag of Purina.

Outside, my chest loosened up as I tore open the donuts and stuffed three into my mouth at once. Snake *woofed*—something I hadn't heard before—and I gave him a donut, too. He gulped it down and threw his head back, once, in a distinct gesture that let me know he needed more of that.

I tossed him another as we crossed the parking lot back toward the fuel islands and the red pickup truck and the lanky man in the blue shirt.

Is it possible? I had to find out. I skirted the man. He appeared to have fallen to the pavement on his knees first, then onto his side. His upper body was twisted as if he'd tried to shield himself from the sound of the universe shredding. I crossed around to the passenger door and opened it up to look inside. The empty ignition mocked me.

I shoved all eight bottles of water and the snacks inside my backpack, and then placed it, the Mountain Dew, and the bag of dog chow on the pickup's seat before striding directly back around to the dead man.

Standing over him, I wished I hadn't scarfed down those donuts. Just the thought of touching the man made my stomach churn. I was certain the keys would be in his pocket. I just had to get them. I reached down and turned him over. He was surprisingly heavy. Dead weight.

A soft word of thanks—*yes!*—escaped my lips when I saw the leather key fob with a single fat truck key on the ring. The man had collapsed on top of it.

I reached down and hoisted it gingerly.

In my fastidious haste, I turned loose of the man's arm and his body flopped forward, back to its original position. I leapt away terrified he was getting up to take back his key.

Snake sprang forward, but determining no threat, didn't bark, or even growl. He simply looked at me questioningly.

"It's okay, boy." My voice shook. "Let's just pray this guy had already filled the tank." I crossed my fingers, climbed into the driver's seat, and inserted the key. I sat for another moment, hoping it was the right thing to do.

What if I start it, and those creatures come pouring out of the woodwork?

Then we just gun it and leave them, my subconscious answered. *They don't seem all that fast.*

Taking the key back out, afraid to leave it alone for even a second, I walked back around to the passenger side on rubber legs and motioned for Snake to hop in the cab. The big dog gazed at me without expression.

"Don't tell me you've never ridden in a truck before."

Snake just looked at me.

I patted the floorboard. "C'mon, bud. You can do it. You're a big dog!"

He stared at my face with his round boxer eyes but didn't budge.

The parking lot suddenly seemed eerily quiet. I found myself whispering. "Last chance, Snake. Either you get in there or I'm going without you." I touched his head and then patted the seat and floorboard again.

He stood, backed up, and sat down.

"What's this happy crappy?" I felt my anger rising like the red on an old thermometer. I didn't want to leave him, but once I started that engine, I might not have a choice. I leaned over and gave his collar a little tug.

Snake leaned back.

I thought about trying to pick him up and put him in the cab, but something told me that might not be wise.

"Have it your way." I stomped around the cab, climbed back into the driver's seat, stabbed the key into the ignition, tromped the gas pedal a time or two to prime it, and then twisted the key forward.

Nothing happened.

I stomped the gas pedal and twisted the key again.

Absolutely nothing.

It was as if there had never been a battery under the hood.

Thad Stewart's words, about the slime coating the engines in every vehicle they had checked, rushed back to me.

"Idiot!" I smacked my thigh with my fist. "Stupid, freaking, idiot! How could you forget that?" I climbed out and raised the hood with some difficulty.

Everything in the engine compartment glittered beneath a shiny glaze. I glanced back at the man in the blue work shirt. "I thought you were our savior."

Then I went back to the passenger side, jerked out my backpack and stumbled away. At the last second, I reached back in for the Mountain Dew and bag of dog chow. When I felt Snake bump my calf I finally slowed. A fat tear plopped onto the dog's broad head, and that's when I realized I was, once again, bawling like a baby.

CHAPTER FIFTEEN

Church

After leaving the store, I ate the rest of the donuts, sharing them liberally with Snake. "How'd you know it wouldn't start?" Snake didn't answer, he just trotted along on tiptoe until I finally remembered to stop and offer him a drink to wash down all the sugar.

It was nearly impossible for him to drink out of my cupped palm, so I began to watch for something we could use as a bowl. I felt stupid for not picking up something from the convenience store. But he was, after all, my first pet. Except for Goldie, the goldfish. She had lived a surprising number of years in her little round bowl.

We were back to sticking to the shadows of houses, and just like the park, this entire area had been cleared of bodies although I still got a whiff of them every now and then. Also like the park, there were still spots and blotches detailing where deaths had occurred.

Where did they put the bodies? I imagined mass graves like those so often found in war-torn countries. Or the ones that continue to come to light in the land of the drug cartels.

I remembered the way the Takers fell through holes in the sky, and how they had risen from the murky rain puddles, hissing. Then there was the slime-glaze . . . was that some sort of weapon, something that came in as a liquid and then changed its form upon contact? Is that how it got beneath the hoods of cars, was it also a gas, is that what the hissing noise had been? If so, why didn't it seep down into basements? *Maybe it was lighter than air, maybe it dispersed or dissipated too quickly.*

So many questions . . .

Is this a new kind of war? *Can you have a war if you don't know the enemy?*

As my feet led me north, I allowed my mind to whisper thoughts of hope that I would somehow find my father alive, and maybe my Aunt Edna. But my rational side always pulled me back. *Not gonna happen*, it said. *Not Dad, anyhow. Edna, maybe. Not Dad. He would've found me by now. He would've found Mom, too.*

I glanced down at Snake. Hard to believe it had only been two days since I found him. It seemed as if he were part of me, somehow. I touched him again, knowing I could not have left him at the gas pump. *It is well with my soul,* I thought, though the music remained silent.

Up ahead, St. Stephen's Catholic Church crouched in the sun. Pieces of the beautiful stained-glass windows decorated the lawn. The colorful mosaic was almost as impressive on the ground as in the window.

I felt pulled to go inside. *Would there be a bowl in there? Don't Catholics drink wine and eat bread during services?* I wasn't exactly certain what went on during Catholic mass, but I was pretty sure it involved food and drink. Without another thought, we crossed the street, out of the comforting shadows of the houses.

Halfway across the wide avenue, I stopped.

No more closed buildings, remember?

At least the convenience store had plate glass so I could see inside. *Yes, and there were dead people in there. But no monsters,* my conscious mind argued. Besides, this was church. Surely it would be safe.

Sure, my other self answered. And the creatures have sin-words beneath their skin. What could go wrong?

I listened to my internal debate for a moment. Of course, I couldn't go in. What was I thinking? On the other hand, churches were places of refuge. Wasn't it possible other survivors might have gathered there?

We started walking again. Snake stopped and started with me.

There hadn't been anymore Takers. Not since the ones that had been cleaning up the town like Wyatt Earp and his brothers. I almost laughed at the notion. *The Earps and me. I'm Doc Holliday, haha.*

It made me feel better thinking of the old west lawmen who *cleaned up* Tombstone. It occupied my mind so completely I marched right up the front walk to the church. The massive doors were closed. They contained a few narrow panes in shades of gold, purple, and blue.

The silence was unbroken.

I hesitated only a moment before reaching out, grasping the heavy twin handles, and giving them a hearty pull. Snake hung back. The doors opened, and I stood alone, silhouetted in the gap, the light shining behind me.

At the rush of air, every head in the place turned my way.

The pews were packed with Takers.

The one standing nearest the altar wore a large, ornate cross on a chain around its pulsating neck. I could see the sin words there, but I couldn't read them from this distance.

I blinked and blinked again. There were shards of white light hanging near the ceiling, coming in through the now-absent windows. The monster wearing the cross started down the aisle toward me. Its hands were outstretched, palms up, in a sign of welcome. "Amazing Grace" suddenly vibrated the air. Was it in the church, or in my head? I didn't know, couldn't tell.

All I could think was, *Here's the church, here's the steeple, open it up, and where's all the people?*

The Taker-priest motioned me forward by curling its gray fingers in a come-forward gesture. The others rose to their feet.

I let go of the doors and dashed back toward the curb with Snake leading the way. Behind me, Takers poured out of the church like gray salt from an overturned shaker.

This is where they were. This is where they were hiding. But where are the people, where are all the people?

CHAPTER SIXTEEN

Reunion

Eventually I stopped running and bent over at the waist, hands clasping my knees, breath stabbing a hot poker in my side. Somewhere along the way I dropped the bag of dog chow, and it split open like a bomb, pellets of kibble flying outward like edible shrapnel. "Dammit," I gasped. "What's going on?"

I looked behind but nothing seemed to be following. Slipping off the unwieldy backpack, I took out all the bottles of water save two. That lightened the load considerably, but I didn't want to be without water.

Too bad I couldn't strap them on Snake. I measured his broad back and shoulders with my eye. *He needs a pack. No time now, but maybe later.*

We each drank some water, quickly emptying a couple of bottles between us, half of it going through my cupped palms, and then I put my pack back on, and we returned to the shadows of nearby houses.

The day grew hot. I was so confused, and I could feel the beginning of a blister on one heel. *Need to change socks more often. These probably have a hole.*

The houses in this section of town were much smaller than the ones before. But their windows were broken, too. The siding was no longer brick, and the landscaping only hit or miss. Scrawny trees and skimpy bushes bordered scabby lawns enclosed by a variety of fencing, usually chain link.

Inside one house, I thought I saw a curtain move, but when I looked again, I saw nothing but a sliver of sunlight reflecting off a loose fragment of glass.

All the people can't be dead. Surely some were in basements like me. Or like the group that took over my house. I wanted to pursue that line of thinking, I wanted to make sense of the Takers in the church, but to do that I needed someone else to talk to.

Snake was an excellent listener, but he never seemed to have an opinion of his own unless it had to do with protection, or vehicles that wouldn't start, then he could really talk the talk *and* walk the walk.

The two of us trekked on in the noontime sun.

I began to feel exposed. I also felt the beginnings of sunburn on the back of my neck. It would go well with the blisters on my feet.

The lack of birdsong and traffic noise continued to harass me. A few insects were beginning to come back. Those that lived underground or had hatched underground. Every now and then, I heard the buzz of a locust, and it made me search the skies for black rain. But these seemed to be common locusts, or cicadas as my Gran called them, the kind that only came out every thirteen years or so. *Without birds to eat them, would they take over?* I thought of the food web we learned about in science.

Snake seemed to be feeling the heat, too. The dog's long tongue hung out the side of his mouth as he tiptoed along. I began to sing under my breath just to break up the oppressive silence. I started with "Carry On Wayward Son," hoping Dad would chime in somehow, but he didn't, so I changed to "Amazing Grace." I surprised myself with the number of verses I knew. Especially since we only went to church on Christmas and sometimes Easter.

I remembered Gran singing "Amazing Grace," when I was little. It must have made more of an impression on me than I realized.

The sound of my sneakers on the sidewalk was nearly nonexistent. We had to give up walking in the shadowy yards because of the abundance of glass and interruptions of chain link. I began humming the tune to "America the Beautiful" when I ran out of "Amazing Grace," but then a different sound caught my ear.

I stopped humming and listened. *Are those footfalls?* I whirled around but saw nothing. We started walking again, and I resumed humming to throw off anyone following. But I was listening.

The sun beat down, the locusts started up, and I listened.

At the end of the block, I turned abruptly, certain I'd heard them that time. Soft, stealthy footsteps. The kind that meant someone didn't want to be heard. But still, I saw nothing.

We moved on again, and then without warning, Snake took off like a shot, his toenails digging into the surface of the rough concrete.

"Snake!" I called. But of course, he couldn't hear me. *But if he didn't hear the footsteps, why did he take off running? Maybe he saw someone when we turned. Saw them run—*

A mass of snarling preceded a volley of sharp barks. It came from between two of the houses.

"Down, Snake! Down!"

I recognized Thad Stewart's deep voice.

I would've called the dog off, but I couldn't. I rushed toward the sound yelling, "Don't shoot him!" I remembered the handgun the older man had at the house.

Half a block away, Snake had the tall man pinned against the side of a small yellow house. "Call him, Jack. Call him off!"

"Show me your hands, first." I wasn't sure why I said that. I was going strictly on instinct. "And your pockets."

The lawyer slowly pulled his pockets inside out. In one hand he held a set of keys, in the other, a handful of change. His lustrous white hair no longer swept regally away from his brow. Now it hung in greasy mop strings. His eyes were shadowed, and he bore traces of blood on his face and arms. Even his shirt was stiff and black with it. But when I looked down at his feet, I understood why I hadn't been able to hear him.

The man had traded his blister-causing cowboy boots for a pair of New Balance running shoes. They looked like the ones from my dad's closet. I expected to feel angry at the idea of the man taking Dad's shoes, but all I could manage was a sense of amazement that he had changed his shoes but not his filthy shirt. Besides, I'd learned my lesson about being stingy, and I had told him to take the socks, so why quibble over the shoes?

Even from ten feet away, I could smell him. He smelled like a mixture of blood and whisky.

His eyes were red-veined and narrow. "I don't have the gun anymore if that's what you're worried about."

I scanned the area; worried that Marla might be creeping up on me from behind. "Why are you following us?"

Snake rumbled. His forelegs were stiff, his back legs slightly bent, ready to propel his muscular body at any moment. I touched his head to let him know I was there, although I was certain he did know since he'd stopped snarling and barking. I didn't try to pull him away, though. I wanted an answer to my question.

Thad Stewart just shook his head. "Call off your dog so we can talk."

I simply looked at him, waiting. I wasn't trying to be a hard ass—I hadn't really mastered that skill. The thing was, I didn't know what to do. So, I did nothing at all. Snake, on the other hand, knew exactly what to do. He stood his ground. Bob Marley played softly in my head.

Thad started to run a hand through his hair, but at the last second, he stopped, as if leery of making any sudden movements. "Okay, I'll tell you."

I waited. I didn't like standing still knowing there were dozens, maybe hundreds, of Takers just a few blocks away. So, I attempted to hurry him. "Okay, then. Why are you following us? Where are the others?" I tried to sound tough, but I couldn't resist looking over my shoulder. The last sound I remembered hearing when I left my house was Marla threatening to kill me.

"First of all, I wasn't following you." The lawyer's voice wasn't quite as self-assured as it had been. "I'm looking for a set of wheels. If I don't find one that works, I'm headed to the hospital. I know they have underground parking. If that doesn't work, I'll go on to the police department. They also have underground parking. And guns."

Snake's hindquarters began to tremble.

I recalled how the big dog shook hands with Thad when they first met. That trust was obviously a thing of the past. I wondered what the canine knew that I didn't. Or rather, what he sensed. I also wondered how I had so completely forgotten my own plan to try the law enforcement offices.

"Where are the others? Marla? Mo? Lara?"

The attorney hung his head. "I couldn't stay with them. Not after Kevin ..."

He was either a very good actor, or he was playing me for sympathy. "But they were your employees, your friends." I watched his face carefully. "You mean you left them back there to fend for themselves?"

At that, Thad's face contorted. "They asked me to leave. I-I found your dad's Scotch. It was an unopened bottle. I had a few too many."

"They're still at my house?" I'm not sure why, but something didn't sound right. From the short time I spent with Mo, I found it difficult to believe she would give up on her boss over one night of drunkenness.

Thad nodded, but his eyes did not meet mine. He kept his head down. I wasn't sure if he was lying, or simply afraid to take his eyes off Snake. I made a split-second decision. "Okay, then." I placed a calming hand on Snake's back. He ignored me.

I didn't know what else to do. I no longer felt comfortable with this man, but I didn't know how to force Snake to back off. "We've got other plans," I said at last. "You go ahead and go find yourself a car. Maybe you will even go back and pick up Mo and Lara." I didn't mention Marla. As far as I was concerned, she was the cause of all the problems back at the house.

"What about you?" Thad asked. "You're welcome to come along with me. Two heads are better than one, you know."

That was the last thing I expected to hear. "No. I guess we'll just go our own way as the old song says. But thanks just the same." I touched Snake again, and then turned to leave, expecting Fleetwood Mac to appear in my head with Bob Marley, but they didn't.

After a moment, I glanced over my shoulder to see Snake slowly inching away. He didn't seem to want to turn his back on the man.

"Hey, Jack ..." Thad called.

I hesitated. The sun beat down on my shoulders and I was

overcome with the sudden certainty that before the rip, this would have been one of those glorious days when I might've been standing out in right field waiting on a fly ball to grace my glove, or working on the Mustang with my dad, the sun beating down on our backs as we bent under the hood, and I would've known, just known, that life couldn't get any better.

It would have been one of those moments. An epiphany, my mom might've said, a realization about a major life truth. Now, it was nothing more than a future memory.

No. That wasn't right. None of that was right. If not for the rip, I would be at home getting ready for tonight's dance. Getting ready and getting nervous. Instead, Dee was . . .

My feet dragged, and my shoulders sagged.

Snake looked around as if he had felt my mood drop.

"Come with me," Thad called again. "Or I could come with you." His voice sounded a little stronger. "Those creatures are changing. Adapting or something."

That got my attention. I stopped in my tracks, waiting for more.

"Last night, they marched down Sycamore Avenue and gathered up all the bodies. Even the ones hanging from the branches."

"I know." I turned back to face him. "I've seen them, too. They're cleaning up their mess."

Thad stared at me as if I should've been able to divine some hidden meaning from those words. I told him my theory about how some of them might have been successful in gaining new souls by ingesting the souls of their victims. I told him I thought the ones trying to hurt us were still empty.

I wanted to hear what he thought of my theory. It sounded ludicrous when I said it aloud, but I did not want to stand still very long. Standing still no longer sat well with me. I was also afraid if I kept talking, I might tell him how I'd seen my mom stacked against the wall in the library with her hair hanging down and her sweater hiked up. And I didn't want to do that. I wasn't ready to tell anyone about that. I just wanted to get as far away as possible. And I still wanted to find someone who cared about me. Someone I could trust.

But instead of Thad's voice agreeing or disagreeing with me, I heard a familiar shushing sound. It reminded me of the library. It was slightly reminiscent of the sandpapery sound I first experienced in the school basement—magnified a thousand times.

They were coming.

I began to run. I didn't wait on Thad Stewart. Neither did Snake. He passed me, and we left the lawyer to fend for himself just like he'd left the women back at my house. *Even the one who had saved my life.*

CHAPTER SEVENTEEN

Dad

Not knowing where to go, I just ran. My ears strained to catch screams of agony, certain the things would overtake the shaky lawyer easily, but I heard nothing. I couldn't even hear the sandpapery marching anymore.

Everything seemed to have stopped.

I slowed, and Snake slowed too. We'd run out of the lower income section. Now we were back into a mixed commercial/residential area. The creatures hadn't got this far with their cleanup yet because bodies and body parts were everywhere. It looked like an explosion had gone off. The gore was mixed with bits of broken glass. The mess covered almost every yard and sidewalk. Dozens of bodies hung from trees, traffic signs, and fence posts.

The decorative iron fencing around the Eden Dinner Theater had been turned into what I could only think of as a drying rack like the ones Native Americans used. I remembered pictures in our history books that showed strips of buffalo meat hanging on wooden racks in the hot sun. But I didn't think these things were drying their food. Thad said they liked to bleed their meat before they ate it.

Then they went to church.

The image of St. Stephens filled with Takers leapt into my mind accompanied by strains of "Amazing Grace." The image was so ridiculous I had to stop and get my bearings. Dr. D said they came from Purgatory. They had sin-words pulsing inside their skin. They ate only live people, not the ones who were killed by the force of the rip. And even though they sort of resembled humans, they killed without conscience.

And now they're cleaning up their mess and going to church.

My mind spun.

Following Snake's lead, I found a cool, deeply shadowed overhang outside Jim's Gallery. The stench from all the putrefying bodies was horrendous, but the heat and lack of food had made me dizzy and weak. The sugary donuts hadn't helped much at all.

I knocked a large shard of glass off the bench outside the gallery and collapsed. Then the questions assailed me: *Takers from another dimension? Repentance for their sins? Purgatory? Death, cannibalism, eating, eating sins, sin-eaters? Where did that come from, some old story? Some old custom? What is purgatory? Why are they here? And why are they cleaning up?*

I pulled our last bottle of water from my pack and shared with Snake as best I could. That's when I heard the car. I raised my head, shading my eyes with my free hand. It was the first time I'd seen or heard a vehicle since the cops came to the school. Snake watched, too, water streaming from beneath his floppy lips.

I knew Thad would be the driver. I knew it as surely as I knew my own name. And when the old Beatle's song, "Ticket to Ride," blared into my thoughts, I knew I would get in the car and go with him. I just hoped I could convince Snake to do the same.

The white Chrysler 300 pulled up even with us in front of Jim's. The windows were darkly tinted so I couldn't see inside. "Ticket to Ride" played so loudly inside my head I thought it would crack my skull. The window slid down as if greased with butter.

Thad stepped out and opened the back door. "Last chance."

I nodded. It was obvious he'd already had the car when we encountered him earlier. But did that matter? No. Not at that moment. There would be plenty of time to question him later.

"C'mon, Snake." I didn't trust the man, but my music—and the dizziness—convinced me it was time to ride.

I walked over to the car and motioned toward the open door. "C'mon." I didn't have a backup plan if he refused the way he'd done at the red truck. But Snake had his own agenda. He sauntered over and leapt into the back seat, settling his doggy butt onto the pristine leather as if he owned it.

Decision made, I grabbed my pack and scurried around to the passenger door. "We're going to the high school," I said.

Thad climbed behind the wheel. "Fine by me."

I glanced into the back seat. Snake's tongue hung out, and he panted loudly. I scrunched around, pulled down the backseat armrest, and filled the cup holder with the remains of the water. Snake slurped daintily but noisily.

Thad didn't say a word.

"We need to stop for more water. And some weapons. And then I want to hear all about where you got this car." I pushed the button to lower my window. It felt good to be in a vehicle again. I untied my shoes. My socks were wrecked. Through holes on both heels, blisters had formed and broken and reformed until the fabric of the socks was now glued to the broken skin just like Thad's had been.

He drove slowly away. There were vehicles here and there. Some with bodies behind the wheel, but most empty. Some car windows were cracked or blown out, but oddly, some remained whole. It made no sense.

Beneath one broken-branched tree in the median, I saw a handful of coins scattered across the grass, winking in the dappled rays of the sun. I suspected the flayed body had once worn pants filled with pocket change.

I clenched my teeth and began to raise the window when the sounds of bare feet on asphalt infiltrated my consciousness. I glanced at Thad to see if he heard it and then we both leaned over and looked through my window down the avenue.

A platoon of Takers was on the move, plucking bodies from trees and body parts off the ground. Many of them wore what appeared to be church choir robes.

"Drive," I whispered. "Please, just drive."

Thad did.

The Takers didn't even appear to notice us.

As we drove, he told me the car belonged to Mo's daughter who worked in the business office at the hospital. He said Mo had given him the keys so he could find the car and come back for them. He also said they already knew the hospital had been overtaken, it had been one of the first places they'd checked when they left his office. "But today," Thad explained, "the monsters were gone from there. I was able to get the car out of the garage with little problem. There were other cars there, too. But this is the only one I had keys for."

"What about people, though? Any people there?"

Thad shook his head and looked away.

"Why didn't you tell me a few minutes ago? Why did you pretend you hadn't been there yet?"

Thad shrugged. "You snuck out of the house in the middle of the night. I didn't know if I could trust you."

"That's rich," I said. Then I realized it was the same reason I hadn't gone with him. The same reason I'd left him back there at the yellow house just now. "I guess we're even then, 'cause that's why I didn't go with you back there. Didn't know if we could trust you."

He nodded. "It's a brave new world."

I decided that topic was a dead end. "Oh well. At least now we can go back and get Mo and Lara." But even as I said it, I had second thoughts. Not that I didn't want to save the women, I just didn't want to see my house again. And I sure didn't want anything else to do with Marla.

Still, I knew it was the right thing to do. "But we have to check the high school first," I said. "I've got to see if my dad is there."

"That sounds like a plan," Thad replied.

I thought he might insist on going back for the women first, but he didn't, and that made me a little uneasy. Besides, even though I didn't like imagining what it looked like back at my house, I needed to know what to expect. Of course, if we found my dad, the two of us might not go back with Thad. We might have our own wheels. I felt for the Mustang key in my pocket. "What became of Kevin's body?" *Surely, they didn't just leave it beneath the dining table.*

Thad's face paled noticeably. His Adam's apple bobbed up and down as he worked to swallow. "It's been taken care of."

"I just wondered. I mean, when we go back for the women, I just want to know what to expect."

Thad concentrated on driving. He didn't elaborate on exactly how Kevin's body had been taken care of.

I decided not to push it. First, I wanted to hear how Thad was able to get the car, and why, if there was an underground garage at the hospital, there weren't any other survivors driving around.

When I questioned him, Thad shrugged again, as if having the only working vehicle on the planet wasn't that big a deal. "For once, I got lucky. When we were there earlier—when the monsters were everywhere—Mo had told us where to enter and where the car would be parked." He stared straight ahead, a lit cigarette now dangling from the corner of his mouth. "I hurried in and got it. I didn't hang around. The parking garage was full of other cars. I figured if there were any live people, they would've hightailed it out of there. Just like we're doing."

I watched his face closely. He certainly didn't appear very concerned.

"But I thought Mo and Lara turned you out for getting drunk. Why would she give you the keys?" I was rummaging around in my backpack in search of Band-Aids as I spoke. *I should've brought the Peroxide,* I thought, and that reminded me of Mo all over again, and the events at my house. Something seemed very different about Thad, almost as if he had become a different person, and I didn't think it was just the cigarette.

"Oh, we made up after I went back this morning. She never could stay mad for long." He cut his eyes at me as he exhaled. "I promised her I'd find the car and be back for them. Of course, I never thought I'd happen on you before I made it back."

I wasn't completely convinced. I thought it more likely that the attorney somehow sneaked the keys when Mo was sleeping or something. But I didn't want to argue with him, not yet. *I'll bide my time,* I thought. *See how things feel when we go back to the house. After we find Dad.*

We stopped at a 7-Eleven a few blocks from the high school. I went in and picked up several cases of water, enough to fill the big trunk of the car. I barely even noticed the dead people lying about. Since all the windows of this one were blown out, the smell wasn't nearly as bad.

I didn't waste time, though, simply reached over the counter, grabbed some plastic bags and filled them up with food and water. I even remembered to pick up a bottle of Peroxide and some more dog chow.

Thad stood by the car and washed himself off with one of the bottles of water. "Have to find a new shirt soon." He began to load all the items into the car as I brought them out. I saw him lift a small funnel out of the way as he loaded the items, but I didn't realize how important it would become later. I was just glad he was standing watch in case the Takers caught up with us.

Snake got out and stood watch, too. I had a feeling he was standing watch on Thad. The sunshine looked like heaven spilling down to earth. I felt almost guilty for the sense of joy—or was it simply relief—that I felt. Riding in a car seemed so much safer than being on foot, hoping we could outrun the Takers every time we turned a corner and happened upon them again.

When we had stuffed the trunk full, Thad slammed the lid down and got back in the driver's seat. "We need to see about a gas can and some hose. I don't know any other way to get fuel when the pumps don't work."

Back into the store I went, walking up and down each aisle, looking for a gas can. "Guess that's one thing they don't carry," I muttered to myself. But I did find a sack of red plastic picnic bowls. Grabbing them, I headed back to where Thad waited, engine running. "Let's go." I opened the back door for Snake. Excitement flooded my veins. In a few seconds, we were underway again. This time, we were headed straight to the high school.

My excitement was short lived. The streets around the school were jammed with Takers picking up body parts. Baseball practice must have been going on—reminding me of my epiphany earlier— because the streets were lined with cars. The once silver points of the chain link fence appeared rusty and dark. The whole area was thick with Takers cleaning up the mess.

This group, what I had come to think of as a platoon, were dressed in old uniforms they must have found in the school: band uniforms, football uniforms, baseball uniforms, even shiny basketball shorts that hung down to their knees. Some had also donned baseball caps. With their sin words mostly covered, I could almost believe they were human. Nevertheless, I leaned out the window and vomited a stream of water into the street.

"You okay?" Thad asked.

I shook my head. "Can you get around the other side to the faculty parking lot? If my dad's car is there, then I guess I'll know he didn't make it out before they came."

Thad backed the Chrysler up, and we made a wide loop around the practice field, approaching the school from the other side. There were no Takers on this side. The entire area appeared clean. Not a single body in sight.

I pointed toward the red Mustang. "That's it." My throat closed up, and I felt the world turning a little too fast. It was Dad's car all right. The one we had restored together. The one that was supposed to be mine some day.

"You want to check it out? Who knows, maybe it will start."

I shook my head again. I didn't want it now. I didn't think I could force myself to open the door and look inside. It would smell like Dad's aftershave. But "Ticket to Ride" blasted my brain with sound. And then Kansas joined in. Hearing them sing "Carry On Wayward Son" was downright soothing after the jangly Beatles message.

I pulled the silver Mustang key from my pocket. One of Mom's earrings fell out onto the seat. *How'd that get in my jeans pocket? I was certain the earrings were both in my shirt pocket.* I mentally scratched my head. *Okay, okay. I get the message. What could it hurt to try?*

I held the key up, and Thad smiled and made a wide U-turn. He parked right beside the Mustang. "We might be able to jump it if it doesn't start."

I didn't really think so, but stranger things had happened. I exited the Chrysler and looked around. The parking lot appeared normal. A few cars were parked in their respective spaces, but it appeared lots of teachers had already left when it happened.

With shaking hands, I stuck the big silver key into the old Mustang's door. The windows were badly cracked, but not shattered. We'd installed them just last summer. The paint was new, too. It had cost a mint to have it repainted, but Dad said some things were worth doing right so we had scrimped and saved, and I'd mowed a million lawns and finally, we'd put it in the shop and had it done.

I sucked in air, hoping a bit of the heavenly sunshine went in with it, and then I crossed my fingers and said a silent prayer for some sign of my dad.

When I opened the door, it made such a loud *screak* I jumped as if I'd been shot. That was one thing I'd forgotten. We had greased it with WD 40 a half-dozen times, but the metal groan always came back. Somehow, the door didn't hang quite right. It was one of those things we were going to fix properly farther down the road.

The interior of the car was a blast furnace.

I laid my hand on the hard plastic steering wheel and immediately jerked it back expecting to see a fat blister on my palm. Instead, what I saw was a slip of paper on the seat.

Jack and Mom—I was in the downstairs locker room. I'm coming to get you. If you are reading this, we must have missed each other. Stay safe until I find you—Dad.

My legs went out from under me, and I barely caught myself by grasping the scalding metal doorframe. Thad jumped out of the Chrysler and hurried around the hood to where I had collapsed halfway on the bucket seat, halfway on the edge of the frame, my feet on the ground outside car.

I handed Thad the note. "I can't believe it. He was in the basement locker room." I looked at the older man. "Where could he be now?" In my head, I saw the bodies stacked in the library and in the little park. *Was one of those bodies my dad? Had he made it all the way to the library only to . . .*

"Ahh, damn." Thad handed the note back. "He could be anywhere between here and there. Or he could be d—"

"Don't say it!" My emotions exploded. "Don't even think about saying that to me. I should have never stayed at my house. I should have come straight here from school. I shouldn't have messed around w—"

Thad held up one hand. His cheeks grew apple red, then purple as he stood there on the receiving end of my tirade. A large vein at his temple began to throb.

I could see that I was pushing the man to his limit, but I couldn't seem to get a grip on myself, and then I realized Thad was no longer looking at me. Instead, he was looking over me, over my head, and his eyes were huge.

I turned as if in slow motion.

Two Takers were there—right behind me—and they were reaching for me with arms that were impossibly long. Their eyes were garnet red and their skin pulsed with blue-black words that looked like *slaughter* and *death* and *greed*.

Snake must have felt a change in the air. Or perhaps he'd caught their chemical scent. All at once, he was out of the car, a whirling dervish of teeth and fur and solid-as-iron pit bull muscle. He latched on to the nearest Taker's calf and proceeded to rip away chunks of gray meat.

My first thought was *serves you right!* But then I realized the other Taker was no longer reaching for me or even for Thad, now it was going for my dog.

"N-o-o-o!" I shoved the note in my pocket and dove past Thad to make a grab at Snake's collar. For a moment, I had it. But it was like tugging on forever. I lost my grip and fell backwards against the Mustang's open door, slamming it shut with a bang.

Thad grabbed my arm and started dragging me toward the Chrysler.

"Snake!" I screamed.

Thad was attempting to stuff me into the passenger seat.

"No!" I twisted away. "Not without my *dog*."

But Snake couldn't hear me calling him. He had one Taker by the leg, but the other was kicking at him with its bare foot. It made a horrible *thud* every time that foot connected. I couldn't stand it. *The next kick will be to his head. Then it will be all over.*

Snake held on, twisting his body around just like a snake so that the thing could never connect too solidly. As before, there was no blood, not even where the Taker's flesh hung in tatters. Instead, a rivulet of clear, viscous liquid dribbled from the wound.

That's what the sin-words float in, I thought. And then I saw some of the letters. They were scattered across the ground like tiny, blackened earthworms stranded on a hot Texas sidewalk. *Homocidio, muerte, matar.* They appeared to be Spanish words.

I looked up as a third Taker joined the fray. This one sported long, shiny, basketball shorts and it seemed to be trying to catch hold of the Taker kicking at Snake. Plump new words pulsed frenetically beneath the translucent skin of this new creature's scalp. Those words were *epiphany, salvation, rebirth.*

What the hell? My mind whirled. *Did he get religion at St. Stephens? Is that why they suddenly covered themselves with clothing? Is that why their sin words are being replaced with terms of understanding and forgiveness? Or did it simply get lucky and eat someone who had a pure soul? What do they think this is, Heaven?*

"Wait!" I called out. "Wait, what are you—what are you doing?" I knew the monster could easily pick Snake up and throw him away if it wanted. I'd seen them toss grown men into treetops. Why didn't it just kill the dog and get it over with? For that matter, why didn't it kill me, or Thad? This one didn't seem to be after us at all. It seemed to be putting itself *between* us and the other two.

"Stop!" I cried. "Tell me what you want!"

Can they even hear me?

I realized, for the first time, that the creatures had no ears. I didn't know what to think, didn't know what to do. Rushing forward, I grabbed Snake's collar and yanked with all my might. The kicking Taker turned its glittery garnet eyes toward me, but Snake saw his opening. He yanked away from me and leapt toward it but got the basketball Taker instead. With one snap of his jaws, he ripped a huge piece of flesh from the thing's forearm. Clear liquid gushed out of that one too.

Overhead, one of the previous rips fluttered open. Ugly blobs of black slime rained down out of the clear sky. With tremendous effort, I fell on Snake and got hold of him again, dragging him backward with all my might. "Thad," I screamed. "Help us!" But Thad was nowhere in sight. Both he and the Chrysler were gone.

The inky rain fell to the asphalt and squirmed toward the wounded Takers. In seconds, all three were engulfed. None of them had made a sound.

I continued scrabbling backward, one hand tangled up in Snake's collar, the other steadying myself on the ground. In moments, the blackness finished its work and exploded into a plague of locusts that flew back into the thin slit from whence it had come.

The sky-hole sealed itself up. It didn't disappear completely, but it seemed to repair the damage like sudden scar tissue covering a deep wound. I recalled one of Dr. D's earlier programs about dark matter.

Is that dark matter? The doc said dark matter is the glue holding the universe together. Could it be holding many universes together? Could it be repairing the damage? Could it be manifesting as locusts? Could I be insane, and this is all in my head? "Carry On Wayward Son" blew through my mind as if in answer.

I fell to the ground, my dog in my arms.

Whatever it is, that's the stuff of our salvation. That black stuff will save us.

I looked at the sin words drying on the asphalt. A few had escaped the notice of the locust-rain. They were almost dead, but one of the letters wiggled ever so slightly.

With effort, I heaved myself up, walked over to the words and stepped on one, crushing it into dark powder beneath the sole of my shoe. "Ashes to ashes," I muttered as I crushed the rest of them. "And dust to dust."

Another Kansas song, "Dust in the Wind," bloomed in my brain. I knelt beside Snake and let the shakes take over.

Then I remembered where we were and looked around to see where the next Taker would come from. I knew they were all around us, just out of sight. And now we were afoot. Again. Without even my backpack or a bottle of water.

Shouldn't have trusted him. If only the Mustang would run, we could drive back to the house, see if Dad made it there after we left. I felt of my pockets, surprised to find that I had automatically stuck the key back in with the note.

I shambled over and popped the hood. The sun beat down on my head. It glanced off the chrome and the windshield, and when I had the hood all the way up, the sunlight bounced off the engine. Everything was glazed and shiny.

"Dammit!" I smacked the front fender with the heel of my hand, startled to find that the palm was still sore from my fall in the school parking lot two days earlier.

Two days? Only two? I thought of the spread on the cover of my bed and the way Snake had curled up there as if he were home. And then for no reason at all, I felt the hairs rise on the back of my neck. A Taker must be nearby.

I turned around, but there was nothing except Snake, sitting there, licking his wounds. I wondered if dogs bruised beneath their coats.

Looking down the road, I felt certain more monsters must be approaching, but none were visible. But what was *that*? I shielded my eyes with the flat of one hand, like a sailor looking for land. Something was coming . . .

CHAPTER EIGHTEEN

Dead Cars, Dead Bodies

From way down the street, the Chrysler barreled toward us at top speed. *We won't get back in with him. I'll just get my pack, some food and water, and—*

The car skidded to a stop mere inches from my feet.

Snake leapt away.

Immediately furious, I kicked the passenger door with all my might. "What the hell?"

Thad flung the door open. "Get in!" He gunned the engine. "C'mon. You don't know what's coming."

I looked down the road. "You left us—why would we want to—"

"Get in the damn car right now you little punk!" Thad's bloodshot eyes were wild, crazy.

I felt as if I were seeing the real Thad Stewart for the very first time.

"There are thousands of those things—every road is blocked. Now get your skinny ass in this car, or I will leave you for good."

I opened the back door for Snake, and then ran to the Mustang, yanked open the driver's door, and stabbed the big key into the ignition.

I twisted as hard as I could. I had to try.

But it was the same as the old red pickup. Absolutely nothing. Nada. Zip. Zilch. Everything had been rendered inoperable by the glaze.

"Wait," I shouted, suddenly certain Thad would drive off when he realized what I was doing. "Don't go! We're coming." I craned my head around, trying to see all four directions at once.

Snake stood beside the Chrysler's open back door, waiting to see what I would do. I touched his head and nodded toward the interior of the car. He jumped in, and I slammed the door. I was halfway inside the passenger compartment when I heard the *shushing* sound.

I glanced upward, praying for helicopters, but the sky was clear except for the wavery black slits. Down the road, I thought I could see something. It looked like a wall of gray. And it was moving our way.

Thad grabbed my arm and yanked me down into the seat, accelerating as he did. The door slammed shut, and then we were spinning around in a 180-degree turn, headed across the school parking lot in the opposite direction.

I felt Snake bump the back of my seat. "Hold on, boy," I said. Then I reached down and fastened my own seatbelt across my chest and lap.

We flew past the band hall and the field house, past the football practice field and the girls' baseball diamond.

"Where we going?" I yelled.

Thad ignored me. He seemed to be intent on getting us as far away from the Takers as possible. I just hoped we would survive the trip.

With the high school being on the north side of town, it was only logical that Thad would drive straight toward Highway 385, the main highway going north and south. When he didn't do that, I assumed we would intersect the truck loop that led back toward my house.

But when I saw the sign indicating the loop intersection coming up, I realized Thad wasn't slowing.

I tried again. "Where are we going?"

The man still didn't answer.

I began to get worried. "Aren't we getting on the loop?" Not only were we not going back toward my house in the center of town, we were also not going the direction of Abilene. To get there we would need to head east on I-20.

Thad simply kept driving north, skirting stalled cars and big rig pileups. Fortunately, the land was so flat all he had to do to go around *was* to go around. Sometimes we drove on the wrong side of the highway, and for a while we even drove straight down the grassy median.

"Stop," I said finally. "Just let us out."

After a few moments, Thad seemed to realize I was serious.

"What? Why?" His voice was incredulous. "You saw them back there. We need to get as far away from Eden as possible."

We were already a few miles north of town. We'd even left the industrial section behind. Bodies here were all dead behind the wheel. Little metal coffins. But I didn't let myself dwell on them. Apparently, the cleaning Takers hadn't made it out this far.

I wonder where they put all the bodies from the high school.

I didn't let myself dwell on that, either. My dad was not among them. He was alive, somewhere. My hand strayed to the note in my pocket.

"I said, just let us out." I tried to put some steel in my words. "We aren't going this direction. I'm going back to look for my dad—"

Thad kept driving. "Shit, son. Be reasonable. You saw those things." He glanced at me quickly. "We have a car now. We can get away. Find out if this has happened in other towns. Going back now would be *suicide*."

I snorted. "Suicide? Why are you suddenly worried about that? You *left* us back there. I *screamed* for you to come and help me, and you were *gone*." My fists itched to connect with the big man's face. I straightened my fingers and stuck them under my legs.

In the back seat, Snake began to grumble.

I didn't know if the dog could feel the vibrations of my raised voice, or if he simply responded to the tension in the air. Perhaps it was all the same thing. In my head, Kansas played "Carry On Wayward Son." I wished they would stop.

Thad shook his head. His stringy white hair flopped around, and he pushed it off his forehead and carefully maneuvered around an overturned semi. "You've got it all wrong, Jackie-boy." He shot me another quick glance. "I went to the edge of the parking lot to pick up some speed, I was going to mow them down like bowling pins." He steered the car into the oncoming lane and then back onto the correct side of the road. "But when I heard that awful sound, I had to investigate." He wiped one finger across his forehead.

I wondered if that motion was one of those telltale signs that a lie was forthcoming. I'd read an article about forensic body language not too long ago, and the author of the article made it clear that everyone—except maybe true sociopaths—had markers like that.

"I'm not lying," Thad said. *(Often another sign a lie was being told.)* "I wasn't going to leave you. I just made a mistake. When I stopped to listen, hoping against hope that it was a fleet of Black Hawks coming to save us, I looked up and I was surrounded by those things."

I just stared at him. "That's bullshit. You panicked and deserted us. I don't even thing you're telling the truth about Mo and Lara." I sat back in my seat and folded my arms across my chest. *Might have to wait until he stops. We have to leave him. He's worthless. Probably wind up killing us all. Maybe I can find my own car somewhere.*

Thad looked at me again. Then he sighed. "Okay. Okay. Maybe you're right. I did panic—a little bit. But as soon as I got to the street, I knew I had to go back." He hesitated. "That's when I saw them."

I kept my eyes straight ahead. "There's nothing you can say that will convince me we should trust you now."

"Doesn't matter," Thad replied. "We're stuck together. You and me." He pulled a pack of Marlboro's from his shirt pocket and shook out a cigarette, lit it with a yellow disposable Bic. "Me and you. Hell—" he inhaled deeply. "I don't think there *is* anyone else."

I sat like a stone. *No one else? What about Mo and Lara?* I didn't say it, though. Choose your battles my dad always said. *Choose your battles.* At last, I said, "Let's make a deal." I waited for the older man to agree or disagree.

He blew smoke out his window, checked his rearview reflexively. "What kind of deal?"

"I have to find out if my dad is alive. I mean, wouldn't you? Didn't you have a wife or some kids or—anyone?" I hated the sound of desperation that crept into my voice, but I was powerless to stop it. Each mile took us farther from my dad. How would I ever forgive myself if I just left without knowing, especially after the note?

Thad's shoulders drooped. His foot came off the accelerator just a bit. "I did," he said. "I had a family once, but when my wife left, she took the kids with her."

"So . . ."

"So, they grew up on a ranch in Montana with a stepfather." He slowed and made his way around another small pileup. Then he turned across the median without saying a word. "I want to head there now that we have a car." He shrugged. "But I guess we can check for your dad first."

I sat up a little straighter. "We're going back?"

"We'll give it the old college try." He glanced my way. "But if every road is crawling with *them*, we'll just turn right back around." Under his breath he muttered, "We need to find some hose or something anyway."

I felt so happy I wanted to cheer. Then I realized I might be trusting too easily. Maybe the man had an ulterior motive. "Hose? For what?"

"Gonna have to suck some gas, remember?" He indicated the many stalled cars along the road. "And for that, we'll need a length of hose and a container."

I looked at the fuel gauge. It stood just above three-quarters of a tank. "I forgot about the gas can and stuff. But it looks like we have plenty in the tank."

Thad lit another cigarette. "I've been thinking." He exhaled.

The smoke swirled around his head, and I was glad when he cracked open the window. I had to refrain from saying something about *cancer sticks*. My grandmother had died of lung cancer, which made my mom fiercely anti-smoking.

I was becoming aware of just how much my parents had rubbed off on me. But I didn't want to cause more hard feelings with Thad, especially now that we were headed back toward town. "What were you thinking?" I prompted.

Thad opened the window wider. "I'm thinking we should probably avoid big cities. I mean if we had that many in our little town, I wonder how many are in the bigger cities. Know what I mean?"

I didn't. Not really. "I don't think I'm following."

Thad tossed the lit cig out the window.

I opened my mouth to protest—West Texas had been in a drought for years—throwing a lit butt out the window was like lighting a candle. But then I looked around and decided that a grass fire wasn't the worst thing that could happen. In fact, we'd learned in science that fire could be nature's way of cleaning house.

When I thought of all those dead bodies roasting inside their shiny metal coffins, I came to the conclusion that cleansing by fire might be the *best* thing that could happen.

I killed that line of thought and tried to listen to what Thad was saying.

"What I think is this: the creatures, what was it you called them? Takers?"

"Yeah, Takers."

"Yeah, yeah, I get it. Well, these *Takers* fell right out of the sky, didn't they? But did they fall over the deserted prairie? Or did they only fall into populated areas like cities?"

I sat quietly for a moment. "I think I see what you're getting at—we don't really know if they fell into other places, do we?"

Thad snorted. "Look around, Jackie. See any aliens out here in the middle of nowhere?"

Balling my fists again, I tried to remain calm. No one but my mom or dad had ever called me *Jackie*. It didn't bother me then, but it didn't sound the same when Thad Stewart said it. "I see a lot of dead cars full of dead people." I stared up at the huge Texas sky. "And I see some of those dark places where the things might have come through."

"True, true," Thad admitted. "Guess the sonic blast happened all the way out here, but I haven't seen an alien—I mean a Taker—since we left the high school." He let that sink in. Then he continued, "Anyhow, my point is, I think we should get our gas can and hose now, and from here on out, avoid cities altogether. If those things fell mostly into inhabited areas, then cities might be death traps.

If they didn't," he reached down and turned on the radio. "Then we should be picking up a station, soon."

I watched as Thad scanned all the radio stations on AM, FM, and Sirius.

The highway spun out in front of us on waves of heat-mirages punctuated by stalled or wrecked vehicles. I wanted time to travel backward. I wanted nothing more than to be riding in the shotgun seat of the past with my mom and dad, going to Gran's house in Colorado. But when Thad's scan of the radio picked up nothing but nothing, my little daydream came to a halt, and my guts clenched up into a hard mass of anxiety. Again.

Somehow, hearing all that white noise scared me almost as much as seeing my mom's body stacked in a corner like so much cordwood—though I suspected I was still in shock on that one.

Now, I realized that all along, in the back of my mind, I'd been harboring the idea that the attack on Eden had been an isolated event, and that once we were out of West Texas, things would be back to normal. But if even the Sirius satellites were out of commission that was a good sign it wasn't just our corner of the world after all.

Whether I wanted to believe it or not.

CHAPTER NINETEEN

Driving

Aw, hell." Thad's voice was almost inaudible. Nevertheless, the timbre of it infiltrated my brain. I'd been dozing, chin on my chest, for at least a couple of minutes.

I yawned and rubbed my eyes.

Then I rubbed them again.

A large mass of Takers was headed straight toward us. There were so many it seemed as if they'd been formulated on a CGI green screen.

The entire horizon appeared to be throbbing just like the gray wall back at the high school. I thought I could even see their millions of sin words pulsing in the late afternoon sun.

Thad slowed to a complete stop. "I don't really care for these odds, Jackie-boy." His hand hovered over the console gearshift.

"Is there another road into town?"

Thad put the car into reverse and executed a jittery U-turn, careful not to get hung up in the low median. "Only the one by the high school. And we tried that already."

From the corner of my eye, I saw Snake dig his claws into the buttery leather seat and hold on.

Neither of us said a word until the Takers were out of sight again. When they were no longer visible in the rearview mirrors, Thad's foot eased off the accelerator.

"Watch for a semi with a sleeper cab," he said. "They usually have supplies, maybe a gas can, some hose."

I knew the answer, but I had to ask the question anyway. "We aren't going to try another approach into town? I know there are back roads. Farm-to-markets or something."

Thad lit up, inhaled deeply. "I'd like to Jackie, I really would. But I just don't think we have enough fuel to be driving around looking for a back road into a town that now belongs to *them*."

I slumped down.

Snake whined until I dangled my hand behind Thad's seat so the dog could nuzzle it. I knew the man spoke the logical truth. But my dad was back there.

Thad tried to ease the pain. "If your dad made it, he'll head toward his parents—didn't you say that's where you wanted to go? To your grandparent's house?"

I nodded, wondering what Dad would think if he made it home and found Kevin's body lying in a pool of blood beneath the dining room table. I wanted to ask Thad how they had *taken care* of it, but I didn't really want to know the details. I felt certain whatever Thad told me would be a lie. Besides, I didn't trust my own voice. If I opened my mouth, I might start to blubber like a two-year-old.

"Okay, then," Thad said. "He'll expect you to go to the grandparents. He'll look for you there. It just makes sense."

I looked in my rearview mirror. There was nothing to see but endless prairie highway and vehicles parked this way and that in the impartial West Texas sun. I wiped my leaky nose with the edge of my t-shirt, and then faced forward again. What else could I do? The fields on either side of the highway were beginning to show livestock, dead where they'd fallen. One field contained an entire herd of Black Angus cattle bloating in the heat. I thought they might've belonged to the Diamond S Ranch. I knew it was out here, somewhere.

After a while, I was grateful for the hot air rushing in through Thad's open window. It was like a song without words. I song I had to make up for a change. *Song of the road. Song of the plains. Song of the prairie. Song of grief, of death, of terror. Song of tires on pavement. Song of a dog snoring in the backseat.* That was how my mind entertained itself in the absence of my usual music.

I awoke a second time when the Chrysler veered onto the rumble strip along the edge of the highway. Thad jerked the wheel and brought the car back onto the road with an overcorrection that sent us skidding into the opposite lane directly toward a semitruck jackknifed across the median. I planted my palms against the dash and my feet against the floorboard. *Hang on Snake!*

Thad twisted the steering wheel into the slide and let his foot off the accelerator.

The car began to slow, but we were still headed toward the truck.

With the heel of his hand, Thad twisted the wheel ever so slightly back the other direction, then let nature take its course. The car continued to slow, drifting toward the truck at a much slower pace. There was no way we could miss it.

Thad began to apply the brakes gently, barely bumping them with his foot.

I squeezed my eyes shut, not wanting to see the crash.

The next thing I knew, Thad was opening his door.

We had ghosted past the semi with inches to spare.

The white haired lawyer walked over to the truck and began to urinate beside the open—empty—cab, watching in seeming fascination as his stream darkened the dust beside the highway.

I finally found my legs and climbed out of the Chrysler.

"Whoo-hoo, Jackie-boy, scared me there for a minute." Thad's voice sounded jovial, on the verge of hysteria. "Wouldn't mind myself a little drink after that ride. Thought sure we'd survived the aliens only to wind up smashed to a pulp on a deserted stretch of Hwy 385."

I tried to tune out the sound of the man's pee splattering beside the pavement.

"Anyhow," Thad continued, zipping up as he spoke. "Maybe this guy had a gas can or something." He leaned down and gazed inside the open cab.

I shielded my eyes against the westering sun and peered all around. *Where could the driver be? Most of the vehicles contained bodies. Unless he had somehow survived the rip.*

Then I saw something way out in the field. A clump of mesquite trees bent almost to the ground. As if something heavy hung from their thorny tips.

I pulled my gaze away.

Everything stood still. There was no movement save a few blades of wild yellow grass flickering back and forth in the bar ditch and something farther up on the east side of the road, spinning every now and then on the breeze.

"Hey," I called. "Can you make out what that is up there?"

Thad shielded his eyes and looked. "Not really. Looks like a broken sign."

I thought that sounded likely. But highway signs were taller, weren't they?

I didn't know why this particular twisty thing made me so curious. It just looked out of place. It wasn't a plastic bag caught on a cactus. It wasn't an old soft drink cup or burger wrapper blowing across the road. It was something stuck up above the ground, twirling gently, metallically. Every other revolution reflected the rays of the sun right into my eyes.

I started walking toward it.

It reminded me of a pinwheel, one of those old-fashioned toys my granddad gave me when I was a kid. The kind that had a few shiny blades fastened to a wooden dowel like a little windmill. That's what this looked like, only this one had only a single green metal blade going around and around on a short silver pole.

I quickened my pace. Snake trotted along at my heel. He'd jumped over the seat to follow as soon as I stuck my leg out the passenger door.

When I got close enough to see that the object was indeed a green metal blade, I was sorely disappointed. It was only a single-name highway sign barely hanging onto a silver pole by one large bolt. It was just a little taller than me.

I stood staring, waiting for it to complete its revolution in the gusty breeze. But as I was about to turn around and head back to the car, the sign creaked to a stop, and I was able to read the name of the town to which it pointed.

KANSAS
Pop. 1,110

There must be some mistake. Kansas? But we're in Texas.

134

Population 1,110? I guess there could be a *town* named Kansas. After all there's a Paris, Texas. All at once I became aware of the return of my music.

"Carry On Wayward Son," written and made famous by the band, Kansas, had been playing in my head for some time, but I'd grown so accustomed to it I hadn't made the connection.

Kansas. Okay. I guess that's where we have to go. I don't know why, but I know it's true. My heart started to pound. I began to run. Snake streaked along beside me.

When we were close, Thad stuck his head out of the cab of the truck. "Hey, Jackie. Wait'll you see what I found!" He climbed out holding a handful of folded papers.

"What are they, maps?" I wasn't sure how to tell him about Kansas, so I followed him back to the car where he immediately began to unfold one of the maps across the hood. He smoothed the stringy gray hair out of his face and leaned close. "That they are Jackie. That they are."

Looking over his shoulder, I said, "Please don't call me *Jackie* anymore." I didn't press the point, but at least I got my two cents in. "Thank God this truck driver was old school." I thought about the weight in the mesquite tree way off in the field, but I didn't dwell on it. I was getting very good at not dwelling on things. "Hey," I peered at the map. "Do you see a town called Kansas? I think it's nearby."

Thad leaned in. "Nope. Must be too small. Why?"

I couldn't tell him that a song and a highway sign said we had to go there, so I made up a lie. "My mom's younger brother lives there. He's the black sheep of the family so I haven't seen him in a long time. But he's family, know what I mean?"

Thad hesitated. "Black sheep, huh? What makes you want to see him?"

"He might be the only family I've got left. Besides, it's on the way to Colorado, *and* Montana. And I've always liked him. He just didn't get along with my folks. Said he drank too much or something." I really laid it on thick. I hoped it wasn't too thick. The drinking thing had hit me like a bolt out of the blue. I figured Thad would have sympathy for a drunk.

He made a funny sound. "Drinker, huh?"

Got him, I thought. "Yeah, I guess. I don't know. You know how parents are, keep everything a big secret."

He went back to looking at the map. "What's his name?"

Oops. I scanned my brain for a suitable name for a black sheep uncle. "Carlos," I said. The name popped into my mind the same way music always did.

Thad's head swiveled toward me. "Carlos? What's his last name—your mom's maiden name?"

"Ramirez," I said without hesitation. Of course, my mom's real maiden name was Stanton, I don't know where Ramirez came from, but at least I hadn't said Santana.

Now Thad turned his full attention to me. "You don't look Hispanic. Not even half. You speak Spanish?"

I shook my head sadly. "She won't allow it in the house. Said she came over the river, and that's the end of that." God forgive me, I didn't know where this story was coming from.

Thad poked his finger at a fold on the map. "Don't see Kansas, Texas. But here's a spot that says Kansas, New Mexico. Looks like it's barely over the Texas-New Mexico line."

"Are we that close already?" I knew Eden was close to the New Mexico border, my family had often vacationed in the mountain village of Ruidoso, but I didn't think the two of us had driven nearly far enough to cross over yet.

Thad stabbed his finger at the map again. "We got a couple hours to go, looks to me like."

I eyeballed the route he was pointing out. We were nowhere near Kansas, New Mexico. What the heck was that sign doing way out here in the middle of the West Texas desert? The opening strains of "Dust in the Wind" began to play though my head, followed by the unmistakable sound of Dad's voice telling me to get on with it. *Carry on son just carry on.*

"I'm ready," I said. "Let me grab some snacks out of the trunk."

Thad pushed the release button on the key fob, and I went back to rummage through the food. I got the bowls out and filled one with kibble for Snake.

Thad gathered up the maps—two we hadn't even opened—and stuffed them over the visor in the open window of the Chrysler. "Well, one thing's certain, we've got to find gas, soon."

I let Snake in the backseat, and then I climbed in the passenger side and reached across to get the map again. "How long did you say till we cross into New Mexico?"

"Be awhile yet. We'll just stay on Hwy 385 until it intersects 40. That looks like it'll take us right close to Kansas. We'll have to really study it when we get to that junction." He looked at me closely. "Can't believe you thought it was in Texas."

I looked away. "Haven't been there since I was a little kid."

Thad seemed to accept that. "Think you could drive awhile? I'm beat."

My heart flip-flopped in my chest.

Drive? Hells yeah, I can drive.

I climbed back out of the passenger side and sauntered around to the driver's seat. My pulse raced. I didn't tell Thad that until now I'd only driven with my mom or dad on back roads and in parking lots. I didn't even have my learner's permit yet—maybe I would never get it now—but I could drive. Of course, I could drive.

"You sure?" he asked as he stepped out to let me in.

"No problem," I replied as he walked around and got in my shotgun seat. "You just lean on back and get some sleep." I recalled that the reason we'd wound up here was because Thad had dozed off.

On the other hand, if he hadn't dozed off, we wouldn't have found the Kansas sign or the maps. That idea gave me a start. Are we doing the right thing? "Carry On Wayward Son" blasted my brain. *Okay, okay, I get it. But if it wasn't on the way to Colorado, I might not believe it.*

Reclining the automatic seat as far back as it would go. Thad closed his eyes. "The town of Levelland is coming up soon. It's a small town—maybe it'll be safe. We need to find a Wal-Mart or automotive supply store. Get that hose and gas can before we turn off onto 40 at Littlefield. After that we'll hit the New Mexico line. I don't know too much about New Mexico. Things might get sketchy after we leave Texas. But if you see any Takers, you wake me, hear?" He opened one eye and waited for an answer.

I nodded and pushed the starter button. Takers or no Takers, I was going to drive. The smooth engine purred to life, and I backed the vehicle onto the highway. It was all I could do not to turn around and head back to town now that I had control of the car. Even though Dad—and Kansas—were telling me to carry on, I couldn't help but feel I was deserting him and the women at my house.

Then I remembered the hundreds of monsters that had blocked the road, and I tamped that idea down and lowered the back window for Snake. The dog stuck his broad snout out into the breeze.

I grinned. I couldn't help it. *I was driving!*

In seconds I had the car straightened out and headed north. When we passed the crazily whirling sign that said **Kansas, Pop. 1,110** I said a silent prayer that the next person who saw it would be my dad. *He'll make the connection*, I thought. *I'm sure he will.*

But when I glanced in my rearview mirror, the sign had already grown too small to see.

CHAPTER TWENTY

Bite Me

The road unrolled before me like a painting. There were a few cars and trucks like before, but this far north, the traffic had become extremely sparse.

I wished I had a radio or something. This new model Chrysler didn't even have a CD player. Before the rip, I'd already started compiling playlists of driving music. I examined the dash and saw the place where I would've plugged in my iPod or phone. *Lotta good that does now. I'll bet there's one somewhere that works though. That pink one wasn't slimed or anything. Maybe it had just run down.* That idea gave me a glimmer of hope that maybe I'd find another one somewhere. *Maybe Uncle Carlos will have one.* I chuckled at my own joke, and then glanced over to make sure I hadn't awakened Thad.

Just looking at the gore-spattered man caused a deep sadness to settle over me. This was supposed to be one of those first-time days; the kind you never forget. First time driving, first time to kiss a girl—an image of Dee flashed through my head—first time for, well, other things, which I wasn't going to allow myself to think about right now. *But what if there aren't any more girls my age? Wouldn't that be a joke?*

I decided not to think about that either. I felt certain there would be other girls. The Kansas sign was hope. The music was hope. Carry on, it kept telling me. Why would I have to carry on if there was nothing to carry on for? I tried to keep the faith, as my dad would've said. But still, it was tough not to brood. This was supposed to be the best time of my life.

I drove on, the setting sun painting a pink and gold masterpiece out my side window. *I'm still going to have a lot of first times. They just won't be the ones I expected.*

My foot pressed the accelerator, and I let the needle creep up to seventy. I knew it was too fast, but this was North Texas. I could see forever, and there was nothing up ahead.

In my mind, classic rock began to play. It came from my playlist "Driving Music: Classic Vinyl." Kansas was on there, but so was ZZ Top, The Rolling Stones, CCR, and even Bruce Springsteen. Dad was a huge Springsteen fan, comically referring to him as The Boss every time one of his songs came on. I tried to remember the words to "Drive All Night," it seemed appropriate now, but the words wouldn't come. They just wouldn't come.

I didn't slow down until my bladder told me it was time. I'd eaten a whole packet of spicy beef jerky washed down with a bottle of water. I tried to coast to a stop, not wanting to wake Thad in case he insisted on getting back in the driver's seat, but I needn't have worried.

He changed position, then grunted, and went back to sleep.

When we'd come to a gentle stop, I got out and left the engine running. Then I let Snake out. He'd been crunching his bowl of kibble off and on in the back seat, and now he hopped out and headed for the bar ditch to do his own business.

I opened the trunk and got out peanut butter crackers and a bottle of Mountain Dew. I gave Snake a couple of crackers and together we ate and watched the sun go down.

The prairie wind whispered in my ear and ran its cooling fingers down inside the collar of my shirt. The spokes of the dying sun radiated across the land.

I shivered, finished my drink, and poured some water in Snake's bowl. I couldn't help looking around to make sure we really were alone. The big emptiness was frightening. And the silence, the absolute lack of any type of animal or human noise, was even worse.

Every now and then, I thought I heard a cricket in the high

grass, but I never saw one. I thought about the black locusts that ate up the Takers, but I didn't think they were of this world. It still made me shudder, though. I think I was more afraid of them, of the black rain, than I was of the monsters themselves. At least them we might have a chance of outrunning, but if the locusts came, we couldn't outrun that.

I wanted to whoop and holler and run around in circles yelling something at the top of my lungs just to hear the sound of a human voice. But I couldn't think of anything to yell. Every word I might've said would have been a curse word. And that was one more place I didn't want to go.

My momentary euphoria at finding the Kansas sign and driving the car had dissipated. Thinking too much. That's all. Just thinking about everything too much.

Letting Snake back inside, I closed the door gently. The automatic headlights had come on a while back, and I fiddled around, figured out how to operate them manually—just in case—and then we drove on. I began to wonder if Thad was asleep, or dead. But then he let out a gnarly snore, and I laughed under my breath, only slightly disgusted.

The driving had lost some of its appeal. The darkness made everything different. Every now and then the highway would dip just enough to hide a rollover or a vehicle that had simply stopped working in the middle of the lane. They were so few and far between it was easy to forget to watch for them. Twice, I had to swerve to avoid rear-ending vehicles that loomed out of the darkness like prehistoric beasts.

I dropped my speed to sixty-five, then sixty, and finally to fifty-five. That seemed to be the safest speed at which I could brake quickly without slamming Snake into the back of my seat or throwing Thad in the floorboard.

When the sign for Levelland appeared, I heaved a sigh of relief. I knew it wasn't much further to Littlefield and the junction with Hwy 40 after that. Next, I saw the big blue and white sign for the Wal-Mart Super Center. But it had gotten dark already. The huge store would be blacker than a grave inside.

I slowed to a crawl.

The streets of Levelland bore the same haphazard collection of stalled and wrecked vehicles that I had become accustomed to seeing. Bodies dangled from dark trees. Dead birds littered the streets in front of my headlights, and the corpses of pets dotted some of the moonlit sidewalks.

Should I simply go on and hope for another Wal-Mart in Littlefield just a few miles down the road? I skirted a huge pile-up in what appeared to be a main intersection, careful not to look at the bodies hanging out of broken windows or hunched over steering wheels, and then I pulled the car into the Wally World parking lot where dozens of other vehicles were parked, most of them still in their slanted spaces.

If there were any of the "cleaning crews" here, they hadn't made it to this place. The dead were everywhere. Children were the hardest to look at. Several were still in shopping carts that had obviously been pushed by a parent until the sky split open and ended their lives with a supersonic explosion of killing noise.

I parked at the edge of the lot; afraid I'd run over a body if I tried to get closer to the door. "We're at Wal-Mart," I said, hoping I wouldn't have to actually touch Thad to wake him.

From the backseat, Snake whined.

"I know, buddy," I muttered. "Another parking lot outside another dark building so far from home. And we didn't even get to check on Aunt Edna in Abilene."

Thad yawned and stretched. "Good job, Jackie-boy. I mean, Jack. You got us here in one piece." He climbed out, took a whiz, and then dug around in the trunk for a snack of his own. "Give my eyeteeth for a steak," he complained.

"I just wish we had a gun. Or two." I couldn't relax. This felt wrong, as if we were sitting out in the open with targets painted on our backs. "Where do you suppose they are?"

Thad got back in the car. "Probably wiped out the place and moved on down the line." He pointed toward the highway with his elbow. "Maybe headed to Amarillo or some place with more people."

"But how do they know where the people are?"

"How does that black rain know when one of 'em is injured?"

Thad stuffed a handful of chips in his mouth. "I don't understand it, but I've noticed it happens every time. Some sort of E.T. ESP is my guess."

I nodded. "Yeah, I've noticed that, too." I finally worked up enough nerve to get out of the car again. Snake got out with me, and together, with him standing watch, I got more food out of the trunk. Eating seemed to be the only thing I wanted to do.

We got back inside the vehicle with Thad.

The moon was high now. But it didn't shed nearly enough light to push back the silent blackness enveloping the small town. A town that was now little more than an open-air graveyard.

We ate desperately, me working my way through half a box of frosted strawberry Pop-Tarts, both of us making inane comments from time to time, just to break the silence.

When the food was gone, water bottles almost emptied, I pulled my toothbrush out of my backpack and brushed my teeth, using the last inch of water in the bottle to rinse and spit outside the driver's window. It felt good. It was the first time I'd brushed in two days.

Thad leaned his head back. "Gotta pick me up one of those in the store tomorrow. When it's light. Maybe we can figure out how to get a couple guns to go along with the gas can and hose. And some beer. Could use a deck of cards, too." He closed his eyes, adding to his mental shopping list perhaps. "You know how to play poker Jackie-boy?"

"Yeah," I replied. "Little bit." *But it's not something I'm dying to do right now. Maybe in Kansas there will be someone who likes other things. God, I hope so. There has to be a reason for us to go there, right?*

"I'll take first watch," Thad said, not opening his eyes. "You get some shuteye. I'll wake you when I get sleepy again."

I looked at him in disbelief. The guy never opened his eyes the whole time he was speaking. "We could use a couple pillows, too," he murmured before he began to snore.

I sat in the moonlit car wishing for my iPad or my iPod or any damn thing. If I had my tablet and it actually worked, I could pass the whole night playing games and listening to music.

I clicked the button to make sure all the doors were locked, and then I leaned my head back and tried to emulate Thad. But every time I dozed off, I would come awake with a jerk, certain a Taker had me by the throat.

Several times, I got out with Snake and simply stood beside the car or sat on the hood. A few times I found myself running in place out of pure boredom. Once I even fell down on the ground to do push-ups, but that made me feel way too vulnerable, so I jumped back up and looked around to see what might be lurking nearby.

It was a long night. I think the reality of our situation was finally beginning to sink in, and it was killing me. Thad slept well though, only grunting and groaning a few times without waking.

Daybreak crept up as it always does, first black, then dark gray, then a lighter shade, and then miraculous sunrise.

When I realized I could feel warmth on one side of my face, I awoke for the last time; amazed I'd finally dozed at all.

Thad also woke and without preamble, climbed out of the car, drank some more water, and then walked a short distance away to where an empty shopping cart was nosed up against an evil concrete parking barrier just like the one I'd tripped over in the school parking lot an eon ago.

"Got yer list?" The man sounded jolly, a Wal-Mart pirate about to embark on a dry-land raid.

I tapped the side of my head and nodded. I did not want to go in that store, but I knew we had to.

"We'll go to automotive first," Thad said. "That's our most important chore." He lit a cigarette and exhaled. "After that, we'll pick up anything else we need."

I made some noise of agreement. For the first time in my life, the smell of cigarette smoke was tempting. Thad made it look so appealing. As if it gave him a hit of courage somehow. I almost asked him to give me one. *Look Ma, another one of those teenage firsts!* But I figured I'd just choke and look foolish.

With unspoken resolve, we chose the path with the least number of bodies. *The path of least resistance,* I thought grimly. We had to veer out toward the edge of the lot, adding quite a few steps to our journey, but it was okay. Most people appeared to have died instantly, but they always died with their eyes open. Learning that little tidbit was one first I wished I hadn't experienced.

Thad tossed his cigarette on the asphalt and ground it under his boot. "Here we go, Jack." He stepped through the broken foyer doors.

I stepped through behind him.

The interior doors were intact, and the two of us pushed against them together. Just like at Big 5, the trick was to push in, then pull apart.

All at once the doors gave and the stench that filled the gap was so overwhelming, we both rocked back on our heels, covering our mouths and noses, gagging.

Snake backed away, shaking his head.

"Godamighty, that's bad!" Thad shoved the shopping cart into the gap, still covering his nose with his hand.

I couldn't say anything at all; I was too preoccupied with trying to keep my strawberry Pop-Tarts in my belly. "Must be a million bodies in there."

Thad nodded. "Been hot, too." He took off his shirt exposing his mushy, white belly.

I looked away, embarrassed for him.

Backing up even further, he wrapped the nasty, bloodstained shirt around his head, leaving only his eyes visible.

"We aren't really going in there, are we?"

"I don't know any other way to get gas. We need that can and some hose."

I spat on the ground, trying to get rid of the vileness. Then I pulled off my t-shirt and wrapped it around my head like Thad. It did help somewhat. I looked down at Snake. "You can stay out here, if you want."

Thad was already heading back to the door where we'd left the shopping cart. "Maybe it's aired out some," he said.

I laughed harshly. I knew from experience with the Mustang that automotive was always at the very back of the store.

Thad shoved one of the doors open wider and we stepped inside leaving the cart in the gap. Snake wiggled through at the last second.

Bodies and pieces of bodies were strewn everywhere. Some were stuck onto clothing racks and gutted. Others were dead on the floor, untouched. At least some of the Wal-Mart shoppers had survived the initial blast, but then the Takers must've come in after them—maybe all that glass at the front of the store let them see the shoppers.

My eyes began to water. *How'd they get in and then back out?* I didn't have time to think about it now, but later I wanted to examine the problem of how the Takers managed to get out after bleeding so many bodies.

Thad coughed.

Snake sneezed and gagged, and I grabbed another empty cart and ran a crazy path toward the back of the store skirting bodies without looking. I tried to breathe wholly through my mouth, but it was hard to get enough air with the shirt tied on my head. I slowed down to read the aisle signs and that's when the first Taker stepped out of the clothing section.

"Lookout!" Thad yelled.

I veered to the right and kept going. *Getting that hose. Not doing this again.* I heard Snake's claws on the tile so I knew the dog was still with me but in the back of my mind, I began to worry that Thad would try to skip out on us again.

"Thad! You okay?"

No response.

I slowed and looked back over my shoulder just in time to see him duck into another aisle. A Taker lunged at me, and I shoved the shopping cart into its middle. Snake wanted to stay and fight but I kept on trucking, keeping the shopping cart in front of me like a shield.

A couple of times, I thought I heard Thad's boots on the tile. Then I remembered the guy had changed to Dad's New Balance running shoes. "I'm getting the gas can and getting the hell out of here!" I called. The shirt muffled my voice, and I prayed Thad could hear me. I felt of my pocket to make sure the car key was still there. Thad might desert us again, but he wouldn't be taking the Chrysler this time.

I heard the attorney make some sort of grunting noise. I wasn't sure if it was an acknowledgment to what I'd yelled, or something worse. I really wasn't even positive it was Thad. I wanted to go and check on him, to make certain the man wasn't in the clutches of a Taker, but I wanted to get that gas can even more.

And suddenly, there they were, stacked neatly on Aisle 24.

I grabbed two red and yellow plastic containers and flung them into the cart just as another Taker appeared behind me. I raced down the aisle snatching up everything that even resembled hosing and flinging it into the cart, too. Snake stayed right beside me, rumbling as he ran. *Now I know how they got back out—they didn't. They're still here.*

I ran so hard my t-shirt slipped down around my neck and the odor wafted into my open mouth causing bile to come up the back of my throat. I was forced to gag and spit as I ran.

A fat man lay sprawled across the end of the aisle. His dead hands clutched his chest as if he'd died of heart failure. I didn't know what to do. The guy was immense.

Behind me, the Taker's bare feet slapped the tile.

Without slowing, I ran up to the man, put my foot on the back of the cart and pushed down, forcing the nose of it up and over the man's mountainous midsection. The cart came down right in the middle of the guy's huge gut.

All at once the air was filled with an even more noxious vapor as the man's belly deflated and all the internal gasses of decomposition rushed out of his half-open mouth.

Vomit flew from my lips and splattered the dead man and the red gas cans. I shoved the cart onto the other side and it flipped over, spilling the gas cans and packages of hosing into the intersection between the aisles.

The Taker stepped over the deflated body without missing a beat. Its garnet eyes glittered; its sin words pulsed beneath its skin.

I fumbled the cart upright and scrambled for the gas cans. I was close enough to see the Taker's words, but I couldn't read them. I'd never seen that language before in my life.

Snake rushed at the monster, and the thing slowed and reached for him, but Snake was quick. He leapt aside and dashed after me. I'd given up on the cart and simply clutched one of the plastic gas cans and a package of hosing.

Together we raced down the next aisle leaping bodies like Olympic hurdles. I had no idea where Thad had gone, but I knew the approximate location of the front door, and that's the direction we headed.

A Taker reached through a rack of western shirts and grabbed me by the throat. I turned and let the thing have the t-shirt that had fallen down around my neck. It burned when the Taker ripped it from me. I smashed it in the face with the plastic gas can and Snake barked and snarled, attempting to find the monster's legs through the hanging clothes.

I took off again.

Almost there.

Thad came out of an aisle, arms filled with pillows.

I leapt over a little girl lying near the Subway sandwich counter, a bag of Doritos in her hand. Three Takers were shoving the shopping cart back out of the open front doors. Another, this one wearing a bright turquoise Hawaiian-style shirt appeared to be headed there, too. *We just opened it up for them,* I thought. *They were trapped in here until we came.* I remembered how the others had learned to open the doors at the grocery store back in Eden simply by watching me.

We're dead, I thought. But I didn't have time to consider other options. Thad was motioning for me to follow. He put his finger to the place where I assumed his lips were—he still had his shirt around his head—and I slowed and followed him quietly.

Up ahead, I saw the sign for Home and Garden.

Of course. There's always another set of doors in Home and Garden.

We hurried to that exit and pushed at the glass. This time, they didn't open as easily, and I began to suspect they were locked. But when a knot of Takers appeared behind us, Thad found a sharp new strength and shoved the doors apart. The two of us slipped through with Snake right behind.

The doors immediately began to come together again, and I knew we were going to make it after all.

The first Taker to reach Home and Garden shoved the doors apart even before they'd closed all the way. The whole group poured forth like a bad dream.

We ran for our lives.

Snake stopped to bark a few times, and I yelled for him to come on because I could already see Takers coming out of the main entrance, too.

I dug the key out of my pocket and pressed the button twice to unlock all four doors at once. Scrambling to open the back door, I threw the gas can and hose inside and looked around for Snake. He had stopped to bark at the Takers again.

Thad grabbed open the passenger door and fell inside. I jumped into the driver's seat and pressed start. If I had been thinking correctly, I could've started the engine remotely.

I dropped the key into the console; I couldn't bother about it now. Snake wouldn't come. He finally had one of the Takers by the leg, and he wasn't letting go. I gunned the engine hoping the vibrations would alert him that we were leaving.

Still, he didn't come. I looked back. He had finally given in to his canine rage, ripping and slashing at the legs of every Taker within reach. He spun like a Tasmanian devil, biting at each one that came close; releasing one only to latch on to the next when they tried to grab him. Before long, words were leaking out all over the ground.

"Go!" Thad screamed.

I shoved the gearshift into drive and drove toward the melee.

"Not toward them, dammit!" Thad tried to wrench the steering wheel out of my grip. "Go the other *way*."

I pushed him aside and smashed the car right into the nearest Taker. It fell to the ground, a tumbled Colossus, and I drove over the top of it honking the horn and screaming for Snake to come.

The other Takers backed out of the way. Several were holding leg wounds, trying to keep the clear word-fluid from spilling.

I flung open my door.

Snake looked up, and I screamed and motioned at him with both hands.

The big dog headed toward me like a missile.

But the Taker I had just run over appeared out of nowhere, tire tracks on its translucent skin.

In slow motion, it reached through the open door, grabbed hold of my arm and yanked me onto the pavement even while Thad scrambled into the driver's seat, grabbing for my legs.

Snake leapt at the Taker's arms and hands, but it swatted him away and proceeded across the pavement, dragging me toward the line of trees at the edge of the lot.

Thad jammed himself under the steering wheel and smashed down on the accelerator. He steered the car around the huge group of Takers that were still assembling.

Snake recovered from his roll across the asphalt and launched himself at the monster again. The Taker whipped around to face the charging dog, and I both heard and felt the bone in my forearm snap. An unbelievable shriek issued from my throat followed by an image of Cade's face as he'd sat on the patio that day holding his own broken arm.

I struggled to stand but the thing still had hold of me. It flopped me backward like a rag doll. I tried but couldn't get to my feet. My arm burned inside as surely as if someone had driven the tip of a torch right through my flesh. My vision began to darken, and I knew from recent experience that I was on the verge of blacking out.

The thing apparently decided Snake was not a real threat because it turned its back on him and yanked me along the ground. My pain flared in white-hot agony.

Through a fog of pain, I realized the Taker wanted a branch to hang me on. Here, the trees were all heavy with corpses. It lugged me off the pavement onto the grassy strip where the trees marched along in a neatly planted row.

My head lolled to one side. I thought I heard the smooth purr of the Chrysler and I figured it was the sound of Thad leaving. Not that I would blame him, not now. My consciousness began to slip, and I was glad. I welcomed the caul of darkness threatening my vision. In the distance, I could hear Snake snarling and barking. *Go on*, I thought. *Go with Thad. Be safe.*

Just as my world went black, the monster tossed me into the

air and my unwelcome senses returned. I expected to be pierced through the gut at any moment. *Oh my God, what will it feel like?* Instead, I hit the ground, hard.

Missed.

I landed on my back; all the air knocked out of me. Coughing, I rolled over, trying to pull my knees up to crawl. My arm screamed when I tried to use it.

Snake's legs appeared in my peripheral vision, and then the big dog was licking my face.

"Help," I rasped.

Strong hands grasped me under my armpits, and I found myself looking into the glittering garnet eyes of the Taker in the turquoise shirt.

I saw the words *murder and robbery* flicker beneath the thing's skin. Then I saw one more word: *redemption.* I closed my eyes and waited to be stabbed onto a branch.

But this was a different Taker. It wanted me for itself. The two monsters struggled briefly, pulling at me like a piece of meat. I found myself whipsawing back and forth, my arm flopping wildly.

Without a sound, the turquoise Taker slammed the other one to the ground with a huge elbow to the head. Snake was on it in a heartbeat. This time, he had the advantage. He tore at the creature's throat with his strong, white teeth. The horrific sounds reminded me of the first time I'd heard Takers gulping down strips of human flesh.

In moments, foreign sin words were pouring out onto the ground. Almost navy colored beneath the skin, they were stark black in the open air. As before, they wriggled around until the good light of day put an end to them.

I did not recognize the letters that made up those words. They reminded me of hieroglyphics or cuneiform symbols. He must be *ancient,* I thought as Thad whirled the car into the space between the crowd and the dead Taker.

He opened the door, eyes wild, and looked at Snake. It was obvious he wasn't sure what to do about me. The turquoise Taker still held me beneath my arms.

Overhead, a ragged looking spot began to flutter.

Snake looked at Thad but made no move to get in the car.

Thad looked over his shoulder at the crowd moving toward us.

Behind his head, buzzing black raindrops began to fall from the fluttery tear in the sky.

Holding one ear at the sudden change in air pressure, Thad hopped out of the car, opened the back door, and urged Snake to get in. He signaled him with the "come on" motions he'd seen me use. Instead, the turquoise-shirted Taker took three steps and shoved me into the back seat even as the black rain flowed over the fatally wounded monster on the ground.

Then the turquoise one spun on its heel and walked straight to the line of trees and began to jerk the bodies off the branches and stack them neatly on the grass.

Another partially clothed creature broke through the crowd and headed toward the trees. It didn't look back as the black liquid flowed toward the ones that had been bitten.

Without hesitation, Snake jumped into the backseat beside me. Thad threw himself behind the steering wheel and shoved the gearshift into drive. He didn't worry about running over bodies as we fled the parking lot. The black rain rushed across the ground like a buzzing river. We didn't wait to see it change into locusts and fly back into the sky.

By the time Thad slowed the car, we were well on the other side of town. It was only then that he seemed to realize he'd lost his shirt somewhere. Through tears of pain, I saw him feel around in my backpack until he found one of my tees.

This one had *Bite Me!* emblazoned across it.

Thad laughed somewhat hysterically and pulled it over his head.

It was a tight fit.

CHAPTER TWENTY-ONE

Backdrop For Eternity

Moaning in pain, I kicked the gas can into the floorboard and cradled my wrecked arm in my lap.

"Here." Thad handed me the two maps we hadn't unfolded. "Use these to stabilize it."

I took the maps and unfolded the paper enough to roll them around my forearm. "Water?" I asked through gritted teeth.

Thad passed me one of the bottles we had opened earlier. "I also found these." He handed me the bottle of Hydrocodone that Marla had wanted so badly.

I thanked God and Bob Marley when my fingers felt that smooth cylinder. "Open, please." I passed them back to Thad. "Oh my God." I leaned over and threw up all over the red plastic gas can, again.

Thad slowed the car and pulled to the side of the road. We were headed for Littlefield and the Hwy 40 junction. "Here, kid." He wet one of my clean tube socks and handed it to me to wash my face. Then he took the gas can out and poured water over it.

"You'll need to eat something with those pills, or they'll make you even sicker." He dug a loaf of bread and jar of peanut butter out of the trunk and made me a sandwich.

My mind was all jumbled. "Did you see that thing save me? It *saved* me. *Redemption* on its forehead. Did you see it?"

"I saw it," Thad said. "I still can't believe it, but I saw it. And it had on clothes, too. Most of the others didn't. Reminded me of those at the high school."

I tried to think about that, but the pain was getting worse by the second. I couldn't seem to formulate a reply.

Thad handed me the pills and water after I choked down a few bites of the sandwich. "Take two," he said. He looked down at the lump halfway between my wrist and the bend of my elbow. The bone hadn't come through the skin, but it was definitely broken.

"Can you set it?" I stared down at the huge lump.

Thad tried to sound nonchalant. "Nah. Not right now, we'll just splint it up and let those pain pills kick in." He looked around for something better to splint it with.

Across the road sat a minivan full of passengers. With a deep breath, Thad loped across the highway, examined the antenna, bent it back and forth until it broke—it took several tries—and then ran back to the Chrysler. "This oughta do it." He took the maps, rolled them together into a tight whorl, slid the antenna inside to strengthen them, and then bound the skinny tube tightly with the plastic-coated twist tie from the loaf of bread.

Once he'd positioned the splint against my broken arm, he wrapped it gently with another t-shirt and then tied the t-shirt on with two of my long socks.

Thad had somehow made it to the car with one of the Wal-Mart pillows, so he put it in my lap and laid my arm there. "You need a real sling," he said. "But this will do for now."

"We have to set it," I mumbled. "Cade had to have his set or the doc said it wouldn't heal. The ends of the bones have to be stuck back togeth—"

I threw up all over the new pillow. The wads of peanut butter and bread nearly choked me to death coming back up.

Thad clenched his jaw, took the pillow out, shook off the nastiness, and wiped it as clean as possible with the wet sock. He took a plastic 7-Eleven bag from the trunk and put it in my lap. "Next time, throw up in this."

Then he dug down in the backpack in search of something. He pulled out the two other medicine bottles. One held Cipro antibiotics, and the other contained Tylenol with Codeine. Thad looked at them and then stuck them back in the backpack, which he put in the front passenger seat within easy reach. "When your belly settles. I'll give you *both* of those."

Finally, we got underway again. "Getting low on fuel," Thad said. "Watch for an older vehicle. Most of the new ones have that anti-theft device. Might not be able to get a hose in there at all."

He bypassed several until he came to an older model Chevy. "Back in college, we often had to liberate gasoline to keep us mobile. Damn textbooks weren't covered on my scholarship."

I heard what he was saying, and it struck me as quite ironic that while he'd been going to school to be a lawyer, he'd also been stealing to pay his way, but I didn't say anything. The pain pills were making me very sleepy.

"Ready to get out and stretch your legs, Snake-man?" Thad had coasted to a stop beside the Chevy.

Snake stared at him but didn't raise his head from my knee.

"Suit yourself." He tore the new flexible tubing from its package then stepped from the car and tossed the trash on the ground. It took a few minutes of fiddling around with the coiled hose before he was able to get it down into the tank of the old car, but once he did, all it took was a little bit of suction before the gas flowed right into the can.

"We're in luck, Snake." He had rolled down the window since the dog wouldn't get out with him. "This old car seems to have a full tank." He kept talking to the dog as he worked. I thought maybe it was to keep from having to focus on the puffy face of the dead man slumped beside the car. His eyes were wide open, staring at the sun.

When he had judged the can nearly full, Thad tipped an imaginary hat at the corpse. "Thank you kindly." He walked back to the Chrysler under a sky as blue as any I'd ever seen. "I guess if you have to be dead beside the road, that sky is as good a backdrop for eternity as anything. I don't even see any sky scars out here, though I know they must be there, or you wouldn't be dead."

He talked to Snake and to himself and to the dead man the entire time he transferred the gas to the Chrysler. The sound of his voice was soothing. I even heard him thank the makers of Chrysler for including the little fuel funnel inside the trunk. In half an hour, we were on the road again with me moaning occasionally, Snake whining nervously, and Thad driving faster than he ever had before. I think he was determined to find Kansas, New Mexico before dark.

CHAPTER TWENTY-TWO

As Far As The Eye Can See

We made it to Littlefield, but Thad had second thoughts about going on to Kansas. The pain meds made me so groggy I kept falling asleep, but when the car hit a bump or Thad had to maneuver around a wreck or stalled vehicle, I would wake myself with a moan or a cry. Sometimes I would keep on crying. I knew it, but I couldn't help it. The meds took away my self-control. Or maybe it was the pain that did that.

Once Thad screamed at me to *shut up just shut the hell up*—at least I think he did. Another time he told me was going to put me out beside the road if I didn't stop bawling. Then he wiped his scraggly face and said, *kidding, just kidding*. Later he acted so normal that I decided I must have imagined the whole thing.

I couldn't always tell waking from sleeping. When he said he didn't think we should try for Kansas after all, I remember throwing a fit, kicking the back of his seat and screaming until Snake started to bark, and I came to myself enough to realize he was on the verge of leaping over the seat in attack mode.

"Okay, okay." Thad sounded confused. "We'll go on, I just don't see the point—"

Then we saw the Harley. We'd gone through Littlefield, and we'd made the Hwy 40 junction. A sign said we were now in New Mexico. Even though I was in a twilight state, I was pretty sure I knew what I was seeing. The bike was just growling along ahead of us like something from a movie. "Is that real?" I asked. "Is that a motorcycle?"

Thad's voice, when he finally spoke, sounded like a man who'd just experienced a revelation. "It must be real, Jackie-boy. Or we wouldn't both be seeing it." He pressed the button to lower his window so we could hear the engine more clearly.

"Catch it," I said. And then I got an unbidden image of a Taker in a denim vest with a Hell's Angels skull sewn on the back of it. "But make sure it's human . . ."

Thad's eyes caught mine in the rearview mirror. "Hold on to that arm boy, 'cause if it ain't human, I'm gonna ride that sucker down."

I wondered if I was still asleep, or even unconscious. What happened to Thad's lawyer voice? When had he started sounding like the man who ran the used auto parts place? Then it hit me. Wal-Mart sells alcohol. Had he somehow picked up something while I was running for my life?

"Are you drunk?" I asked bluntly, but before he could answer, we had caught up to the Harley.

The look on the rider's face was almost comical. I suspected it was a mirror image of ours. "Pull over!" He gesticulated wildly.

The guy appeared to be grinning, but Thad whipped the car to the side of the road so suddenly I had to grab the armrest to keep my balance and the next thing I knew he was out of the car and the motorcycle man had come to a stop beside us. Like something out of the old west. *Are we in Tombstone after all?* I noted a shotgun stuck in a makeshift holster on the side of the motorcycle. It was partially covered by a rolled and tethered Mexican blanket.

"Hot damn," Thad yelled. "I thought we were the only ones left!"

I wanted to call out, to warn him the man might not be one of us, might not be a good one. I didn't know much about Hell's Angels but what I thought was they took what they wanted without asking. If we lost the Chrysler, I didn't think I'd make it. The lump on my arm was now the size of a lemon and the bruising was creeping out from the inside like one of the Taker's internal tattoos.

"Hey!" I heard a voice call.

Leaning forward, I pressed the button to roll down my window. Snake growled, and I rolled it back up. The man walking toward the car was slope shouldered and stout. He reminded me of a boxer for some reason; maybe it was the way he walked, leading with the side of his body. Simon and Garfunkel's haunting melody crept into my skull.

As my eyes focused, I realized he didn't have on a Hell's Angel's vest at all. He had on a t-shirt and jeans. He looked like my dad on his day off. Except for the shotgun that is. It was still visible beneath the colorful blanket. At least he hadn't grabbed it when he got off the bike.

I watched as he approached Thad smiling and holding out his hand. I could hear him through Thad's open window.

"Name's Carlos," he said. "Carlos Ramirez."

Thad took his hand and yes, sure enough, when he leaned forward to grasp it, he stumbled a bit. "Thad Stewart. Pleased to make your acquain'unce."

He is drunk, I thought. I don't know how, but he is. I looked over the back of the seat and there in the center console was a flat silver flask with SUPERTEACHER engraved on the front. My mom had given it to my dad one year for Christmas. "To keep you warm at the Friday night football games," she'd joked. "That way you won't be tempted to cozy up to Miss Blunt, the science teacher." As far as I knew, he never used the flask. It just stayed on top of the fridge year after year.

No doubt about it, though, Thad had something in it now, probably Dad's good Scotch. *And what's with the manners again?* I'm dying here, and he's acting like it's a tea party. *Pleased to make your acquaintance? Seriously?*

I laid my hand on Snake's quivering back. The man looked okay to me, but if there's one thing the last few days had taught me it's that looks can be deceiving. My mind flashed back to the turquoise Taker standing in the dappled sunlight beneath the gory trees. Looks can definitely be deceiving.

Hauling my mind back to the fuzzy present, I heard Thad tell the stranger—Carlos—about me. "—in a bad way," I heard him say. "Looks like a serious break, and I'm no doctor. Saw some action in Vietnam. Set a few bones back then helping the medics."

I closed my eyes. Maybe I'd be better off dead. The thought of Thad pulling and twisting on my arm made my stomach roil.

"Hydrocodone," I heard him continue. "Tylenol 3, and some Cipro antibiotics, that's about it."

Then I heard Carlos' voice. It was musical, with an accent so slight I wasn't even sure it was there.

"—done a couple. It's going to hurt like hell, though. I've got a place up ahead. I'm a realtor. I was set to show it to a family before the rip. It's on the historic register even though it's been deserted for a while. Built by Bitty Sloan, an old gangster from the 1930s."

He stopped talking as if to give Thad a chance to intervene. When Thad said nothing, he continued. "Bitty ran moonshine all over the state, stored it in the underground tunnels of this old house. Even has a water well in a secret basement kitchen where he made his own 'shine."

"Sounds pretty ancient," Thad said at last. "But it prob'ly saved your life. I'll bet you were down in that basement when the monsters came. Just like we were down below. How far is it?"

The man nodded several times while Thad was speaking. "I thought that's what saved me. When I first heard the big noise, I went straight to the basement. I thought a tornado was coming." He hesitated for a moment.

"And when I came out, it was raining—*them*."

Thad's head bobbed to beat the band. But it was what the man said next that got my attention.

"It's not far from here," he said. "Just up the road in a little wide spot called Kansas."

I looked at Thad just in time to see his mouth fall open comically. "That's where we were headed. The boy's got an uncle there." Then it dawned on him. "He said his uncle's name was Carlos."

If he hadn't been half-drunk, and if I hadn't been almost obliterated with pain, we both would've made the connection earlier.

Thad knocked on my window with the knuckle of his middle finger. Snake leapt over the seat and dove out the driver's window. I thought he was going to kill Thad, or the new man, but instead,

Carlos held out his hands, and my big brown dog stopped and looked at him with his head cocked to one side.

"This your uncle, Jack? This man says his name is Carlos Ramirez, just like you said." The look on his face was such that I expected him to cock his head to the side like Snake.

"Hello, Uncle," I muttered. "It's good to see you." After that I must have lost consciousness because the next thing I knew, we were on the way to the house, and I had awakened screaming in pain.

"Sorry, Jack, I'm trying to keep up with the Harley—didn't see that dip in the road. Almost there now."

We hit another bump, and I screeched. I couldn't help it. Tears were running down my face. I'd never experienced pain like that. Each time we hit something, the bones in my forearm moved and the feeling was liquid fire sluicing though my entire body.

For a split second I wondered how much worse it must have been, what Dee and the others had gone through, but then Thad made a sudden turn into a bumpy dirt drive, and I fell to the side, and it hurt so bad I begged for God to make it stop. The next time I threw up, there was nothing left but stringy, yellow bile.

"Slow down, please slow down. Just let me out. I'll walk just please don't do any more bumps or turns."

Thad slowed to a crawl. The road was red dirt in the headlights. Humpy and bumpy and curvy and before I knew what was happening, our lights picked out the house standing tall against the horizon. It was three stories; with a gabled roof so steep it might have been pointing at Heaven. Elaborate gingerbread trim laced the front.

"Must've had a woman in mind when he had this built," Thad said. "Certainly not what I expected the house of an old gangster to look like."

"Have you ever heard the story of Hansel and Gretel?" I asked. "This is how they described the witch's house. I wonder if she had the windows all boarded over like that? She probably did, to keep the kids from escaping."

"I don't know," Thad said. "But I'm damn glad they are. Carlos must've done that recently. Most of the boards look they were taken from other things. Look, that one is a chair leg or something. He's been busy."

I tried to see, but tears of pain blurred my vision.

Our headlights lit up the figure of Carlos as he hopped off his bike and manually opened an overhead garage door. He motioned us forward with his hands. "It slopes down, be careful."

Thad drove us inside, the headlights illuminating the bare concrete interior that seemed to go down and back forever. "Amazing," he said. "Guess that's why his bike still runs. Garage goes right down under the house."

I didn't care. At this point, I was teetering on the brink of consciousness—again.

"We're in Kansas, Jack," a voice said.

I reached out my hand and there was Snake, smashed up against my legs with his soft, flat head just in reach of my fingers. "Snakeman." I smoothed his wrinkly skin and drifted away.

In my dreams I heard the Kansas song "Dust in the Wind" and saw hordes of monsters roaming the plains, thousands upon thousands, as far as the eye could see. Just like the painting of bison that hung on the wall of the post office back home. That famous painting showed a herd of buffalo stretched out from horizon to horizon grazing peacefully before a setting sun.

Even in the dream I recalled my dad telling me the setting sun was a symbol of the bison's demise. He said the painting was done by a man who had actually seen that last immense herd before the great white hunters had come with their Gatling guns and slaughtered them all, leaving them to rot in the harsh western sun.

I remember being horrified, asking why the hunters had done that, and Dad said it was to get rid of the Native Americans, to force them onto reservations by taking away their main source of food.

That horrified me even more, knowing our government did that to an entire race of people. I woke in a sweat, dream half-remembered. *Was Dad trying to tell me something about buffalo and Takers? What was he trying to make me understand? Take way their main source of food? But* we *are their source of food—or so it seems. Except for the one that saved me. What does he—*

"Here, Jackie-boy, try to drink some of this." Thad pushed a spoon against my lips.

Chicken noodle soup dribbled down my chin but enough got into my mouth that I tasted salt, and it was good. My belly cramped, and I opened my mouth wider, a baby bird in a nest of blankets.

"Attaboy," he said. "You've been out for a while. We need to get some liquid in you." He pushed another spoon at me, and I nearly broke my neck trying to raise my head high enough to take it all in.

Thad chuckled. "Slow down, there's plenty."

I heard the metal spoon scrape against a metal pan. "The previous owners were nice enough to leave us a couple of pots under the stove."

Bitty Sloan, I remembered. "They must be old," I croaked. "From the thirties."

Thad shook his head. "There've been several owners since then, just none recently." His breath was fragrant with the smell of warm beer, the foamy smell that had always made me beg to take the first sip of my dad's when he opened one out back, standing at the grill.

I took a few more sips of soup and then lay back, exhausted. My arm didn't hurt as much as before. I tried to hold it up, to see how it looked, but it seemed to weigh a ton, so I just felt of it with my other hand. It was wrapped in bandages.

"He's not really your uncle, you know."

My eyes opened, and I looked for anger in Thad's face. But I saw none. "I'm not sure about that," I said. "How did I know his name—"

"And the name of the town," Thad interrupted.

I started to tell him about that. I had a Dorothy-of-Oz moment in which the green Kansas road sign twirled madly, hard enough to take flight and smack me upside the head, knocking me out the way the spinning-tornado-house had knocked Dorothy out.

But I couldn't tell him anything. Just then the words to "Amazing Grace" drowned out all thoughts.

And grace will lead you home . . .
and grace will lead you home.

I wanted to ask if Carlos' name was really Grace, but I knew that wouldn't make any sense, so I let the music lull me until my eyelids were so heavy I couldn't force them to stay open no matter how hard I tried.

In my dream-state I overheard Thad telling Carlos all about the scene at my house and how Mo had saved me, but we couldn't save Kevin. He didn't add that he was the one who shot Kevin, but when he got to the part about the fire, my foggy brain halted its downward slide, and I listened, holding my breath so I could take in every word.

Fell asleep with candles going, he said. Curtains caught fire. The house went up like a torch, I barely escaped, the women didn't make it, didn't make it, didn't make it—the words curled into my ear like smoke and into my head and into my brain, and I didn't know if I was asleep and dreaming or awake and hearing it for real.

I touched my eyelids, and they were closed, so I started to breathe again. And I dreamed of buffalo being ridden by Takers. They were trying to outrun a prairie fire, but there was a problem up ahead. They couldn't see the cliff. Or the black rain that would turn to a plague of locusts, waiting to devour them.

CHAPTER TWENTY-THREE

Talisman

Feeling stronger, I sat up from the narrow bed and tottered on jelly legs to the hallway to figure out where I was. Snake stayed beside me every step of the way. Instinctively, I reached for him with an arm that was bound to my chest with strips of what appeared to be one of my own t-shirts. I wanted a bathroom, but I doubted there would be running water. Sure enough, in the corner of the room, I spied what had to be a chamber pot. I'd read about them in history books and seen them in movies about the old west.

The house felt huge. Hallways meandered off this way and that, doors lined up like dominoes waiting to fall, and windows, everywhere there were windows. Built before central air conditioning, the old home's windows were being put to good use now, just as in the past. Up here on the second floor they were all opened to the breeze. I stood in front of the one at the end of the long hallway and breathed like someone coming out of a deep coal mine. The air was clean up here, just a hint of dust from the cakey windowsill. I leaned out, my soul and my senses drinking in the spring day.

The clouds in the sky were white, puffy, and harmless on a background of purest baby blue. Amazement kept me standing there. How could anything be wrong? The world seemed perfect. This *could* be Heaven. Except there were no birds flying, no planes in the distance, and if I looked hard, I could see those peculiar looking places where something awful tore through from another dimension.

Baby blue. The color of a newborn's softest blanket. A few shades north of turquoise. What about turquoise? What was my slippery mind trying to get me to recall? *Mom's sweater, hiked up. The color of the shirt on the Taker that stuffed me in the Chrysler.* Turquoise. Favorite stone of Native Americans—the sky stone according to some. Sky stones and buffalo. *Why buffalo? What about buffalo?*

I turned slowly, afraid of making myself dizzy. My head felt lighter than the air around me, lighter than the breeze coming in through the window. Stuffed with so much, and with nothing at all. Last night I should have been dancing with Dee—*or was it two nights ago?* This morning my only worry should be wondering if she was now my girlfriend.

Snake touched the back of my leg, and I spoke to him like always. "Hey, boy." I rubbed his head with my good hand. "Hey—how'd we get here? To this place, to this bedroom—"

"Thought I heard movement." The voice belonged to Thad. He seemed to be climbing the stairs slowly, he wasn't young, but again, I wondered about booze.

"Hey." I stood still to keep my head from spinning. "Where are we?"

He grunted, holding onto the newel post on the landing. "We're in Kansas, my boy. We made it. Your *Uncle* Carlos led the way, and we carried you in. How's the arm?"

"Doesn't hurt as much, that's for sure."

Thad nodded. "We set it. Took both of us. Had to lock Snake in the basement. Thought he would tear us limb from limb when you shrieked—"

I looked down at my friend, rubbed his head again. "Do we have food?"

Thad chuckled. "Yep. Do you want some more soup, or something a little more substantial?"

I tried to understand what he was saying. "You mean I've eaten once already? Soup?"

Thad was beside me now, taking hold of my good arm. "I think you'd better come on back to bed, son."

"Why?" My voice was a little shrill.

Thad let go when he heard the rumble in Snake's chest. "Boy, we've been here three days already. I've been feeding you soup since we got here. You spiked a fever that first night—talked out of your head a lot. Stuff about your mom and the color turquoise and Indians and buffalo, you even sang a few bars of "Amazing Grace" and "Carry On Wayward Son." Man, you were out of it. But the Cipro helped. I think we got you on the mend now."

"I really appreciate everything you guys have done for me," I said. But in the back of my mind, I felt deprived. As if losing even a couple of days was too much. I wanted to savor the time I should have spent with Dee at the dance; instead, I missed it completely. Stupid idea anyway—you can't savor something that never happened, never will happen.

"It's no big deal," he replied. "We did what was needed. You're just fortunate you had the pain medicine and the antibiotics in your backpack." He didn't say anymore, thinking perhaps of what it had cost for me to have them.

"Yeah, guess we better stock up next time we hit Wally World or CVS."

Thad laughed uncomfortably as he helped me back into the bed.

"These are nice accommodations," I joked. "Is Carlos here alone?" Snake leapt up on the bed beside me. "Hey, by the way, you are feeding my dog, right?"

"Of course," Thad said. "I have to bring his when I feed you. He doesn't leave otherwise, except to go outside every now and then, you know, to do his business."

The idea of Snake outside without me gave me pause. "How is it, outside? Are *they* here?"

"They've been and gone, just like back home. Only this house is outside town, so there wasn't much to keep them around here, thank God."

From the hallway, a new voice, the musical one I heard in my dream-state. "Thank God is right." The man rapped on the door-jamb with his knuckles. "Mind if I come in?"

"Carlos?"

"At your service. How ya doin, m'ijo?" He walked over to my bed and sat beside Snake, giving his head a quick rub the way I always did.

"I'm better, thank you." I looked at his face without reservation. "Are you Hispanic and Native American?"

Carlos laughed lightly. "Somewhere back in the past, yes. Before our country and Mexico got divided that is. Back then, the border wasn't the border, you know what I'm saying?"

I nodded. "I understand exactly. But are you from one of the plains tribes? Or your ancestors?"

"Jack, I—"Thad wanted to interrupt. Him and those darn manners.

"It's important," I said, though I couldn't say exactly why.

Carlos looked into my eyes, and I did not look away. That was something adults never did—look into your eyes—unless you were in trouble, then maybe. "I'm sorry, I don't know for certain, Jack. But I had a grandfather in the Amarillo area, so I'd say it's a possibility. He's been gone a while, though." A veil of sorrow shadowed his face, and then it was gone.

I liked this man. "I'm sorry I said you were my uncle." I looked at Thad. "I had to get here. There was a signpost that said Kansas, but it was way back in Texas and I—well—I just knew we had to come." My good hand had a strong grip on the extra skin around Snake's neck, but he didn't seem to mind. If I didn't know better, I would think he was hanging on my every word.

"That's good," Carlos said. And then he pulled a small turquoise stone from his pocket and laid it on the blanket between us. "It belonged to my grandfather," he said. "Why don't you keep it a while?"

It was blue and lumpy and cool, about the size of a quarter, and shot through with a broken line of gold. When I picked it up, it grew warm in my palm. "It's a talisman." I closed my fingers around it. "Yes. I don't know why, but this is where we were supposed to come."

"Do you believe in God, Jack?" His voice was that of a hypnotist on a small stage. His straight black hair clung to his forehead, and his dark eyes were locked on mine.

It wasn't a hard question. "I do. I always have."

"Big church-goer?"

I shook my head. "Not so much." I debated telling him my parents didn't think it was necessary, but it seemed disparaging to them now, so I kept it to myself. "But I do believe. I want to believe. I saw a professor on the Internet right before the sky broke open. He said these things were from Purgatory. He said they want new souls." I thought of all the things I'd seen them do. "I think it may be true. They don't eat the dead because their souls are already departed. They don't eat animals because, you know, animals supposedly don't have souls."

I glanced at Snake; thankful he couldn't hear me. "And the thing I keep going back to is this—the ones with the ancient looking words are not the ones trying to dress themselves or clean up. The ancient ones are the real killers. It seems like the younger ones—the ones with the more modern words under their skin—have some memory of this place. Of us. Or maybe just of being human."

Carlos studied the ground for a minute, and then shrugged. "Makes as much sense as my theory, I guess. Though I don't really see how it could fit in with what I learned in Catholic school."

Thad cleared his throat. "What's your theory?"

The room seemed dim. I assumed the sun had gone behind a cloud. Since there was no electricity, daylight was the only source of illumination.

"Global warfare," Carlos said. "Our country has always kept its best weapons secret from the people. Stands to reason other superpowers do, too. And don't the creatures look just a little bit robotic? Have you seen them up close?"

I pointed to my arm. "Up close and personal."

I understood what he meant, the way they moved, the way they all looked the same, but still, they weren't all the same, that much I knew for certain. "I don't know—I understand why you say that, but one saved my life. Would a weapon do that? Even an organic one?"

His eyes went away from mine. I don't think he believed one had saved me.

"Artificial intelligence, maybe? I always heard about it, saw the movies that said machines would one day take over once we made them capable of learning. Even Stephen Hawking liked that theory. I read *that* on the Internet. Who knows, maybe these things do learn." He fingered a small gold cross that lay in the hollow of his throat.

He probably thinks I'm lying to him and to myself. It would be so much easier if everyone were on the same page. But then, hadn't that always been the way—that old free will thing—free to believe what you want to believe? "You're right about the learning part. They learn and adapt very quickly. But the one that saved me was different. Thad was there, he saw it."

The attorney nodded. "It's just like he said. One of the Takers—"

"You call them *Takers?*"

Thad indicated me with a nod of his head. "Jack's word. Says they have taken everything from us. I'd say that's accurate—though from what I've seen, the three of us, here in this room, have been pretty lucky—"

Carlos interrupted. I don't think patience was his strong suit. "And then what happened? Tell me the whole story of the broken arm, please."

Thad was a study in patience, now that he'd been drinking. He went back and started over. "We'd gone into Wal-Mart to get the gas can and some hosing, and they came out of nowhere. I think they must have been back in the stock room or something. One minute it was clear and the next minute there were a hundred of them." He glanced down at me, and I could see he was reliving the thing in his head.

"Anyway," I took up the tale, "we made it all the way back to the car. I had to run over one to get away, but I didn't kill it. Didn't even hurt it. That's the one that got me. Just reached in the car window and yanked me out. Broke my arm right then. Took me to the trees, tried to stick me on a jagged branch."

I swiped away beads of sweat pooling in the sunken places beneath my eyes. "Snake came to help. Then a Taker in a turquoise shirt knocked the first one to the ground. Then the turquoise one scooped me up and stuffed me inside the car, and Thad got us out of there." I lay back, trembling.

"That's exactly right," Thad agreed. "The thing just walked over to the car as pretty as you please and gave the boy back to me. Back to Snake and me. It's like you have a protective veil around you or something, Jackie-boy. First, at the house, when Mo saved you—that one had you in a death grip, too—and then at Wally World." His eyes rested on the broad brown back of my dog, the only creature in this room said to be without a soul.

I didn't lie when I said I believed in God. But I didn't know if I believed everything I'd been told *about* God. And I sure didn't believe I had a protective veil around me. "If I'm under protection, I guess you are, too." I looked at Thad's face. Surprise made him appear momentarily younger, smoothing out the deep trenches bracketing his mouth.

"I guess you're right, Jack. I never thought of that." He looked up at Carlos. "Maybe it applies to all of us."

For the first time I felt a connection with Thad, this man with whom I had already shared so much. I glimpsed, once again, something inside him, something good, like trying to save Kevin and his girl from drugs. Like trying to save *her* from the Taker, then trying to save Kevin's life on the dining room table. I thought about the ways I had judged him and found him wanting—and I thought of how he might be judging me in return.

The light grew dimmer, no longer even strong enough to make our shadows on the walls. "Is something wrong outside?"

Carlos strode to the window. His voice was incredulous. "Madre de *dios*, the black rain is falling."

CHAPTER TWENTY-FOUR

Goals

I struggled from the bed, Snake right beside me. I grabbed his collar to steady myself. The four of us crowded in front of the narrow window looking over the western prairie. The sky was dark in that direction.

"It's the black rain," Carlos said. "Have you guys seen this stuff?"

We both nodded, but Thad snorted and waved a dismissive hand in the air as he turned aside. "It's a long way off."

"It comes down as liquid," I said, wobbling on my feet. "And then it slathers the injured Taker before bursting into a cloud of black locusts and flying back up into the void."

Carlos laid a steadying hand on my shoulder. "The void. Yes, I guess that is where they come from. Like the Bible says, 'In the beginning God created the heaven and the earth. And the earth was without form, and void; and darkness was upon the face of the deep. And the Spirit of God moved upon the face of the waters.'"

I let the verse sink into my drug-addled brain. "That's beautiful—and very frightening. I don't know much about the Bible, but I've heard the most popular parts. Still, to think about nothing out there . . . just void. It sounds like deep space, doesn't it? Or dark matter."

"I don't know much about deep space—except no one can hear you scream—" Thad arched one brow comically, "but the whole *concept* is terrifying if you ask me. I don't know so much about God or the Bible, either, but it seems to me that black stuff might be some kind of savior."

I saw Carlos make the sign of the cross when Thad said that.

"I mean, look," he moved to the other window, "if the black rain is falling on a bunch of the Takers over there, that would mean they're injured, right?"

Carlos leaned further into the breeze outside the window. "I think that's right. I shot a couple of them with my shotgun the day I was coming to show this place. Thank God, I had it with me. It's so remote out here, you know? Anyhow, after I shot them, the clear stuff leaked out and all those words, too—"

"Their sin words," I said.

"Right." Carlos looked at me for a second as if he would say more, but then he continued. "Anyhow, that's when the black rain descended and rolled over them. But look how large *that* blackness appears to be. That would be a *lot* of them. So what could be injuring them over there? More people, survivors like us?"

"Survivors?" My voice was small and tight. I'd earlier thought of us that way, but now? It seemed somewhat pretentious to call us survivors. It had only been a few days—and we hadn't actually done anything except run away. When I thought of survivors, I thought of fighters, scramblers, warriors. Not just hiders. Like us.

But Carlos liked the word. "Survivors, yes. We are survivors." He gripped the windowsill. "Can you hear that sound? That buzzing? I think I hear it, and then it fades away. But I feel it," he patted his broad chest, "in here." He stared out at the western horizon. "Maybe it was that buzzing sound that ripped open the sky when they first came. But look, the sky is almost clear again. The blackness is already gone."

In my head, The Eagles began to sing "Already Gone." My legs were suddenly weak. I tried to stay and watch—could I hear them buzzing from way over there, or was it the power of suggestion? Or was it maybe the helicopters I thought I'd seen before? Nah—I wasn't even going to kid myself about that anymore. If the military was coming to our rescue, they were being pretty darn slow about it.

I couldn't stand any longer. I steadied myself on Snake and made my way back to the bed, falling onto it ignobly. I didn't care.

I seemed to have used up my store of nobleness, my store of bravery, my store of survivor-ness.

"Let's let the boy rest," Thad said. "I'll take the first watch up here, at the hall window." He grabbed a ladder-back chair and walked toward the door. "It should be a good spot. From here we can almost see tomorrow. That blackness out there encourages me. Someone is fighting back, by God. But we'll still have to make a run to town. Or at least to that farm you mentioned, the one with the greenhouse full of vegetables."

Carlos agreed. "It is encouraging, isn't it?" He stroked his chin. "At least it means we aren't completely alone. And look, from here you can also see the cliff half a mile away. But to get to the farm we must go the opposite direction. Your car will be a lot better than my bike. I can't *wait* to explore that farm. I tried the Piggly Wiggly in Kansas, but with the electricity off all the meat had already gone bad. I brought as many vegetables and canned goods as I could haul, but that greenhouse really beckons. I'll bet they have fuel, too. Most farms do."

"Colorado," I mumbled.

Both men turned back toward me just outside my doorway.

"I'm going to Colorado as soon as I can drive . . . need a car." My eyelids closed as the words left my mouth. My falling asleep dreams were full of the lyrics to "Simple Man" by Lynyrd Skynyrd, and "Jesus Just Left Chicago," by ZZ Top. But the last song I remember as I tumbled down the well was "Ramblin' Man" by The Allman Brothers.

When I awoke later that night, with no one in the room save my best buddy, Snake, all I could think was, *What are you trying to tell me now, Dad? I know it's you because this is your music, the songs you always played while we worked on the car together, the songs I learned to love because of you. Does that mean you're gone, too? Just a spirit now, like Mom? Or does it mean you aren't? I've always had the song-flashes so I guess that's nothing new—except now they come all the time. Are they coming from you? What about "Carry on Wayward Son?" I haven't heard that one in a while. Is that one done now that we're here, in Kansas?*

I waited for a response, but nothing came. The songs never came just because I wanted them to. They came when I needed them, or when someone thought I needed them.

When I examined that idea, I decided it meant my dad was still alive. Maybe this mess, this apocalypse, had strengthened our connection, which was always strong, even more.

In the beginning I'd kept thinking we were going to drive out of the madness, that it would be relegated just to Eden, or West Texas, or then as we got farther from our home, maybe even *just* Texas.

But this was New Mexico.

So, it's widespread, national, maybe even global. Don't think about that—it's out of our control. Instead, think about a cliff. Carlos mentioned a cliff. Just like in my dream.

I wondered where Thad and Carlos were, and I wondered how safe this place was if those things came looking for us. A deep snore arose from the hallway. *That has to be Thad. Sound asleep. Some look out. Just like in the car on the way up here. Maybe I should stop taking the pain pills. Can't leave it up to the others—gotta take care of myself. And Snake.*

It was late the next day when they gathered in my room again. I had overdone it, Carlos said. Stayed up too long. Then I'd slept away the night and most of today.

I waved away the pain medicine he offered and asked for plain old Tylenol or Motrin instead. Carlos was good. He'd stocked up on both at the Piggly Wiggly.

We'd eaten the last of the ripe veggies and canned ham with Chips Ahoy cookies for dessert. There was bread and peanut butter and tuna stacked in the kitchen pantry, but it would go fast between the three of us. Snake still had some Purina, but he looked at us so beseechingly when we ate the ham that we each fed him when we thought the others weren't looking.

We had all the sweet water we could drink from the basement well, which I had ventured down to see earlier in the day. Everything was cozy. But every now and then, a gusty wind whined at the door, begging to be let in. On it I could smell something strange, something chemical, like ice before a hard storm.

"We'd be fools to leave here," Thad said. "Except to bring in more supplies from time to time."

What about your kids in Montana, I wanted to ask, *aren't you even curious to find out if they are still alive?* But for once, I didn't let the words out before I thought them through. Mom, the librarian, always told me to "couch" my words. Check them first, she explained, before you let them out into the world. Try to make sure they really belong there.

I did try. I pictured my words sitting on a couch waiting for me to give them the thorough once over the way Mom had always given *me* the once over before school when I was small. "Let's see those hands," she'd say, examining my nails to make certain they were clean.

But I'd never been very adept at examining my words. My way had always been to speak first, think later. What came out of my mouth this time wasn't much better than what I'd originally thought, but at least it wasn't directed at Thad personally.

"We'd be fools to stay here," I said. "I mean, what's to say a whole army of Takers isn't marching this way right now?"

Carlos touched his little gold cross. It was a gesture I'd already come to recognize as his way of thinking things over. "We're safe here, *m'ijo.* We have the tunnels, the garage where our vehicles are safe underground . . . and the water well. That is the most important part."

But I have goals, I wanted to say. I *have* to have goals. They're the only reason I'm alive. Without them I might never have left the school basement. Might never have found Snake, or my mom—but I still hadn't told anyone about that except for the mutterings when I was nearly unconscious with pain—or even the note from my dad. The one that let me know he was alive and looking for me. Or had been at some point at least.

My next goal was Colorado. My grandparents. Not hunkering down like a scared little rabbit, the way I'd done in those first surreal moments at school. *But it saved you,* my subconscious said. *Hunkering down below ground like a rabbit saved you. Never forget that.*

I looked at my splinted arm. "You guys did a great job fixing me up." My jaw was still a little sore. Thad said it was because they'd stuck Carlos' leather belt between my teeth for me to bite down on. "But as soon as I'm able, I'm going to need a ride to town. There must be other cars in underground garages. I need to find one."

I leaned back, sick at my stomach from exertion or from a buildup of pain meds, or maybe both. "But first, I think I'll take another little nap." I tried to make it sound lighthearted and funny, but it didn't quite come out that way. Even to my ears it sounded just on the edge of pathetic.

"Let *us* worry about things for now, buddy." Carlos always called me buddy or m'ijo—which sounded like *me-ho* in English—which I knew from my Hispanic friends back home was a shortened version of *mi hijo*, a term of endearment, like saying, *my son*. I kind of liked it, but I didn't want him to think just because I was young that I was going to simply go along with whatever he or Thad said. I had goals.

He continued, "When you are healed, we will find a set of wheels. Every teenage boy needs his own wheels. No doubt about it."

I opened my eyes and smiled. We'd been extremely lucky to find him—and his perfect house. The opening lines to "Dust in The Wind" floated into my head, and I knew for certain it *wasn't* luck that got us here to Kansas. Not luck at all. We were somehow meant to find Carlos. And this place.

Thank you, Dad. Now please, come and find me. We'll go to Colorado together.

This time when I dozed off, I heard John Denver singing "Rocky Mountain High," his Colorado song. But even though it was one of Mom's favorites, I didn't think she sent it to me. This time, I was pretty sure I was sending it out to her—and to my dad—wherever they, or their spirits, might be.

Carlos and Thad remained in my room as I drifted away. I could hear them comparing stories. Carlos talked about his family in Ojinaga, Mexico, and how he wanted to go there and check on them.

"But you don't want to leave the safety of this place?" Thad murmured.

Carlos was quiet for a long time. Then his calm voice wound its way into my sleeping ear. "Right. I'm afraid of what I will find if I get there. My brothers lived near my mother, so she wasn't alone, but it's me. I'm an orphan. I feel it in here."

I could imagine him patting his chest again, maybe fingering the tiny gold cross. But I didn't open my eyes to see. I was too close to sleep. Down in the deep.

The next day, I wondered if Thad had ever told Carlos about his kids in Montana. But I didn't have time to ask. I felt so much better I got right out of bed and accompanied Carlos on a tour of the *entire* house.

It was after we'd toured the basement tunnels—each one leading to a different dirt-floored room like the water-well kitchen or the still-fragrant beer storage rooms—that I'd learned how the entrance to the tunnels was through a *secret* paneled-over door in the hall.

Since Thad had been on watch the night before, I wound up following him back through the main floor kitchen and into the living room—what was likely called the parlor back when the house was built.

"'Scuse me," he said, as he trudged past me to open the front door and stepped out onto the porch.

I assumed he was going out to smoke a cigarette or check the weather. We'd been talking about trying to make it to town for gasoline before going to the farmhouse, but when he came back in, zipping his fly, I realized he'd just been peeing off the porch.

The Taker walked in behind him as if it, too, had merely ventured outside to answer the call of nature. The dark red eyes seemed to focus on me over Thad's shoulder. At first, I had the idiotic idea that he'd befriended one of the monsters and brought it home. But then the creature reached for Thad's head.

"Look out!" I screamed.

Snake lunged forward and snared the thing by its ankle. I could see the silvery skin stretch before it broke. Thad—with the unbeliev-able luck of a drunk—fell sideways and flipped over the camelback settee, part of the period staging Carlos had arranged before listing it on the market.

Carlos rushed in from the kitchen. "Stay down!" he commanded when he saw where Thad had landed. He raised the shotgun he always carried, and before I could get Snake away, he blew the monster's head clean off.

Fluid gushed out all over my dog. He staggered away in the opposite direction, shaking his head and whining. "We have to get it out of here," I yelled. "There may be others."

"That black stuff will come," Thad said from behind the settee. "In fact, it's coming now." He had risen to one knee and was peering through the boards on the front window.

Carlos grabbed the Taker by the arm. "Help me push it out the door."

I positioned myself on the other side and got a grip on the thing with my good hand. Its flesh was cool and rubbery, like touching a dolphin. My feet slipped in the words and liquid still pouring out of its ruined head.

"Be careful, Jack," Carlos said. "That fluid may be toxic. Thad, get your ass over here."

Thad staggered over and began to push at the heavy body. I saw words like *lust* and *greed* and *murder* disappear beneath his shoes. *Cardinal sins,* I thought, *the seven deadly ones. Are they all the same?* I didn't know, didn't have time to ponder. I copied Thad, got down on the floor, and braced my feet on the wall. Then I pushed my back against the Taker with all my might.

In this manner, with Carlos pulling and the two of us pushing, we managed to get it out onto the porch just as the black rain came.

It fell in one spot like an ominous Charlie Brown cloud parked overhead. Then the inky drops massed together and came slithering across the yard.

"Shove it!" Carlos yelled. And we did.

The Taker rolled down the steep porch steps and landed on the hard packed earth with a solid thud.

Carlos ushered us back inside and slammed the heavy door. We all watched through gaps in the boarded-up window as the dead Taker disappeared into the black ooze.

"Look," I pointed across the yard. More than a dozen other monsters milled about, obviously avoiding the dark slime.

"I thought they were gone," Carlos said. "I thought we were safe."

I didn't say anything else. Nor did Thad. We just stood silently as the blackness finished absorbing the Taker and then burst into locusts before rising in a cloudy swarm back toward the ragged-edged hole in the sky. I covered my ears against the loud buzzing hum.

That's when I remembered Snake. "I hope that stuff isn't poisonous." I started through the house to find him.

"We need to talk," Carlos called behind me. "You're right, Jack. We need a plan."

"A goal," I called back. "We need a goal."

CHAPTER TWENTY-FIVE

One more epiphany

I found Snake in the kitchen still shaking his head and pawing at the back door, probably wanting to get out and roll in the dirt the way dogs always do.

Glancing through the slats nailed across the window, we could see the monsters everywhere. They weren't getting too near the house, thanks to the black cloud of locusts that had just taken one of them, but across the yard they were as thick as flies at a picnic.

Snake pawed at the door more forcefully. His sharp nails left werewolf-looking marks down the freshly painted face of the wood. I grabbed one of the gallon jugs of water we'd brought up from the well and sloshed it over his head. The clear liquid coating his fur seemed as waterproof as the oil on a duck's back. The water sluiced right off. It smelled antiseptic, like the inside of a doctor's office.

I grabbed a stack of red and white cup towels off the counter—more of Carlos' pre-sale staging—and used those to scrub at Snake's wet head. I dislodged several squiggly letters from beneath his fur in the process, smashing them with my foot when they fell to the floor.

Snake picked up his feet when the letters fell near them on the linoleum, as if he knew they might burrow back into his fur if they could.

I poured another gallon of water over him, and then Carlos was there, scrubbing as I poured. Together, we got the mess off him before it could harden into a glaze—which I was certain it would do—and I checked under his tawny hair for any sign of blistering or other skin damage.

"I think he's okay," I said at last. He'd stopped pawing and shaking his head and stood patiently. "I think the water felt good to him."

Carlos kept rubbing him, and I recalled the almost instantaneous bond they had exhibited when we first met. "I had that stuff splatter on me when I shot them before, and it didn't hurt. But they were only drops. I thought it might smother Snake the way it gushed over him."

I nodded. "I was worried about his eyesight, too."

"Guess it isn't toxic—"

"Just full of monster-pheromones—"

Thad joined in. "Yeah, like bees or hornets, but instead of calling other Takers, it calls down Our Savior, the dark stuff."

I saw him take a nip from the flask after he spoke, then he tucked it in his back pocket and wandered off to the parlor where we heard him collapse heavily onto the sofa.

I jerked my chin toward the boarded-up window. "Did you see them?"

Carlos leaned over and glanced out. His fingers were touching the small cross in the hollow of his throat. "I don't like this. They haven't congregated like this since I've been here. I thought they were moving on." He turned from me and walked into the parlor. From his gait, I could tell something was wrong. I followed him quietly.

"What do you mean, *Our Savior?*" he asked Thad. His posture reminded me of Snake when he went on high alert. He didn't stand *over* Thad, who was reclining on the sofa, but he didn't sit down either. He simply stood in the center of the room and demanded an answer.

Thad cracked open one eye. "Wha—?"

"Our Savior," Carlos repeated. "What did you mean by that remark?" His face grew tomato red. "Are you saying that black stuff is Jesus? 'Cause I'm pretty tired of people taking potshots at my religion. If God sent this plague down on us, and I'm not saying He did—I still think it's man-made—then it's because we turned our back on Him."

For a moment I wondered if Carlos had been drinking, too. Then I realized I didn't really know him. As if on cue, a stray beam of sunlight arrowed in through a gap between the window-boards and lit up the gold cross at Carlos' throat like a pointing finger from Heaven.

Christianity, I thought, *Native American talismans, the science of pheromones?* Maybe the fabric between the dimensions wasn't the only thing fraying and growing thin. Everything began to seem possible, and jumbled, as if it were up to each of us to choose which set of beliefs to embrace, which path to follow.

But that's nothing new. That's how it's always been in the USA, those were the principles our country was founded upon. *Not quite,* my mind replied. *Native Americans and Africans were forced to toe the European line, regardless of their previous beliefs.*

I rubbed my forehead. Carlos' outburst made me nervous. Could he be mentally unstable? I had no doubt about Thad. When I'd overheard him telling about the fire at my house—which I still hadn't confronted him about—it made me even more certain I couldn't trust him.

Carlos stood in the center of the room a moment longer.

Then Thad grunted. "Ain't dissing your religion, son. I don't even know Jesus—" He sighed and took another nip from the flask.

I could see Carlos' jaw tighten at the word "son."

"You're drunk," I said. I wanted to go over and snatch my dad's flask away from him, but the memory of the pill-bottle fiasco stopped me. "What's in that, my dad's Scotch?"

In answer, Thad tilted the slim silver container forward as if in a toast.

Carlos turned on his heel.

"Hey, don't go away mad," Thad called after him. And then under his breath he said, "Just go away." He giggled at his own juvenile insult.

Snake looked from me to Thad to the retreating back of Carlos. Confusion was evident on his damp face. "I don't know," I said aloud. "I guess Kevin and Marla weren't the only ones with substance abuse problems at that office." I didn't think the attorney would've taken up serious drinking this quickly. Backslid into it, maybe.

I decided to let him sleep it off. I had no experience with this. He'd been tipsy earlier, but this falling-down drunk thing was different.

"I'm going upstairs," I said. "I'll take the first watch—"

"Yeah," Carlos said. "And maybe by tonight sleeping beauty will be awake again. We wouldn't want him to miss out on his rest." There was venom in his voice.

I touched Snake on the head so he would follow me. He'd stopped in the hallway and turned back.

Carlos nodded. "I'm going to watch from down here." He glanced toward the slatted windows. "Maybe they will move on if we stay quiet for a while."

I walked softly up the stairs, not wanting to make any more noise than necessary. Snake tiptoed as always, his nails light upon the wood.

My arm wasn't too bad, but it certainly wasn't good. Carlos had talked about looking for plaster to make a real cast if we ever got into town, but I thought it was healing pretty well with just the splint and bandages, although it had begun to itch down inside, beneath my flesh.

I went into my bedroom and checked the view from every window. The curtains were new and frilly—not the dusty remnants from the past one would expect in a house this old. These were what Mom would've called eyelet. *Don't go there*, my mind whispered, *don't open that mom box yet.*

Running my hand down into my jeans pocket, I pulled out the little blue stone Carlos had given me. "Carry On Wayward Son" began to play softly in my head. I thought about the word *son* for a moment, trying to understand why it had angered Carlos when Thad said it.

I decided it must have been the tone of the man's voice; sort of condescending, the way Cade's had been when he told me he'd left something for me in the basement. Even without the accompanying hand motion I would've understood. *But thanks for saving my life buddy*, I thought. *Even though in reality you were just trying to embarrass me.*

Is that what Thad had been trying to do, save us? I replayed his little half-remark about Jesus, but the music grew louder in my ears, drowning it out. Only this time the lyrics were in Dad's voice—*Carry on, son,* he sang. *Carry on.*

I did. I carried on by checking and rechecking the view from every window on the second floor. And when I grew weary of doing that, I sat for a minute or two in the ladderback chair and worked the muscles in my good arm by leaning forward and then pushing my upper body back from the wall, sort of a modified wall pushup, over and over.

And then I went up to the third floor, making the rounds from window to window, stopping to rest in another chair and doing the wall pushups again.

From the southern windows, the view was clear to the horizon. Only a few wayward clouds graced the pale blue. In the distance, waves of heat radiated up from the ground, a harbinger of summer. Just looking at the wavy lines of warmth caused a rivulet of sweat to inch its way into my collar. I reached around to wipe it away and was surprised by the hank of hair touching the back of my neck.

I ran my good hand over my head. My hair felt stiff, filthy. Time for a shower and a trim. Funny the things we took for granted. How long had it been since the start of this mess? Four days, five, six? *Could it be more?* I was spaced out on those painkillers for a while. Time might have flowed around me like a river flowing around a boulder. Panic began to burrow into my gut.

Carry on, son, Dad's voice said. *Stop obsessing and carry on.*

I stood and began another circuit. It was getting warmer. Heat rises. We'd learned that in fire safety week in elementary school. In case of fire, crawl on the floor where the air is better.

Maybe that's what I'll have to do here, crawl around on the floor.

I began to feel woozy, in need of water. The image of the cool water in the basement convinced me it was time to let Carlos take over. I wanted to talk to him about the heat. All the downstairs windows were boarded up, and summer was coming. One more reason to keep going. One more reason to carry on.

I checked the view one last time. To the west I could barely make out the edge of the cliff Carlos had mentioned. What would happen if the monsters fell off the cliff? Would they break their legs? Would words leak out and cause the black rain to fall? Is that why I dreamed about it?

It didn't matter. The Takers weren't moving in that direction. They were moving to the north at a leisurely pace. Every little while a knot of stragglers would stop and look around as if gauging their whereabouts. I could see two more that had come up with articles of clothing and put them on. One wore a billed cap, and the other wore a heavy shirt, like a work shirt. I thought the cap and shirt probably came from the same victim. Maybe the truck driver whose maps we'd used to get here.

I turned away. *What are they?* The question lived in the back of my mind in its own little box—not the box where images of Mom lived, but a separate little box nearby.

My throat tried to close.

I won't think about that right now . . .

Instead, I imagined a box labeled TAKERS. The lid was barely askew. The question, What are they? was typed on a single sheet of paper, awaiting examination. The second sheet of paper asked, Why are they here? And a third sheet at the bottom of the slim stack asked, What do they want? But I'd already answered that one in big red letters—THEY WANT OUR SOULS—to move on to Heaven.

One more paper lay in the box. Typed across the top of it was the biggest question of all: How do we kill them? I moved that paper to the top of the stack. How do we kill them was another way of asking "How do we get rid of them so we can survive?"

Treading lightly back down the narrow staircase to the second floor, I wiped another bead of sweat from the back of my neck. It felt like an insect crawling around back there, and that reminded me of our pheromone theory. But I didn't want to examine that right now. Stick it in the box labeled TAKERS.

My rumpled bed looked inviting. I lay down. How could I be so tired? It was still morning or near noon at the latest. Maybe it's stress, and this. I looked down at my arm. Maybe healing takes more sleep. Mom always said sleep and laughter were the best cures for any illness.

I clenched my fist. No matter what I did, her memory box wouldn't stay closed; the cardboard lid kept slipping sideways so that one small triangle of darkness was exposed, and inside, in the gloom, the tiniest glimpse of turquoise.

It reminded me of the blue rock in my pocket, and of Carlos with his gold cross. I touched the battery-operated lantern beside my bedside table. Carlos had found them in the kitchen pantry along with fresh batteries. Apparently, the electricity had been spotty out here even before the apocalypse, he'd said.

As I sunk into the comfy bed and down into slumber, something kept nagging at me. *Why are some of them cleaning up as if to stay? Why are they wearing clothes like Adam and Eve in The Garden?*

I come to The Garden alone,
   While the dew is still on the ros-es . . .

The old hymn was so loud it almost fried my brain. I sat up; uncertain how much time had passed. One hour—two? My neck felt incredibly stiff, as if I'd napped for quite some time in an unnatural position. The song came again.

I come to The Garden alone . . .

Oh my God. I leapt from the bed and raced down the remaining stairs almost tripping over a startled Snake in the process.

Carlos reclined on the big couch in the second living room, what might have been called a library, if gangsters like Bitty Sloan had such things.

He opened his eyes when I came pounding in. "Maybe *this* is the real Eden—you know, The Garden? I don't mean this house or even my little hometown, Eden, Texas. I mean the Earth. This whole thing. Maybe this is the true Garden!" My voice was strident, I knew it, couldn't help it. "Instead of trying to get *back* to the Garden, maybe they've already arrived."

CHAPTER TWENTY-SIX

In The Garden

Carlos rubbed his face. "This can't be biblical Eden. That was a perfect place—"

"Right, right, right," I said. "What I meant to say is maybe *they* think this is the real Eden. Or Heaven. Aren't they the same thing?" As the words left my lips, I knew they didn't sound right.

"Anyhow, if the monsters really are from the dimension of Purgatory, and they've been waiting eons for new souls or clean souls or whatever—"

"I'm with you part of the way." The tone of his voice was hesitant. "But Eden was a real place here on earth before the flood. It was the place where Adam and Eve condemned us all to mortality."

Thad grumbled from the other room. "Ain't *Heaven* a real place?"

It amazed me how uneducated he sounded when he was drunk. "It's only the booze making him sound so stupid," I apologized.

Carlos nodded. "He brought some with him. I don't drink anything stronger than beer. Didn't bring any here, unless he found some in a cabinet or something."

I nodded. "That flask belonged to my dad. Thad brought it from my house, but he must be refilling it from something."

Carlos stood and abruptly announced, "I'm going to the farmhouse. I can't take much more of this sitting around. Besides," he indicated the window with a tilt of his head. "The black rain is gone, and the creatures are all headed north. I watched the last of them moving past about an hour ago."

"I wish they'd all fall over that cliff. Then maybe they would break their legs and the dark stuff would come down and take them back up into . . . wherever they came from."

Carlos looked at me, and for a moment I was afraid I'd said something to offend him. After all, I'd also called the black stuff *our savior* at one point.

But he wasn't thinking about that. Instead, he said, "Like a buffalo jump. Yeah. A Native American buffalo jump. I'll bet the cliff *was* one before. Maybe that's why God chose this house for us."

My hand went to the turquoise in my pocket. *Oh, give me a home, where the buffalo roam* . . . began to play in my head.

Thad snorted from the other room. It sounded suspiciously like a laugh. At first, I thought it was because of the crazy old song in my head, but of course he couldn't hear that. I glanced at Carlos.

His face was like the underside of a storm cloud just before the lightning flashes through it. He balled one fist beside his thigh. I could see the other hand clamped around the shotgun that had made such short work of the Taker in the parlor. If Thad hadn't begun to snore just then, I'm not sure what might have happened.

"Is the Chrysler's tank full?" he asked.

I followed him to the kitchen door that led down to the garage. "I'm not sure. I was out of it by the time we got here. Do you have the key?"

Carlos held it up. "Thad left it on the coffee table."

I wondered about that, but it was so similar to the story Thad had told me about how he'd gotten the key from Mo, that I wasn't about to question it. "Are we going to wake him? Take him with us?"

Carlos had just picked up one of the battery-operated lanterns from the kitchen counter and was halfway down the steps when he stopped so suddenly, I almost crashed into him. His shoulders sagged, and he turned to face me. "I wasn't going to. I was going to leave him sleeping it off, but I suppose you're right. That wouldn't be very nice, would it?"

"Dangerous," I said, thinking of a rogue Taker pulling a board off the window while Thad lay snoring, unarmed.

Carlos pushed past me and stomped back up the steps.

Snake and I trailed along behind.

"I'm beginning to think you are our moral compass, Jack."

I didn't argue, but I thought, *he wouldn't say that if he'd seen me sneaking out my bedroom window that night.*

Back in the parlor, Carlos didn't stop to chitchat.

Thad lay on his back, sound asleep, one foot hanging over the end of the short settee, the other foot flat on the floor beside him.

Carlos lifted his motorcycle boot and kicked the bottom of Thad's—*my dad's*—New Balance sneaker hard enough to wake him. "Hey—we're going to the farmhouse. C'mon." He turned and stepped around me, headed back toward the kitchen. Snake looked from me to him, uncertain whether to stay or go.

"Come on," I said, shaking the attorney's shoulder. "We're going for food and fuel. You can sleep in the car."

Thad brushed my hand away and turned over showing me his back.

I tried again, pushing at his back with the tips of my fingers. Below ground, I heard the Chrysler start up. "He's leaving," I said. "And I don't want him to get crazy and go off in the car without us. Come on!" I shoved him a little harder.

"Goddammit, boy, leave me alone. He'll be back. This is his house—sort of."

I straightened up and put my hand on Snake's head. I really didn't like the idea of leaving the old man there, defenseless, but I wasn't about to let Carlos go without me. I kicked the bottom of his shoe the way Carlos had done. "Suit yourself. But I wish you would at least go down to the basement while we're gone. We're taking the shotgun you know."

Thad snored deeply, and I couldn't tell if it was real or fake. With a heavy heart, I led Snake back down to the garage. It's nearly impossible to help someone who doesn't want your help. One of my new *lessons learned.*

It was dark underground, but Carlos had set the lantern on top of the car and was wiping out the backseat with a wet rag. "Little smelly in here." He chuckled, and I recalled how I'd vomited all over the place.

"We should have cleaned it better," I said. "And left the windows down."

"I've about got it," he replied. "You know, my old man was a drunk." He didn't look at me while he talked, just kept wiping down the leather seats and floorboard. "That's why he died young. Left my mom to feed us all on her teacher's salary."

Ahh, I thought. *Maybe that's why he hates alcohol so much.* "I'm sorry," I told him. "My dad really doesn't drink. He's a teacher, too. He teaches music at the high school." I wanted to say more, but my voice wouldn't go there.

My fist went to my pocket. I pulled out the note and showed it to him. "I have to get to Colorado," I whispered. "But I'm wondering if I shouldn't try Eden one more time, first."

Carlos read the note and handed it back to me. "Damn, kid. That's tough." He was quiet until he finished his chore. "So y'all are from the town of Eden, for real, huh?"

I laughed. "Yeah. Pure coincidence, I'm sure." I let Snake in the back seat and sat in the passenger side with the door open. The note went into my wallet and into my back pocket. The turquoise was in my front jeans pocket with Mom's earrings and Dad's key. If I kept collecting stuff, I was going to need another backpack. I was struck with a sudden longing for the pink sparkly iPod, too. As if all the things I'd gathered since the rip had—for some reason—taken on monumental importance.

Carlos leaned inside. "You ready?"

I nodded; glad he had already repositioned the car so that it could be driven out instead of having to be backed out in reverse.

"Here's the thing," he glanced at the overhead door. "Without electricity, this door has to be opened manually. It's heavy. I didn't see anything out the windows, but there could be one right outside and we wouldn't know it until it was too late."

"I'll open the door. You hold the shotgun—"

Carlos grimaced. "That's the problem. There's no way you can open it one handed. And if you re-break that arm, we might not be able to fix it." He stood beside the car, thinking. "I can open the door if you can level the shotgun out the window like this—"

He showed me how to lay the barrel out the open car window. "If anything is there when I get the door up—you will see its legs—then you blast it. Don't shoot me, though."

I moved around to the driver's seat. "You sure are a trusting soul." I adjusted the seat and the mirrors. It already felt right, sitting there again. "Be ready to jump in if nothing is there."

Carlos laughed. "I think you're enjoying this too much." He turned the lantern down to its lowest setting, put it in the passenger side floorboard, and then walked over to the door, leaned down, and began to pull.

I leveled the shotgun out the window but didn't have a clear view, so I opened the car door, stood outside, and balanced it on the roof instead. Carlos grunted with effort and then I saw daylight below the edge of the huge door. It reminded me of the night I saw the shadows of feet in the narrow slit beneath our garage door at home.

"How is it?" Carlos whispered.

"I don't see any."

Snake whined from the backseat.

With a giant shove, Carlos raised the door all the way and rushed back to the car. He'd left the passenger door open, so he simply fell inside and slammed it shut.

I handed in the shotgun, slid behind the steering wheel, and goosed the pedal. The driver's door closed beside me as I drove out of the garage.

Carlos pushed the button to raise his window, and I pushed mine with my elbow.

"Not too fast," he said. "There's a big dip in the driveway right below here."

I let my foot off the pedal, and we coasted to a stop.

Carlos hopped out—there were no Takers anywhere—and lowered the overhead door. I got out and dashed around to the passenger side. "I think I would feel better with you driving."

He nodded and got behind the wheel. The land was empty as far as I could see. "How long will it take to get there?"

Carlos craned his head around, attempting to see all directions at once. "Twenty minutes, maybe fifteen if we don't encounter any difficulties."

His concern was catching. I felt my gut tighten up right along with the muscles in my sore jaw. The skin on my good arm crimped into gooseflesh, and I rubbed at it with my other hand, the one in the sling. "It's really quiet, isn't it?" I tried not to whisper, but the vast emptiness almost demanded it.

Carlos nodded. "It was better on the bike 'cause you've got the wind rushing through your skull, keeping your thoughts in check." He rolled down the windows. "There," he said. "That feels better. White noise and all that jazz."

I understood exactly what he meant. The sound of the wind was just enough to keep the memory boxes closed. "Wish we had binoculars." I pointed off in the distance. "That looks like a horse, and look, there's a rabbit!" I almost broke myself twisting around to get another glimpse of the two animals. "Did you see them?"

"I saw the rabbit, which reminds me of us, fleeing down in the tunnels to survive like a bunch of meek little bunnies—"

"And the meek shall inherit the earth," I murmured.

Carlos looked over at me, perhaps to see if I was dissing the Bible, but of course I wouldn't do that. I was only repeating one of the few quotes I knew.

"And so, we shall," he said at last. "Matthew 5:5. And if we play our cards right, we just might inherit the whole enchilada. What do you say to that, m'ijo?"

I tried to picture a huge world with only the three of us in it plus Snake. "I can't really imagine it, to be honest with you. I mean surely a few *girls* were meek, too."

He roared laughter. "Amen to that, Jack." He slapped his thigh. "Amen to that!"

As we drove on down the road, I began to feel lighter than I had in days. Nothing had changed. The land was still bare and empty except for a few vehicles scattered here and there. Mostly trucks hauling freight and feed, but a few passenger cars also roasted in the sun. "Couldn't pay me to open one of those," I said.

Carlos glanced at an SUV as we passed it. The driver was pressed against the side window, face swollen and dark. "Me neither. No way, José."

Small herds of bloated animals also graced the fields, and the occasional spindly mesquite tree still rattled its skeletal wind chimes with every little breeze.

"It's a different world, now. I don't think I like it, but what can we do except carry on?"

My head snapped up. "What did you just say?"

Carlos must've heard something in my voice. "What do you mean? I just said we have to carry on, no matter what."

The song played softly in my head as if it had been there always, and always would be there. "I guess it's nothing." I couldn't tell him the truth about the music. "It's just that saying, *carry on*. It's what my dad always tells me."

He shrugged, seemingly embarrassed by the comparison. "Maybe we'll find him one of these days. Or he'll find us." His voice went soft. "I can't imagine a father who wouldn't keep searching for his kid in a mess like this."

An image of Thad came to my mind. He didn't seem to be in much of a hurry to find his kids. I started to tell Carlos that but thought better of it since he already had a problem with Thad and his drinking.

After a few more moments, Carlos said, "You know, if that really was a horse you saw back there, then it must've somehow been underground. Have you ever heard of such a thing? The rabbits, moles, ground squirrels, all those little critters, I can see them surviving—they naturally live under the ground—but how could a horse survive?"

"I hadn't really thought about it." I scanned the horizon again. "I don't know, I just thought that's what I saw."

We skirted a small truck that had gone sideways in the road as if the driver had simply let go of the wheel to grab his ears. "Is the driver in there? I don't see him."

Carlos shook his head. "I don't see anyone. Guess he survived, too. Hope he found some place safe—"

"Look!" I pointed down the intersecting farm-to-market road

where a two-story farmhouse nestled between two immense cottonwood trees, both of which were oddly devoid of human remains but sported several broken branches. The pale bark of the broken branches pointed skyward like accusing finger bones.

The white clapboard house appeared to float on undulating waves of prairie grass. It reminded me of something we'd read in school. Something about covered wagons being called prairie schooners. I guess this was why.

A few dozen yards behind the home, a good-sized greenhouse sparkled in the sun. "That's it, isn't it? That's the farmhouse. It has to be."

Carlos nodded and slowed to negotiate the ninety-degree turn from the highway onto the adjoining road. Soon we came to a cattle guard across a red dirt drive like the one at the Bitty Sloan house. It wasn't up on a hill like the Sloan house. Here, the road was flat and even except for a gentle rise behind the house.

We drove across the cattle guard, our tires *blump, blump, blumping* over the iron pipes. "Why aren't there any dead things here? There aren't any animal carcasses or anything."

As if on cue, several rabbits and what appeared to be a large field mouse dashed out of an overgrown garden. Snake bounced from one window to the other when he saw them, and I wondered if I should leave him in the car when we got out. *That's all I need*, I thought, *for him to take off across the field with no way for me to call him back.*

But I needn't have worried. Once they were out of sight, they also seemed to be out of mind. I gazed at the garden. "Boy, what a feast." My eyes flitted from one amazement to the next, trying to take it all in.

Even from the driveway, I could see heavy ears pulling the corn stalks down, and I figured the profusion of vines sported melons of some kind. The chorus of *In the Garden* drifted though my head like a soft prayer of thanksgiving, and I nodded in agreement. A sweet ear of corn roasted over an open fire sounded downright heavenly. "This is wonderful."

Carlos nodded and eased the Chrysler right up next to the

garden so we could pick the fruits and veggies and load them directly into the car. "Good set up, isn't it? Garden and green house side by side this way. I bet they would start plants in the green house and then transfer them to the garden when the weather was right."

We sat still, watching, and waiting to see what might appear before we opened our doors. "You seem to know a lot about growing things."

"Back in Mexico we always had a vegetable garden behind our house. *Mi abuelita*, my granny, grew every pepper you can imagine. She would put them up in Mason jars and line the shelves of our pantry with them. The colors were amazing, a million shades of red, yellow, green, and orange. Some were even black. When I was a little boy, I would stare at those jars. When the light hit them, they looked like stained glass." He looked around the yard. "This really takes me back."

I heard the catch in his voice, so I said, "It might be a good place to live once the Takers are gone." *Assuming they are leaving.* I exited the car and scanned the area for movement. Snake hopped out, too. But he didn't take off, just nosed around the rows as if viewing everything by scent. "One thing bothers me, though."

Carlos glanced up.

"Do you think the Takers might already be here? Like, maybe they've cleaned up all the dead and claimed it for their own?" I stared at the house. "Maybe they're watching us from the windows, one wearing an apron and another holding a pitchfork like in that famous painting."

Carlos stepped out and stood in the vee of his open door, one hand on the top of the doorframe, the other holding his shotgun. I'd seen him fill his pockets with shells before we left.

"Damn," he said. "I never thought of that. But I didn't know they were cleaning up until you told me about it." He gazed around. "I'm still not convinced they aren't bombs of some sort."

"What makes you think so? They sure don't look like bombs, they could be weapons I suppose, like the ones in those old *Terminator* movies . . ."

Carlos walked over to the first row of corn and began pulling ears off the head-high stalks. He seemed to be considering his words the way Mom had tried to teach *me* to do. "That's exactly what I mean. Maybe it's so high-tech we don't even know the extent of it yet." He shot me a look of appraisal. "I think some terrorist organization is trying out a brand-new technology on us. I mean, come on, take over the good old US of A and you might as well say you own the freaking world, right?"

I stood, quietly pulling ears of corn, watching for worms in the silk. When he said it all together like that, it sounded extremely plausible. "I'll admit you make a good case for it. But I know I saw the things cleaning up in Eden, and I know the turquoise Taker saved me. If it weren't for those things—and the church-goers— then I might be tempted to agree with you." Did all that come out of my mouth? It sounded like my dad talking, or my mom.

"Maybe they were programmed to clean up at a certain point," Carlos murmured. "No one wants to live in a mausoleum, right?"

We had both reached the ends of our rows and stashed all the ears in the back of the car. He'd given me a lot to think about, not the least of which was the fact that I, a non-church-goer, assumed the apocalypse had a religious basis, but he, who wore a golden cru- cifix around his neck, could see nothing but man made destruction.

Unable to wrap my head around the irony, I stashed it in the Why? Box in my mind. First things first. "Do we go in the farm- house now? Or check out the greenhouse?"

"Let's get some melons," he said. Then he showed me how to pull up the huge leaves of the vines to look for ripe fruit.

It was like Christmas every time I pulled aside leaves and found the sweet green and black stripes of a watermelon or the rough gold skin of a cantaloupe. There were only a few that hadn't been damaged by critters, but those few were heavy and fragrant.

"Look here," Carlos called.

I hurried over.

He grinned and held aside a giant leaf so I could see the little orange pumpkin nestled beneath. "They won't be ripe until fall. Maybe we'll come back."

Thinking of being at the Bitty Sloan house all summer with

nothing to do but survive sent a chill across my skin. I shivered and rubbed at the nape of my neck.

Carlos took out his pocketknife and dug into a small hill of soil. "Let's see if any of these potatoes are ripe yet." He held up a tiny brown lump. "I think I'll just tuck it back in and hope for rain. The carrots on the other hand might be just right." He walked over to a flat spot, but all I could see were chewed up green tops in rows. "Looks like the bunnies have been working on them." Once again, he dug down into the soil with his pocketknife while I held the shotgun.

The carrots were small and hard like the potatoes. "Not enough water," he said. "Pray for rain." He thought about what he'd said. "But not black rain and certainly not that silver stuff that brought us the monsters." He shook his head as if to clear away the memories, then the two of us walked around to the cracked glass door of the greenhouse and peered inside.

Plants crowded every surface and smashed their leaves against the glass walls, smearing the panes with moisture.

"Wow! It's a room full of food."

Carlos laughed. "It *is* a room full of food—fresh food."

I took a deep breath. "Look, they even left us some sacks." I picked up an empty tow sack from beside the door and waited as Carlos opened the screen.

When he pulled it open—a regular looking storm door, all cracked glass and shiny aluminum—a wave of wet heat washed over us. Wet heat, and the smell of good, well-fertilized soil. We stepped inside as if into a shrine. Even Snake tiptoed in—but then he almost always tiptoed when he wasn't charging after something.

Once the door closed behind us, I immediately had to wipe my forehead with the tail of my shirt. Though it was only June, spring in this part of New Mexico must be very warm and the green-house gave everything a jump-start. There were several varieties of tomato plants, loaded with fruit. There were squash plants, a whole row of spinach and lettuce, and even a row of cucumbers in a long rectangular planter.

"Look at the peppers," Carlos crowed.

It was an echo of what he'd told me about only minutes earlier, red bells, yellow bells, green bells, and dark, glossy, nearly black, jalapeños. There were so many other kinds of peppers I didn't even recognize them all. *Jackpot,* I thought, spying a square container of spiky green onion tops.

Sweat poured down my brow. I pulled the tail of my shirt up and mopped my face again. I thought I heard the unmistakable buzz of a bee but if there were any, they didn't come near me. I sure hoped a few survived. I'd been taught that without bees there would be no life on earth.

I looked around at the abundance of food. *What a great place this could be to set up housekeeping. If no one lives here*—I glanced out at the big house dubiously—*maybe it was meant for us. Besides, if someone doesn't move in and take care of this greenhouse, everything will begin to rot. But does it have a sweet well like Bitty Sloan's house? Or secret tunnels to safety?*

Eyeing the tomato plants crushed against the glass, I noticed the edges of some of the leaves had already begun to curl and turn brown. They need to be moved, or trimmed, or something. I didn't know much about growing things in a greenhouse. But I knew how to find out. Every town in America has a public library brimming with books on gardening.

I pulled a bright red cherry tomato and popped it into my mouth. The warm, sweet juice dribbled down my chin, and I began to smile. After this, I wanted to explore the barn, look for that fuel Carlos mentioned. He said all farmers kept fuel on hand for their tractors. I tucked several of the tiny tomatoes into my sling to eat along the way, and then a strange noise caught my ear. I looked down.

Snake's tongue hung out the side of his mouth, and his sides were going in and out like a bellows. He appeared to be on the verge of a heatstroke.

I rushed back to the door, yanked it open, and urged him outside. My tow sack was already half full of tomatoes, onions, and cucumbers. If I put much more in, I would probably crush the tomatoes.

Carlos' sack also appeared to be half full. He'd been gathering the greens and peppers. "You ready to go?"

I nodded and pointed at Snake who was already outside the door. I noticed Carlos carried several cherry tomatoes in his shirt pocket. *All we need is a saltshaker,* I thought. We went out, and Carlos pulled the aluminum door closed. A large triangular shard of the glass fell out at his feet.

We looked at each other comically. "Thank God that didn't hit your foot." I imagined blood filling his shoe. What would I have done, bandaged it with his shirt? "We have to be careful, don't we? More careful than ever before."

His bronze face paled as he thought about the consequences of a serious cut. "You're right." He looked at the big gap in the glass door. "And now all the moisture will escape."

"Maybe we'll find something to repair it with. Every house has duct tape, right?"

Carlos nodded. "I hope so. Let's stick these in the car and then drive back to the tractor shed." He indicated a curiously open structure behind the big hay barn. "I think the fuel might be there. They certainly wouldn't keep it in the same barn as the hay."

"Makes sense to me," I said. Though in reality I never would have thought of it that way. If it had been left up to me, I probably would have stored it next to hay bales and matches. I laughed inwardly at my own little joke. "Can we get a drink first? I think we still have some bottled water in the trunk."

Carlos stuck his sack in the back floorboard with the other vegetables and then thought better of it. "I guess we'd better put as much of this as we can into the trunk, so Snake won't tear them up on the way home."

I started to protest. Snake would never do anything like that, but then I realized he would trample them if he got excited about something, and yes, his claws could do some damage. Especially to the thin-skinned tomatoes. I didn't say anything though, only nodded. Hearing Carlos refer to the old Bitty Sloan house as home struck me right in the melancholy—again.

We took off toward the tractor shed. "I can't wait to check out the kitchen before we leave," I said. I imagined sweets and things that hadn't gone bad yet. "Maybe they've even got a root cellar." I thought of Carlos' granny. Maybe someone's granny had lived here.

We got in and drove down to the tractor shed where, sure enough, there was a large fuel tank. It was marked DIESEL in big black letters.

"Most tractors run on diesel," Carlos said. "I knew that." Disappointment shadowed his face. "Well, let's go check the rest of the place while we're here. Maybe they've got a car or pickup truck in the garage."

I picked up a plastic red and yellow container. "Hey, here's one that's marked GAS. And it feels full." I turned around. "Here are several more. I guess something runs on gasoline." I started toward the car with it.

Carlos followed with two more.

We loaded the three containers and drove over to the big barn. Neither of us said it aloud, but we were afraid to get too far from the car.

I looked at the strange building. The front of it looked like a normal barn complete with big, weathered-gray doors, but the back portion appeared to be built into the side of the small rise. "I remember reading about houses built into the sides of hills because the pioneers couldn't find enough trees to build with, but I never heard of a whole barn being built this way."

"Might be how a horse survived." Carlos shrugged. "Stranger things have definitely happened."

I felt excitement in my gut at the prospect. "Maybe there are horses inside. Or a cow!" But when Carlos pulled open the big doors, the smell of death was there to greet us. It wasn't as bad as Wal-Mart had been, this building wasn't nearly that tight, but it was still bad.

Carlos backed away with his hand over his mouth.

CHAPTER TWENTY-SEVEN

Carlos

Over Carlos' shoulder I glimpsed dead cows and what must have been the farmer. He wasn't ripped to shreds at least. It appeared he had died while milking.

"Stay here," Carlos said. "I'll be right back." He pulled his shirt up over his nose and walked bravely into the stench.

I assumed he was going to check out the lower portion of the barn. I motioned Snake back to the car, and we got in and started it up, thankful we had left the key lying in the cup holder.

In moments Carlos came running out at a hard clip and jumped in beside me. He reeked of death. "They have a generator down there." He paused to catch his breath. "And it's *running*. We have to come back again in a few days—maybe it won't smell so bad if we leave those doors open until then."

I drove slowly back to the house. "No more live animals? Or people?"

Carlos shook his head, stripped off his shirt and flapped it out the window to air it. He also gagged and spit a few times. I was a little confused.

"How is the generator running if no one is here?"

"There are several stalls and tack rooms built into the side of the hill—just like being underground. I guess the generator was spared that way. It's probably designed to come on and run for a few hours when the power is off. That's all I can figure out." He spit out the window a few more times. "There were three horses in the regular part of the barn. And more people."

"Carry On Wayward Son" swelled up and took the place of "In the Garden." I let the music rise. It sounded like a low-voltage warning urging me not to stop for very long. "Guess we'd better carry on, then."

Carlos nodded. His face was red and splotchy, the skin beneath his eyes pale, as if he'd seen something. A ghost, perhaps.

"You still want to go in the house?"

He nodded again so I nosed the car right up to the edge of the yard. Flowers grew in abundance around the old-fashioned front porch. Some were beginning to wilt and turn brown, but the ones in the shade held on to their color. I could imagine Andy, Opie, and Aunt Bee sitting out here with a glass of lemonade.

"Stay here," Carlos said. "Keep the car running. I'll only be a few minutes."

I liked that idea—something had changed—maybe it was just the taste of death reminding us why we were out scavenging. "Okay, I'll honk the horn if I need you. And if you aren't out in a few minutes, we'll come in."

"Don't come in," Carlos said. "Watch the clock. If I'm not back in five minutes—no, make it ten in case I find a root cellar—then you and Snake hurry back to the Sloan house."

Something must have rattled him. "What did you see back there, in the barn?"

He ignored me, climbed out of the car, shook his t-shirt out a few more times before slipping it back on, and then he walked up the steps and onto the wide-planked porch. He led with his shoulder as always. I watched him go, uneasy but alert.

Snake paced in the backseat. As usual, he could sense my trepidation. Whatever was in the barn must have been bad, so why would Carlos insist on going in the house?

The music in my head grew quiet. For once, I sort of missed it. I marked the passage of time on the dashboard's old-fashioned analog clock. Five minutes passed. I played rhythm on the steering wheel with my good hand. The smell of the freshly picked veggies was beginning to replace the smell of death inside the car. I ate another cherry tomato. *On the way back to the Sloan house, I'll roll*

*down all the windows and turn off the AC. Seventy miles an hour down
the highway, windows wide, blow the smell right out—*

Ten minutes gone. Time to make a decision.

Kansas tuned up. I didn't even wait for the refrain. "C'mon, boy."
I opened the door—making certain to pocket the car key just in
case—and took the porch steps two at a time before my courage
could desert me. The door had not shut all the way. The trim was
immaculate, farmhouse white. The doorknocker was brass. There
was no bell. I saw everything with supernatural clarity. Snake had
hopped over the car seat and followed me out the driver's side
before I had a chance to open the back door. He stood beside me
now, tongue lolling. He didn't seem overly concerned, but still . . .

What if Carlos lay dead? Or dying? What if one of *them* had
made a little monster nest in the farmhouse and was now having a
soul-snack in the kitchen, or worse yet, down in the cellar? Would
I be able to go down the cellar stairs if necessary?

"You'd know if one were in there, right?" I touched Snake's head
for luck. I didn't expect a reply, but I'd learned to trust his instincts.
Kansas sang a little louder. *Carry on,* they said. *Carry on.*

So, I did.

We went in quietly. I wanted to call out, but I didn't want to call
out. I stood for a moment, looking, listening. Snake waited, too.
After a moment, we tiptoed across the wide space. An ancient carpet
covered the hardwood. It was country blue with faded vines and
flowers. The edges were frayed. But I didn't see any blood. *Carry
on Wayward Son.* The music was not yet urgent.

Snake followed me through the house. The living room, dining
room, and kitchen were empty. I stopped at the foot of the wide
stairs going up to the second floor, but I thought it would be best
to finish searching the main floor first.

Sunlight painted each open area in a swath of luminous yellow.
The old house sported windows on every side. Most were intact but
cracked. There was no odor like we'd encountered in most closed-up
places. That gave me a moment's peace, but then I felt a flicker of
breeze and realized it meant there were probably windows open,
or knocked out, somewhere.

A short hall led away from the dining room, but a pair of doors begged inspection. The first, just inside the kitchen, was slightly open. It was a well-stocked pantry. My eyes drank in mason jars filled with beans, tomatoes, and something that had to be corn relish. I vowed to take as many as I could carry, but not until we found Carlos.

The second door didn't go outside. The outside door was at the rear of the kitchen. The top half of it was glass, completely broken, its long shards glittering on the floor. It appeared no one had been out that door since the rip.

That left the hallway and the one remaining closed door. I knew it had to be the cellar door. And I knew I would have to open it. The music of Kansas grew in my head, but even as I reached toward the knob, Snake traipsed down the hall toward the rest of the house. He didn't seem to be in a hurry. I'd seen him in attack mode when the Takers were near; he was nowhere near that. Curious. That was the word to describe him today. Just curious.

"Snake? Carlos?" I spoke in a normal tone of voice, but I couldn't seem to get my feet moving. Then Snake disappeared into an open door at the end of the hall.

The sound of sobbing came to me at the same instant "Amazing Grace" washed over my senses.

> *T'was grace that taught my heart to fear*
> *And grace my fears relieved . . .*

I hurried down the hallway and peeked inside. Snake stood in the center of the room. Carlos sat in the floor with his back against the wall. He held a teddy bear in his arms. In the corner stood a white crib with pink bunting.

"Carlos?" I couldn't imagine what had happened. "Amazing Grace" settled into background music between my ears.

Carlos didn't look up. Shotgun across his lap, he reached out to Snake, and then started talking. "In the barn, in the tack room. Hooks where the bridles hung." His glance strayed toward the empty crib. "Babies don't belong in tack rooms." He clutched the teddy bear with one hand, Snake's wrinkly neck with the other. "There's no God, Jack. No loving and merciful God would let this happen. That baby was innocent. She hadn't sinned. Her soul was pure."

I sat on the floor beside him. His small gold cross lay on the floor in a patch of sunlight, the chain broken. "And yet *we* survived. Us. With souls sullied and *im*pure." I hesitated, not wanting to sound like a preacher but knowing I did. "If there is a God, and I believe there has to be because I can't wrap my head around the idea that everything started from nothing, then there must be a devil, too."

My voice faltered. "And if there's a devil, then there is evil. The world seems cloaked in evil now. That's all I know. I can't say why, but I believe it's so. I also think it's possible God is turning the evil ones around one monster at a time. Like the Turquoise Taker." I shoved my good hand into my pocket and brought out the small blue stone.

In the back of my mind, in a What If Box I'd never opened, was that hidden thought. What if the *good* Takers had ingested souls so pure they had turned around on the spot? Souls so pure they overcame the evil instantly— Would God do that? Would he use babies as ammunition in the greatest war of all?

I smashed the lid closed on that unthinkable box of *what ifs.*

Snake wriggled his way into Carlos' lap. I saw him swipe his black tongue across our friend's salty cheek. Carlos reached into his pocket and pulled out his wallet, flipped it open to a photo of a little brown-haired girl. She had his dark, dark eyes.

"She looks just like you." I didn't have to ask what happened to her.

He broke down as surely as if I'd jackhammered a dam. I put my arm across his shoulders, and he hugged the teddy bear to his middle and moaned.

"It's okay." I didn't know what else to say. It wasn't okay. It would never be okay, but his pain was my pain.

He sobbed.

I left my arm where it was, but I kept one eye on the shotgun and the other on the window looking over the yard. I wanted to stand so I would have a better view, but I didn't. He needed time.

At last, he wiped his face on the bear and patted my hand on his shoulder. He picked up his wallet and stared at the beautiful photo. "I left so early. We lived in Yellow Bend, in the mountains, but a friend hooked me up with the deal on the Sloan house. It would've been a hell of a commission." He glanced at the crib again. "I left before daylight."

I squeezed his shoulder and took my arm away. But I didn't stand. My ears were on high alert, though. *If they come through that door,* I thought, *I'm going to shoot first and then go through that window before the black rain falls.*

Carlos continued, "The sky split open after I got to the Sloan house, while I waited on the buyers to show up. I went down to the tunnels. I didn't get back to my place in Yellow Bend for three days." He gazed out the window at the calm blue sky. "My wife must've grabbed her and ran outside. I was 200 miles away." His voice took on a dreamy quality. "There are all kinds of trees in Yellow Bend. Our little house was surrounded by them."

Tears formed in my eyes, and I let them spill over unchecked. Then I threw open the turquoise Mom Box and told him how I'd found her stacked like a piece of firewood in the library. I told him about her beautiful hair hanging down and the shadows of the Takers crawling up the walls, and I told him how Snake had led me to safety.

For a long moment we sat there and cried together. Oddly enough, the Mom Box seemed to close after that.

Carlos wiped his face and stood, pushing Snake off his lap in the process. "Thank you, Jack." He closed the wallet gently, and then stuffed it back in his pocket. He rubbed Snake's sympathetic head. "I know we've all had everything taken, but I didn't even kiss Addie goodbye. I didn't want to wake her." He picked up the shotgun. "I blew her a kiss from the door of her room and told her how everything was going to be different when Daddy got back. I was going to pay off some bills—start a college fund—take a vacation, maybe Disneyland." He held out his hand and pulled me to my feet. We walked out of the nursery together.

On the way out, we detoured to the pantry and grabbed as many Mason jars as we could handle. Carlos didn't mention the summery colors. All the wonder of the place was gone. As we headed toward the front door, I set my jars on the dining table and ran back to the kitchen where I went directly to the drawer farthest from the sink and pulled it open. There, amidst the junk of everyday life, lay a roll of silver duct tape. We had a drawer like this at my house, too.

I grabbed the tape and looked around for something to use on the broken greenhouse door glass. True to farmhouse style, someone had tacked a sheet of plastic behind the old-fashioned stove to keep grease from splattering the wall. I yanked it down and hauled it outside. We stashed all our jars in the trunk of the Chrysler and then, together, we taped the plastic over the broken glass door. Carlos' heart wasn't in it, I knew that, but I also knew the only way to carry on was just to carry on. Kansas played through my head on eternal repeat with "Amazing Grace" and "In the Garden" filling in the gaps.

Later, I would ask Carlos if any of the farmer's people had been upstairs. I couldn't imagine why they would've all been in the barn otherwise, and then it hit me. They'd probably tried to run underground when the sky split open. It was probably their safe place like the school basement had been mine. Like the tunnels had been for Carlos.

CHAPTER TWENTY-EIGHT

Guns

Relief filled me when Carlos automatically got behind the steering wheel. My arm ached with a deep pain that meant I'd used it too much. I pulled a few cherry tomatoes out of my sling and ate them immediately. They were still warm and sweet.

I come to the Garden alone,
    while the dew is still on the roses—

Carlos interrupted the latest song in my head when he threw on the brakes and shoved the shifter into park. "I'm an idiot," he said. "Farmhouse. There must be guns. Farmers need guns. I'll be right back." He tucked the teddy bear into the center console and closed the lid reverently. Then he rushed back into the elegant old house.

I wondered if he would have to go past the baby's room in his search. I hoped not—but maybe he had exorcised that demon-memory. I know I felt better after letting mine out of the box. Sort of like exposing sins to the light.

Snake had his broad head stuck out the back window. With my side mirror angled just right, I could watch him. He never ceased to amaze me—always on guard, always alert, and always ready for action. I know he slept because he lay on the foot of my bed, and sometimes right beside me, but if I woke, so did he.

I came awake with a jerk. Thinking about sleeping had put me right under. I was exhausted. When my head fell forward, it woke me. I looked at the clock, but it did me no good because I hadn't looked at it when Carlos went in. I had no idea if he'd been back inside one minute or ten.

I rubbed the back of my neck. It was stiff. I *must've been asleep longer than a minute or two for it to feel like that again—*

A deep rumble filled the back seat.

I glanced at the side mirror, but Snake's big head wasn't visible anymore. I looked in my rearview and he was a statue staring out the back glass.

"What is it?" I couldn't see anything, but my stiff neck prevented me from turning completely around.

His rumble grew louder, and I knew from experience that ferocious barking would soon follow. Only one thing could make the Snake act like that.

I threw open my car door and stood beside it, one hand shading my eyes as I scanned the area for danger. "Carlos!" I yelled. "Are you coming?" I couldn't see any movement anywhere, but Snake still had his snout pointed toward the highway. If I let him out, I knew he would take off in that direction. I half expected him to come out one of the open windows. I got back inside and leaned across the console to push the automatic window buttons. All four went up smoothly.

Snake's rumbling vibrated the back of my seat.

I did the 360° scan again. Still nothing. Whatever it was must be invisible or so far away I couldn't see it yet. I honked the horn and then immediately regretted it. If something were coming, the sound would give them a good reason to hasten our way.

"Carry On Wayward Son" replaced "In the Garden."

I climbed over the console—no easy feat with the sling—and got behind the wheel. I did a three-point turnaround and positioned the car, so we were headed down the drive toward the farm-to-market road and then the highway. I was as close to the front door of the house as I could get without driving over the landscaping.

Snake's rumbles changed to deep growls.

I slipped the gearshift into reverse and backed over the lovely flowerbeds and into the yard. My driver's side door was now even with the porch steps. I opened the door, stepped up on the bottom step and yelled for Carlos again.

He still didn't come.

Shading my eyes, I stared south, the direction Snake was look-ing. And then I heard it. The sound I'd grown to know—the one I hoped I'd never hear again—the shushing sound of hundreds of bare feet on asphalt. It was just like the day we left Eden.

I made my hand into a tube-shape and looked again, hoping to focus the light to help me see more clearly. But it turned out I didn't need the tube after all.

They came up out of a low spot on the highway. There weren't hundreds of them, though. There were thousands.

At first, I was so stunned I simply stood and stared, then adren-alin shot through me like wildfire, and I dashed up the porch steps, jerked open the farmhouse door, and screamed for Carlos to come.

He rose out of a shadowy pocket like a specter. His arms were full of guns, his eyes were wild, and he had blood trickling from a cut on one hand. His shirt and pants pockets bulged with the shapes of small, heavy, boxes. I assumed they were bullets. Surrounding him I saw a puddle of broken glass and splintered wood. He'd obviously broken into a gun case.

I pointed toward the south. "They're coming."

We crashed down the steps and fell into the car. I got behind the wheel even though my arm was singing with pain almost loud enough to drown out the music in my head. But since I couldn't really load a weapon that easily, nor did I know one from the other, I figured it was the best option.

I slammed the shifter into drive and hit the gas. For a moment, our wheels spun uselessly.

"Let off a little," Carlos commanded.

I did, and the big car shot forward. Our tires had been spinning, churning up the soft, loose, earth of the flowerbeds. I had a sudden, absurd image of a woman in a straw hat planting those flowers with loving hands. "Carry on," my song shouted. "Carry on and get the hell on that road ahead of them."

I got a grip on my emotions and drove back down the red dirt road toward the cattle guard. The platoon of Takers appeared to be less than half a mile away. They were close enough that I could see the sun glinting off their garnet eyes and moist skin. I couldn't see their tattoos, but I could sense movement beneath their flesh, like shadows dappling them from the inside out. Once or twice, I caught a flash of color, as if some were clothed, but then the sunlight reflected off the mass of baldheads and bare skin and the colors disappeared.

Hank Williams' old standard, "I Saw the Light," bloomed in my skull. I shook my head to dislodge it, but it did no good.

As I *blumped* back across the iron pipes of the cattle guard, I thought I heard one of the plastic containers of gasoline fall over in the trunk. I hoped it wouldn't spill all over the produce we'd stuffed in there, but if we didn't make it to the Sloan house before the platoon overtook us, it wouldn't matter.

Just as I hit the junction with the Interstate, a veil of turquoise drifted across the front of the car and disappeared beneath the tires. It might have been a shirt, or it might've been an illusion. With the music growing louder and louder in my mind, I was having trouble telling reality from fantasy.

"Carry On Wayward Son" fought for dominance with "I Saw the Light," and then over the top of everything, a Native American flute broke through.

In the back seat, Snake was going ballistic. He could see the Takers now, and he wanted them. His barking and growling climbed to a fever pitch as he threw himself from side to side across the back seat. That noise, coupled with the crazy cacophony of music filling my head, suddenly became too much and I pounded the steering wheel and yelled, "Stop!" I didn't know if I meant Snake or the music or both.

Carlos looked at me but kept on loading the weapons. He'd made it out with some sort of revolver, a deer rifle, another shotgun, and several boxes of ammunition. "Can you shoot this thing if necessary?" He held up the pistol.

I nodded. I'd do it if I had to. I was pretty sure I could load it with my bad hand. It would be easier than trying to cock a shotgun, but I doubted if it would be very accurate. Better than having nothing at all, though.

The craziness in my head started to subside as we put some distance between the car and the mass of Takers. Even Snake began to settle down, although he still barked and growled incessantly.

Carlos glanced at me. "You okay?"

I nodded. This was no time to try and explain the madness in my mind. I was really beginning to think I'd suffered some sort of brain injury. The turquoise veil was a first. I supposed the music in my head could be a form of auditory hallucination, but the visual one was a new thing.

I held the steering wheel with my knee and ran my hand into my pocket. I wanted to make sure I still had the rock of turquoise. It was the exact shade of the blue that had drifted across the front of the car. Add in the sudden Native American flute and I knew I was either going mad or getting some sort of message. But what I pulled out of my pocket was not the rock of turquoise; it was one of Mom's turquoise earrings.

The lid of my memory box flew off and I was treated to a vibrant glimpse of her red-gold hair against the shoulder of her turquoise sweater. I thought of her Native American heritage. A missing back had stopped her from wearing those earrings to work that last morning. But where had it gone? And what left them there for me to find? Was it Fate or God? I didn't know for certain, but I knew it was no accident—just as scooping up Dad's Mustang key had been no accident. *What is it, Lord, what are you trying to tell me?*

CHAPTER TWENTY-NINE

Overrun

We made much better time going back to the Sloan house than we had coming. I didn't let the speedometer drop below eighty the whole way back. I opened all the windows and let the air rush through just like I'd planned. "Wish we could call Thad and tell him to open the garage."

Carlos nodded, but when we topped the last rise before the house, we saw that it wouldn't have made any difference.

The yard was overrun with a sea of gray.

"Oh, my God." The words slipped out of my mouth as my foot slipped off the accelerator. "Too late."

Carlos made the sign of the cross. "Maybe he got into the tunnels before they got inside the house."

Two of the first-floor windows were open to the elements. The bed slats Carlos had nailed up were broken or missing. "Maybe he did." But in my mind, I saw the awful image of how we'd left him passed out on the parlor sofa.

Behind us, in the rearview mirror was another unbelievable sight. A new group of monsters were coming at us from the east. It was as if the Bitty Sloan house had somehow become the center of the universe and every gray creature on two legs was now converging upon it.

I looked at Carlos. "I don't know what to do."

"Carry on," he yelled. "Just carry on!"

I felt paralyzed, just like back in the old farmhouse. "There's no road past the house. Do I go back to the highway?"

He shook his head. "There's a path—" he pointed to the wide-open field behind the house.

The music of Kansas played in my head—with Dad's voice singing the lyrics—but "Amazing Grace" was there, too, as well as the Native American flute.

And grace will lead me home . . .

I felt like beating my skull against the window. *Who is Grace? I don't know any Grace. Just tell me what to do and stop sending me all these stupid song lyrics and hallucinations.* I didn't mean to, but I think I shouted those words out loud. Carlos looked at me with a worried expression.

"Drive on," he shouted. "I'm going to shoot one and see if the black rain comes."

My head went blank, and a new song flared to life. "A Hard Rain's A-Gonna Fall." Bob Dylan. Yes. Branches bleeding and kids with guns. I didn't know the real lyrics, but they were something like that. *Bring down the rain, son.* That was Dad's voice. *Bring it down before the things drown the whole, wide, world.*

"Bring down the rain," I cried. "Bring it down now!" I drove toward a knot of Takers waiting to get inside the house as if they'd been invited.

Snake was going berserk. Carlos lowered his window and leveled the shotgun barrel at them. I worried Snake would leap over him and get in the way, get shot the way Kevin had done.

Ka-Boom!

The noise momentarily drowned out the song in my brain, and for that I was thankful.

The blue sky opened, and the edges of a dark scar fluttered as the group of monsters scattered away from the one Carlos had hit. Cloudy fluid gushed down its back from the hole in its head. Sin words tumbled one over the other and littered the earth like black confetti. The creature took another half-step and fell to the ground.

The sky darkened and thick black rain fell in a straight-down torrent. Takers opened a pathway as the raindrops coalesced under the torn sky and flowed across the prairie toward the injured creature in welcome rivulets of ink.

"More!" I shouted. "Shoot them all!"

Carlos fired the other barrel and hit two more. Another sky rip began to flutter as the scarred edges reopened and unleashed a second downpour. "It's working," I shouted. "Do it again!"

He grabbed the deer rifle and began to fire. The monsters were so close together it was impossible to miss. He wounded five more before I could blink an eye.

"Drive away," he called. "We don't want to be in the rain. I need to reload."

I drove toward the cliff. It was the only place clear of Takers. I knew there was a chance of getting trapped between them and the edge, but the three other directions were blocked. They were all moving from the south and east toward the north. I didn't see any other option; besides, all of a sudden James Taylor was singing about "Fire & Rain." That must have been one of Mom's songs.

As if in answer, the Native American flute started up again. *My God! Isn't it enough I'm trying to survive, do you have to serenade me, too?*

The black rain fell thicker and thicker across the Takers near the house. So much rain fell it momentarily blocked out the sun. And after the blackness expanded and covered the monsters, it exploded into buzzing locusts, completely blackening the world. Except for a brilliant strip of turquoise all along the edge of the cliff.

The gorgeous color separated the brown prairie from the black sky as vividly as a swash of bright paint. "Look!" I jabbed at the color with my forefinger.

Carlos stopped loading long enough to check it out.

I wanted to pull out the talismanic turquoise in my pocket, but I didn't dare let go of the steering wheel. The prairie floor was rough with cacti and stout clumps of buffalo grass.

When I looked in the rearview, the horde of monsters reminded me of the famous post office painting from my dream.

Carry on, my dad said. He didn't send me the song; just spoke the words right into my ear. Mom's "Fire & Rain" melody played beneath it. The Native flute was audible, but just barely.

All at once I became aware of a thunderous noise coming from the south.

Without meaning to, I allowed the Chrysler to slow as I tried to determine the source of the noise.

Carlos craned his head around.

We saw it at the same instant. The wall of Takers was on the move. For the first time, they were running. The other group was busy trying to avoid the black rainstorm, and having very little luck, but this huge herd seemed to have a different agenda. They weren't simply moving toward the house—they were coming after us.

"Parallel the cliff," Carlos commanded. "We've got to have more space."

James Taylor crooned about "Fire & Rain," and I wanted to tear my own head off just to shut him up. I drove west near the edge of the cliff. The beautiful turquoise color seemed immune to the dark storm. It glowed as if lit from within.

Ding ding ding...

"What's that sound?" Carlos yelled.

At first, I didn't know what he meant. The music in my head was so overwhelming that the dinging just seemed part of it.

Carlos' eyes grew round with disbelief. "*Low fuel?* We're almost out of *gas?*"

I stared at the gauge. How had we let that happen? We had liberated three containers full of gas at the farmhouse but failed to put any into the car. The dinging continued. It seemed to be speeding up.

"We have to put some in," I said. "We don't have a choice."

Carlos nodded. "Okay. But hurry. I'll stand guard."

I rolled up all the windows and stopped the car. I didn't want Snake to jump out and take off. I pushed the key fob button to open the trunk, then grabbed a container of gas and the funnel—which we'd been careful to keep on top of the produce—and began to empty it into the tank using my one good arm and a knee for balance.

Some of it splashed on the ground, but I couldn't help that. The things were running. They weren't loping, and they weren't jogging—they were running! They shook the ground. I thought Snake was going to tear the windows right out of their frames.

"Come on," Carlos said. "That's enough. Get in!"

I closed the gas container and slapped the Chrysler's fuel flap shut. The monsters were almost upon us. From here, I couldn't see any colorful clothing, only gray skin, garnet eyes, and black sin words squiggling beneath their flesh. I stowed the can, slammed the trunk lid, and dashed back to my door, yanking it open with my good hand.

Snake shot over the seat and crashed out my door without ever touching me. He hit the ground on all four feet and headed toward the mass of Takers like a bullet fired from a gun.

"Snake!" I screamed. But of course, it did no good. His tawny coat disappeared between the legs of the monsters, and I heard the unmistakable sound of tearing flesh. "Give me a gun!" I reached into the car and Carlos slapped the revolver into my palm. I fired wildly, James Taylor incongruously droning on and on.

"Get in the car," Carlos yelled. "We'll try to outrun them."

"Not without Snake!" I kept firing until the hammer clicked on nothing.

Carlos stepped out and gave them both barrels of the shotgun. Takers fell and Takers scattered. The sky holes fluttered, and the air vibrated, and black rain began to fall. Sin words skittered across the brown dirt as "Amazing Grace" fought with "Fire & Rain" and Dad cried *Carry on*. I reloaded the revolver while the monsters tried to outrun the rain. The Native American flute hit a shrill note and Carlos fired again.

"Watch out for Snake!" I couldn't see him, but I could still hear him ripping and tearing, barking and snarling. I was afraid if the Takers didn't kill him, and the black rain didn't drown him, Carlos would shoot him by mistake.

Raindrops slithered across the ground, slurping up sin words as they came. I watched in fascination as tendrils of blackness climbed over the wounded monsters and melted together, covering them in big oily sheets, absorbing them as if they were nothing. I fired my pistol into the melee and more sky holes fluttered as even more monsters fell.

Locusts began to explode from the midst, but a thousand more Takers were coming on. "We've got to go, Jack." Carlos scrambled back into the car.

I looked for my dog. I couldn't see him, but I saw a dozen feet kicking at something and then I heard the yelp and saw his body fly through the air.

He landed with a terrible thud. I expected him to roll over and get back up like he had done so many times before. But before he could, another clump took up the fight, kicking him with their horrible toeless feet.

I rushed to his aid, firing my revolver, trying to make sure I didn't hit him, but I was too careful. The things didn't even budge.

I shot the nearest one and saw the fluid spill over Snake. Crinkly black letters spelled out words I couldn't understand. They oozed to the ground and Snake rallied long enough to shake his head the way he'd done before. I hooked my fingers into his collar just as another monster tried to pick me up from behind. I stuck the barrel of the revolver through my sling and under my armpit and shot it in the midsection.

Words and letters exploded from its gut, spraying out in all directions. I wiped the mess off the side of my face and carried on, dragging Snake backward with all my might as the other monsters scattered away from the incoming rain.

Snake seemed unable to rise when I got him away, and I was afraid they'd broken his spine, but just before I got us back to the car, he rippled his entire body and tore himself from my grasp.

I hugged my screaming arm to my side and prepared to follow him back into the fight, but Carlos appeared out of nowhere and grabbed me. He slung me into the back seat before I could protest. "You load," he said.

The last time I saw Snake he was slashing through the forest of gray legs in his blind canine rage, and the black rain was falling faster and harder than ever. I was certain I'd never see him again.

Locusts still obliterated the sun. Their buzzing blocked out every noise except the crazy battle of the bands inside my head.

Carlos drove away from the huge herd. "We'll get to safety," he said, as if the cliff didn't exist. But James Taylor—or was it my mom? —had other ideas. Like an old record stuck in a groove, the words *fire and rain* were reduced to *fire, fire, fire*. I tried to plug my ears but of course that did no good at all since the music was inside me.

I looked at the big barrel of the revolver. I didn't know if I wanted to go on without my dog. He'd been the one I depended on. The one I trusted above all others. I steadied the gun and looked down into the barrel. One bullet and this would be all over—one shot and I could have peace.

The music came to a crashing halt. Silence filled my skull.

I closed my eyes. *Did I do it? Am I dead?*

The gun felt heavy in my hand.

Carry on with fire and rain, my father whispered. *And grace will lead you home.*

I hadn't done it. The gun was still heavy in my hand. It was a momentary weakness; everyone was allowed one from time to time. *Carry on, kid. You can do this.*

"Thank you," I whispered. "Stop the car, please."

Carlos looked at me in the rearview. "Snake's gone, Jack. It's too late . . ."

I nodded. "I know. This is for us. Look around. The sky is filled with help. We aren't the meek. We will have to help ourselves. Let the meek inherit *after* we're gone."

He let the car roll to a stop.

"Load everything you've got," I said. "And then get ready."

Something in my voice must have convinced him. He loaded all four guns and laid the remaining ammo on the seat within easy reach. "Makes sense," he said. "We'll just keep pegging away at them, and let the rain fall where it may."

Yes, I thought. *That would work if we had ten times the ammo we have now.* I had another plan. I hoped it would work. Kansas, Dad, James Taylor, and my Choctaw ancestors assured me it would.

A new tune entered my brain. It was the Native American flute playing "Carry On Wayward Son." I shook my head much the same way Snake had done when the Taker's sins drenched him. *Put that image away. Put it in the* Snake Box—*close the lid.*

"Okay. Drive on. We need to get behind them." I expected Carlos to balk at that, but he seemed to like the idea.

"Good idea if we can. I'd like to get away from the cliff, too." He glanced that direction. "I'd say it's about fifty feet straight down to the rocks. I think the Native Americans really did use it as a buffalo jump."

"Yes." I looked at the amazing strip of turquoise still illuminating its edge. If not for that otherworldly strip of blue, we might have driven right off the edge to begin with. But if Carlos saw the turquoise, he didn't mention it. "I'm sure they did," I continued. "It was the only way they could take down an animal as powerful as a bison. And when the creatures fell to their death, the rest of the tribe would be down there to finish off any that happened to survive."

I saw understanding dawn in Carlos' eyes. "Now I get it. The black rain will finish off any of these that survive. But how will we get them to go over?"

"Start at this edge," I said. "First the fire, then the rain."

Carlos did as I asked. One thing about the end of the world, neither of us stopped to question what the other was doing. We didn't have time.

Carlos made a wide loop to the south. Most of the closer Takers were busy trying to avoid the black rain slithering across the ground. The main body of the group still pushed forward, intent on catching us, unaware we were going the opposite direction now. "Thank God for this darkness," Carlos muttered. "I guess everyone we shot got its own special downpour and its own personal plague of locusts to carry it away."

The light was so dim, I couldn't see if he did, but I wondered if Carlos touched the spot where the small gold cross had hung around his neck when he said, "Thank God." I rubbed my own personal talismans—the turquoise rock, the turquoise earrings, even Dad's Mustang key.

I looked out at the mass of gray. "They appear never-ending. If they weren't such a light color, we wouldn't even be able to see them."

"Good for us they like to bunch up like that—"

"Yeah. Like a platoon. But I don't see any in clothing, do you?"

Carlos shook his head.

Johnny Cash began to croak "Ring of Fire" and I knew it was

time to start the plan. "Okay," I said. "Let me out. I need to get the rest of the gas from the trunk."

Carlos stopped the car but let it coast forward when the nearest group of Takers turned their heads our way. They had slowed when the rain started to fall. Now they were back to marching. "What are you doing, Jack? I can't help you if I don't know . . ."

I laughed. "I guess I thought you could read my mind." I quickly told him my plan to pour a line of gasoline behind the entire platoon and then light it so they would be forced, by the ring of fire, toward the cliff.

Carlos nodded vigorously. "Great, great. There's only one problem—"

I was walking to the back of the car. "What?"

"How are we going to light it?"

I stopped with a fuel can in each hand. My bad one held the can that was only partially full. I stowed them both in the back seat and retrieved the last one from the trunk.

Johnny Cash continued to sing in his deep baritone, and now the flute was playing the Kansas tune, again. *I am,* I thought. *I'm carrying on. I promise.* "God will take care of that part," I told Carlos. "Maybe a bolt of lightning will flash down and set it on fire; or maybe you'll find one of Thad's old Bic lighters in the console—"

"Or maybe we'll get Thad himself." Carlos pointed to the south. "I never thought I'd be so glad to see someone else riding my bike!"

As if on cue I became aware of the growl of the Harley plowing up dirt.

A second Johnny Cash song, "I Walk the Line," burst into my head like the bolt of lightning I'd wished for. I didn't even have time to wonder how Thad had escaped.

He seemed to grasp our plan because he pulled up beside me, drew out his yellow Bic lighter, and flashed it triumphantly. I gave him the thumbs up, got in the back seat of the Chrysler and held the gas can out the window with the yellow nozzle pointed at the ground. "Ring of Fire" and "I Walk the Line" played on a new loop in my head. Mom's Native American flute faded away.

Carlos shot an opening in the nearest bunch of Takers so we

could get behind them. The front line tried to turn and follow us, but Carlos kept shooting into them every so often to make the black rain fall and obscure us from view. In moments we had emptied the partial can of fuel and one of the whole ones, too. And we still had a long way to go.

"Give me the other one," Thad called.

I handed it out the window and watched him tear away, the gasoline blowing back on his legs and feet as he let it dribble onto the earth. I hoped he knew to go ahead and light it at the other end—not to wait for us.

I scrabbled around in the cup holders looking for another lighter. I had the sudden idea that we should light the line in several places, not just from one end or the other. That might take too long to close the circle. "Will the Circle be Unbroken" filled my head.

> *Will the circle be unbroken,*
> *by and by, Lord, by and by,*
> *Is a better home awaiting,*
> *in the sky, Lord, in the sky?*

The new song played as I searched for another lighter. But there was nothing in the cup holders or the seat backs, so I pulled up the lid to the console and dug down in there. All my fingers encountered were the teddy bear from the farmhouse and a pair of eyeglasses that might have belonged to Mo's daughter.

For a moment, I couldn't think for wondering what had become of Mo and Lara, but then a second new song burst into my thoughts—The Doors, "Light My Fire"—and I pushed the Mo/Lara question away.

"Light My Fire" grew and grew as I slowly began to close the lid on the console. I pressed my hand against my temple as a moan escaped my lips.

"What is it, Jack?" Carlos twisted in his seat. I'm sure he thought a Taker had reached in through the window or something.

"It's my head," I admitted. The music grew louder and louder, knocking about in my brain. *Light my fire, light my fire, light my fire*, mixed with *Will the Circle be Unbroken, broken, broken* until the mashup pounded through me like a ballpeen hammer on bone.

"I'm trying," I yelled, holding the lid up with one fingertip. "I don't know how—I need a lighter!"

Carlos looked at me again. "Jack?"

I almost dropped the lid closed, but the music banged into the backs of my eyeballs, and I saw what I was doing. If I opened the console lid, the music lessened, if I made as if to close it, the music overwhelmed me.

I yanked the lid up and The Doors grew quiet. The old hymn grew quieter, too. "It must be in here," I murmured. "Something I can use to start a fire . . ." I pulled everything out and laid it on the passenger seat. When Carlos saw the old glasses, he grabbed them and shoved the car into park.

"These," he said. "We can focus the sun on a puddle of gas . . ." He snatched a gas can from the backseat.

I glanced up at the murky sky, but Carlos wouldn't be deterred. He touched the place where his little cross had been, and I was surprised to see it wrapped around his fingers. I didn't even know he'd gone back and picked it up. "It's like you said, Jack. The Lord helps those who help themselves."

He handed me the shotgun. "It's locked and loaded. Just fire it away from me." He knelt on the ground and poured a small amount of gas on a tuft of buffalo grass. He then angled the glasses lens toward the place where the sun should have been.

I stepped out of the back seat and stood guard. I'd accidentally kicked the gas can with my foot. Would it explode if I shot it? I didn't have a moment to wonder, Carlos whooped and hollered, and I looked up just in time to see a laser beam of sunlight shoot down through the murk directly into and through the curved glass lens.

In the space of a dozen heartbeats the small puddle of gas bloomed into a fierce blue flame that quickly spread down the already-poured line of fuel. The fire streaked along as if it had simply been awaiting instruction.

In the sky, Lord, in the sky . . .

CHAPTER THIRTY

Fire & Rain

Several Takers appeared out of the gloom. A couple started toward the fire and immediately thought better of it. Tough clumps of buffalo grass caught and handed their prize on to the next clump. Some of the monsters stomped at the fire-clumps with their bare feet, then quickly jumped away.

"Whoohoo!" I crowed. "It's working."

"Yeah," Carlos said, "except it's going to burn out before the monsters get anywhere near the cliff."

He's right, I thought. The fire might prevent them from turning around, but we'd set it way too far back. They were not running toward the cliff as I'd hoped, they were simply marching in a parallel along the length of it.

Time for plan B.

I grabbed the stray gas can and slithered in behind the wheel. "I'll drive, you shoot."

Carlos climbed into the passenger seat.

"Can you throw this can into their midst and then shoot it?"

He picked up the bigger shotgun. "I can try."

I was looking down to make sure Carlos had access to the remaining shotgun shells when I hit the wall of Takers. The car knocked down the first few and drove over the top of them easily.

And then we were surrounded.

This group seemed intent on pulling us from the car. They didn't seem to care that the sky rip overhead was beginning to flutter. It signaled the portending downpour of rain, but they seemed to have adapted—in fact, they seemed to be resigned to their own demise—they were not clearing away from the car.

"Roll up the back windows, Jack!"

I didn't even know he'd rolled them back down.

Carlos fired into the crowd and two staggered away, leaking words all over the place.

I pushed the buttons to roll up the windows, but it was too late. I heard the glass crack as one of the monsters grabbed it before it got up. The thing pulled it down and broke it off and stabbed its big ugly head into the opening. The garnet eyes were unblinking, the mouth open wide. Bright teeth glittered in the dim interior of its mouth.

I tried to accelerate but it was no use, something had us hung up, either the bodies beneath us, or the ones grasping us on all sides.

My window was up, but both back ones were now gone. A multitude of hands had hold of the glassless frames. In a few more breaths, they would be inside with us, or they would simply yank us out of our little tin can like a couple of tasty sardines.

Carlos fired every weapon we had. Takers fell back out of the windows and the black rain spattered down on top of us.

At last, they began to back away.

"The black rain will put out the fire," I yelled.

Carlos tossed the empty gas can full of fumes as far as he could and shot it with the big shotgun when it hit the ground.

Whomp!

The explosion was impressive. Monster limbs flew through the air, black words spilled across the earth, and half a dozen sky holes opened up.

"Way to go John Wayne," I yelled as I drove straight through the welcome gap. "Do it again!"

Carlos grabbed the second empty can and my music sprang to life. Eric Clapton began to sing "Let it Rain," and I almost laughed out loud. I took it to mean we weren't supposed to worry if the rain put out the fire. Kansas joined Clapton. *Carry on wayward son. Let it rain!*

I drove like a bat out of hell while Carlos studied the eerie black sky. Millions of locusts buzzed through the crowd as the black rain ate up the Takers and ascended back into the sky.

Oddly, the mini explosions had gotten the Takers running again. This time they did run toward the cliff. James Taylor strummed his guitar. I looked to the east and saw the reason why. The second large wave was not headed toward the cliff yet. They were still coming for us.

"We need more fire." I jerked my head toward the mass.

Carlos held up the last gas can. "I hate to be without any way to carry more fuel. If we get past these things, we're going to need gas for the car."

That's true, I thought. I hadn't been able to pour much into the car earlier. Another glimpse of movement caught my eye. We both looked up as the Harley miraged out of the smoke. I could see Thad's face hanging over the front wheel. He wore a maniacal grin with a Marlboro stuck right in the middle of it. He had the other shotgun and he cocked it one handed like Sarah Connor in *Terminator II.*

When he shot the first Taker near the edge of the cliff, several more went over just trying to get away from its spatter. Another bunch went over when the black rain came down.

Taking heart from that little scenario, I drove the car directly at the platoon running toward us. As the first line of monsters grew near, Carlos tossed the gas can into their midst and shot, but somehow missed.

I couldn't believe we'd wasted our last gas can. "Shoot it again!"

He tried, but it was too late, the can had disappeared the same way Snake had done. Carlos began firing wildly, hitting and wounding several. The black rain poured down and the mass parted the same way I imagined the Red Sea had parted for Moses.

"Just keep shooting. It's all we've got." I drove parallel to the huge group to get behind them and force them toward the cliff the way Thad was doing. He was like a cowboy on a cutting horse, rounding up the stragglers. We all knew if he got too close to the big group they would overwhelm him, but one on one, the Harley's powerful engine could easily outrun them.

Even though he was only getting them one at a time, when any of the monsters went over the edge of the cliff, the black rain came down in response to their injuries. And when he injured one *before* it went over, that was even better. Then the rain fell on the injured one and any others nearby. That was enough to keep them from regrouping.

I took my cue from Thad and began to ram the legs of the nearest ones. It was tough to judge how close to get—if I didn't veer off fast enough, it would be the end of Carlos and me.

But old Thad wasn't quite finished. Once he'd got the stragglers out of the way, he pulled *his* gas can out of the roomy saddlebag and began to pour another line.

"Look!" I pointed out what he was doing. "We need to run interference for him." I drove the car toward him. I was dismayed to see the bulk of the herd turning with me.

"I don't think this is good, Jack," Carlos yelled. "They're following us instead of going toward the cliff!"

"Fire & Rain" bloomed in my head. "Shoot them," I said. "Make the rain come."

Carlos began to fire randomly again.

We were almost to Thad when a rogue Taker charged out of the lingering smoke and tackled him like a linebacker. Carlos fired at it from too far away.

"Hold on Thad!" I pressed the accelerator to the floor. We humped and bumped over the prairie ground as Thad attempted to maintain control of the big bike and fight off the monster at the same time.

I could see his face as he fought for his life. Terror etched new lines on his craggy features. Unable to reload on time, the cocky Marlboro-man was no more. Now he was just a frail human facing mortality.

We hit the monster doing sixty. It flew up on the hood, shattered the windshield, and bounced over the top of the car before crashing to earth behind us. With superhuman strength, Thad straightened the wobbling Harley and tried to pick up speed. I could see him scrabbling to reload the shotgun on the fly.

"Look out!" Carlos aimed at another Taker, and another, and then another, but it was no good. As many as he hit, that many more took their place. They all seemed intent on taking Thad down. It was as if some silent signal had been given.

Behind us, the viscous black rain covered the ones we had hit. The others paid the rain no mind. I aimed the Chrysler at the nearest Taker and Carlos reloaded his big shotgun, but before we could get close, another dozen monsters joined the fray. Suddenly they had hold of Thad and were intent on dragging him off the bike.

Carlos fired and hit two of them. I ran them over and clipped a third. The black rain sent tendrils of darkness shooting across the earth.

Thad got loose and gunned the bike in the opposite direction, straight for the cliff. He was flying. The monsters charged him full out, but they couldn't keep up. The distance between them and us widened considerably. He glanced at us over his shoulder, and I saw the look on his face. "Nooo!" I screamed.

"Turn," Carlos yelled. "You're getting too—"

The Harley's brake lights never even flared when Thad went over. One moment he was looking at us over his shoulder, and the next moment he was airborne. At least two-dozen Takers shot off the edge of the cliff behind him. They were all going too fast to stop.

I threw on the brakes and skidded an interminable length of time before finally coming to a stop on the dusty edge. A small mountain of scree showered down upon the canyon floor.

Carlos threw himself out of the passenger side. I slammed the car into Park and followed from the driver's side. Together we peered over the edge just as a tremendous explosion shook the ground. We grabbed each other and fell back.

The strip of turquoise glowed incredibly bright as an astonishing fountain of orange and yellow flames shot skyward. It was as if a kettle of fire had been poured upward and outward. It shot so high into the air it began to fall back down on us and on the exposed heads of the Takers. We could hear it sizzle when the flaming drops landed on their moist skin. "Fire & Rain" continued to flow through my mind.

The flames fell onto the prairie, too, igniting clumps of buffalo grass everywhere.

More Takers dashed off the cliff to get away.

Carlos beat at his clothing as he pushed me back to the car. I fell into the driver's seat, and he dove inside his own door and grabbed the shotgun. I caught a glimpse of myself in the rearview mirror and saw that my hair was smoking. I smashed at it with my hand and then shoved the gearshift into Reverse hoping to get far away from the growing firestorm shooting up out of the canyon.

For one terrifying moment, our tires would not grip the earth. I looked out the window dismayed to find a river of blackness beneath us. "We're in the black rain. We have no traction!"

Carlos looked out his window and made the sign of the cross again.

"Carry on, Jack!" my father shouted in my ear. I put the car in Drive and tried to move forward instead of in reverse.

Carlos' face was white, a vertical line of worry between his brows. "Rock it!"

I tried going forward and then backward to no avail. "It's not working," I cried. "Just shoot one."

Carlos seemed to understand. He grabbed the deer rifle and sighted on a knot of Takers thirty yards away. They were so close together he was able to hit one of them.

The thing was injured, but not severely. It came at us on the run. The others followed. I could see the cloudy fluid seeping from its chest wound. It must have been full of pheromones. The river beneath us surged toward it, a dark miracle. In seconds the blackness flowed up the thing's legs. Its garnet eyes latched onto mine. Its sin words swam across its bald skull like minnows darting beneath the surface of a cloudy stream and then it was gone. Swallowed by black.

With the course of the river turned, our front tires were able to grip. I gave the engine gas and we shot off toward the thick line of smoke growing behind us.

In front of us, the firestorm that had mushroomed from the canyon floor grew even brighter and flamed even higher. We suddenly found ourselves traversing a narrowing corridor between the cliff's edge and the line of flames that were a result of Thad's efforts and the falling fire from the canyon. Thad had done well with the gas cans. The flammable border he'd drawn continued to eat its way across the grassy field, leaping from clump to clump, eagerly joining the numerous smaller fires that had rained down out of the canyon. The flames herded the rest of the monsters in front of it just the way we had planned. Behind it, as the prairie fuel gave out, a magnificent cloud of white smoke pushed toward us.

"I can't believe that explosion." I drove madly down the length of the cliff's edge. "No way the crash of the Harley did that." I looked at Carlos for confirmation, but he was busy reloading our weapons.

"I don't think so," he replied. "But maybe the Harley's gas tank and the gas can were both full of fumes. All I know is we got lucky. Very lucky. Now we just have to make sure the rest of those things keep moving toward the cliff."

All at once a mass of Takers appeared at the other end of our corridor. They were in front of the fire line, which hadn't reached its full potential on that end.

I hit the brake. I didn't know any other way. The cliff's edge was to my right, the wall of flames Thad had created was to my left and behind us, and now we had this impenetrable wall of monsters in front of us.

"Don't stop," Carlos yelled. "Drive straight at them. It's our only chance." He lined his guns up on the seat between us. "I'll shoot as many as I can, just don't stop for anything! The black rain will come and help us."

I nodded and hit the gas pedal again.

We closed the gap as a gigantic plague of locusts took over the sky behind us. I knew it was from the river of blackness we'd just left—the one that had almost been our undoing. For a moment the cloud of insects was so thick it even blocked out the geyser of flames still shooting up out of the canyon.

"I can't see where I'm going. Don't let me run off the cliff!"

Carlos shook his head and stuck the big shotgun out the window. He fired both barrels and several Takers fell. Apparently, he'd learned it was best to shoot their legs out from under them and let the black rain do the rest. If he shot them in the chest, they didn't always go down.

A new collection of sky holes rippled open, and a cascade of darkness poured down even as the plague of locusts flew up. Behind us, and to our left, the wall of flames grew in intensity. The rushing sound of the fire, coupled with the deafening buzz of the locusts, drowned out every other sound. Even the music in my head was obliterated for a second.

Carlos emptied every weapon we had into the crowd. Within minutes, the torrent of dark rain turned into a deluge as it tried to cover and absorb every wounded Taker. They now lay everywhere. I was uncertain how to proceed. The "Fire & Rain" melody bled through the noise. The tremendous buzzing grew.

I was on the verge of giving myself mental high fives for following my musical direction when our tires began to slip. Once again, we'd driven straight into the black ooze. The liquid was moving so fast I had absolutely no control. "Start shooting again," I told Carlos. "Shoot some that are farther away." I hoped to turn the tide the way we'd done a few moments earlier.

Sweat stood out on his forehead as he struggled. "I'm reloading as fast as I can."

REO Speedwagon's rock anthem "Riding the Storm Out" whooshed into my mind. I shook my head. Storm, flood, river, what did it mean? Ride this river and see where it takes us? Already the car seemed to be moving forward of its own volition. All I could do was turn the wheel and try to steer. Neither brakes nor accelerator did anything other than cause us to slide and fan up black gunk behind the tires.

And then it happened.

As we were concentrating on the weapons and the car, another rogue leapt onto the hood and punched his hand through the already smashed windshield. It grabbed Carlos by the throat, and I saw his eyes bulge. The Taker dragged him from his seat up onto the dash and attempted to pull his body through the broken glass. I could see the black sludge creeping up the monster's legs.

The shotgun fell to the floor as both of Carlos' hands automatically went to his windpipe, his fingers curling under those of the monster in an attempt to loosen them.

"*Jack*," he rasped. His face had gone the shade of a ripe eggplant. I saw the little gold cross still wrapped around his fingers.

I stomped the brake in a desperate effort to dislodge the thing from the hood. It didn't work. The big car simply slid to one side causing Carlos to be swiped across the dash. I could see scrapes and gashes as the glass cut through his shirt and connected with his skin.

Where was the gun? I felt in the floorboard. I wanted the handgun; I knew I could fire it if it had bullets. I wasn't so certain I could cock the big shotgun, but it didn't matter, I couldn't find either one.

And now the car was being rushed along on the black river straight toward the remaining cadre of Takers stomping toward us. The only question seemed to be . . . would they get us before the black river-rain got them?

"Ride the storm out, Jack," my father's voice said. "Be ready to carry on. Grace will lead you home, just ride the storm out."

I hooked my good arm around Carlos' lower legs and held on. He grunted and turned loose of the thing's hands while also making a feeble attempt to grab the edge of the dash so it couldn't pull him any further. It was obvious he was almost out of air.

The monster's teeth were silver and small and as pointed as a row of tiny daggers in the back of its black-slash mouth. Carlos shrieked when it bit off his ear. I thought of Van Gogh's *Starry Night*.

Carlos' shrieks became garbled as his breath ran out. The thing continued to gnaw at him even as it was being pulled down into the river of sludge beneath us.

I couldn't do much with my broken arm, but it didn't matter as far as steering was concerned, the control of the car was completely out of my hands.

Then two things happened at the same time. First, the monster lost its battle with the sludge and slipped off the hood, dragging poor Carlos right along with it, and second, a thunderous, freight train vibration shook the air and flattened my eardrums, threatening to burst my eyeballs like two ripe grapes.

CHAPTER THIRTY-ONE

Forgiveness

*I*t's happening, I thought. *Just like at school. The universe is tearing open again.* I fell over in the seat, clapped my hands to my ears—not an easy feat with the sling—and squeezed my eyes shut as hard as I could. But the darkness was even worse.

I opened my eyes, and the car windows were glowing a brilliant shade of red orange tinged with yellow. The rushing sound of the flames from the canyon intensified at least a hundred times and then the whirring noise came again. It sounded like a freight train racing through the air. This time it was loud enough to shatter the back windshield and whirl the big car around and around and around in a tight little circle.

Tornado!

I let go of my ears, grabbed on to the steering column, and tried to focus on something—anything—outside the broken window. The whirling winds that had spun the car turned it loose and picked up even more speed as they moved on across the prairie. I couldn't hear any music at all.

The storm turned the world black and blue and flaming yellow orange. The twister whipped across the land picking up Takers by the dozens. There would be no stopping it now. It seemed to be gaining strength as it neared the turquoise edge of the cliff. Monsters scattered and old wounds rippled all over the sky, but none of it was any match for the storm.

Sin words shot out all over the world as the tornado picked up monsters and flames. It sucked up all the sounds and all the Takers and even the black sludge. It made another pass close by, twirling the car the other direction—counter-clockwise—the same way my old buddy Cade used to twirl a basketball on the tip of his finger.

"Riding the Storm Out" crashed into my skull discordantly and I welcomed it back. I was on the verge of being sucked out the window when the winds began to abate. The tornado jumped away from the Chrysler and joined forces with the flaming geyser still shooting out of the canyon. I saw what appeared to be parts of the Harley whipping about in the rotating winds. I pushed my hand down on the brake—I was half on and half off the front seat—and was surprised to find a bit of resistance.

I hauled myself up by my good arm.

The tornado hung over the canyon. The sounds were loud, but not quite so killing-loud. Debris and detritus fell into the flames arising from the canyon floor. I saw Takers and cacti, pieces of the Harley, and even lumber from what I was afraid might be the old Bitty Sloan house.

All of it rained down into the flames just past the turquoise edge. Even the black sludge was spat out into the fire. When it hit the flames, an oily cloud of buzzing smoke obliterated the northern side of the canyon.

I watched as the tornado moved on toward the horizon leaving the firestorm to burn itself out. Both Thad and Carlos were gone. Even Snake. I was alone. But at least the Takers were gone, too. Most of them anyway. I figured some were still lurking about, somewhere. They couldn't have all been sucked up and annihilated.

My foot jerking like a puppet on a string, I pressed down on the accelerator. The car jumped forward and I twisted the wheel to see if I could steer. I knew it was a miracle I hadn't been sucked out over the canyon with the tornado, but I didn't have time to think about it now. All that mattered was that I was still alive.

My foot stopped jerking and I crept the car as close to the edge of the cliff as I could. It was like being in front of an open-air furnace. The firestorm still burned even though the black rain continued to fall. The canyon floor was an undulating wave of burning sludge as another downpour of black-rain-slime covered yet another writh-ing pile of Takers and then burst into a buzzing plague of locusts.

I was amazed to see that even the locusts dripped fire on their way back to the wounded sky. It was biblical in a twisted sci-fi sort of way. I thought of the lake of fire that was supposed to be Hell. I thought of the locusts that had once threatened to decimate the earth, not save it. And I thought of the strange fact that I seemed to be the only survivor. *What could that possibly mean?*

My dad's voice cut through REO Speedwagon. "Carry on, son. Carry *on*."

Maybe I'm not the only survivor. Maybe Dad is out there somewhere, looking for me. I backed away from the strange scene spread out below. The bluish edge of the cliff was beginning to pale.

I half expected Thad to somehow come roaring back up the slope, as if he were Superman. I drove the length of the cliff and back again—just to be certain. But he didn't magically appear. Of course, I'd seen pieces of the disintegrated Harley, so I knew it was wishful thinking. Still, I couldn't seem to make myself leave.

Carry on, Jack. Grace will lead you home . . .

I drove away from the brink through tattered smoke toward the place I knew the house had stood. Home? I had no idea. All the grass was burned away, and the land appeared to have been skinned, or scalped. The fire was lower now, down in the canyon, but it had eaten up almost all the grass and brush as far as I could see. I thought of all the vehicles out on the Interstate—metal coffins on wheels—and I hoped they had burned, too.

"Fire & Rain" played softly in my mind. It was soothing this time, not urgent. I could see the place where the Bitty Sloan house had been. At least part of it appeared to be standing. Maybe some of our provisions had survived in the tunnel rooms. Maybe I could still get to the well. The idea of that cool, clear, water was like a beacon pulling me onward. I couldn't wait to drop the bucket down in it and pour the whole thing over my filthy head. Then I might drink until I puked. Anything to keep from having to think about the fact that I was alone.

I glanced in the rearview mirror. The strip of turquoise along the edge of the cliff appeared to be glowing brightly again. *That's odd*, I thought. And then I saw it. If I hadn't looked back for the turquoise, I might have driven right on past.

It was a body, blackened and still. It lay beneath a scorched mesquite. I knew it had to be Carlos. He looked as if he'd been inhaled and then spat back out by the firestorm.

Putting the car in reverse, I backed toward him carefully. His clothes were burned, and the side of his head was ragged and torn. It appeared the fire had cauterized the places where the Taker bit him.

I wasn't going to get out of the car. I knew he was dead; he had to be. Then he sat up and pointed at something off in the distance. He had no hair. If he'd had a hoodie on, I would have thought him a specter, maybe the Ghost of Christmas Yet to Come.

With a feeling of complete and utter dread, I turned toward the direction he pointed, and there I saw a postage-stamp-sized rectangle of flawless turquoise blue trudging across the alien landscape toward us. The color perfectly matched the glowing strip along the cliff's edge.

It was the Taker that had saved me back at the Wal-Mart store. I knew it, and yet I knew it couldn't be.

I opened the car door and helped Carlos to stand. His face was charred, one eye swollen closed like that of a boxer after a losing match. "Kill it," he rasped, pointing. But I didn't know if I could. Not this one.

Laying Carlos in the back seat, I climbed in behind the wheel. He was in bad shape, but at least he was alive. I would go to the nearest drug store and get antibiotics and—

The creature seemed to be making a beeline toward us. Maybe it knew we were the last humans on earth.

I revved the engine and tried to make myself drive toward it, to end it like Carlos said. But the thing was wearing turquoise, my mom's favorite color. And if I hadn't been looking for that color in my rearview mirror, I never would have seen Carlos lying there. Besides, my heart said it was the same one that had saved me.

The Native American flute crept into my consciousness. Very softly, I began to sing the words:

Amazing grace, how sweet the sound
That saved a wretch like me
I once was lost, but now am found,
T'was blind, but now I see.

Carlos waved his arms at me from the backseat as if telling me to go on and do it. Instead, I dug around under the seat until I came up with the handgun. I opened it up, relieved to see it still held four rounds.

Carlos sat up when I clicked the cylinder closed.

"Can you see what I see?" I asked.

He nodded, and we both stared at the Taker as it grew closer, tattoos rising and falling beneath the gray skin of its skull. *Forgiveness* the words said. *Absolution. Mercy.*

Carlos made the sign of the cross on his chest.

I didn't see his gold one anymore.

I stared at the Taker's squiggly words as they appeared and disappeared. And then I held up my hand.

The monster approached the car as slowly as a prisoner approaching a firing squad. It held up both hands, and then lowered one to my open window.

Its garnet eyes glittered as it cocked its head to one side in a movement reminiscent of Snake. I think it was that movement that decided me.

I laid my good hand on the window's edge. "Can you understand me?"

The thing simply stared. Its eyes were like gemstones. Like insects.

I pointed at its shirt to let it know I recognized the color. "You saved me once." I held up my splinted arm.

It nodded. At least I think it did.

"Are you human?"

The Taker did not respond. It reached for my hand, and I knew it could yank me from the car and kill me in an instant.

I pointed at Carlos' burned and swelling face. "Don't hurt us."

The thing touched my hand and the word *Believe* swam down its arm and into its long, gray forefinger.

"Yes," I agreed. "Yes." I put the car into Park and opened my door. I was putting my life into its hands, but I couldn't *not* do it. "Dust in the Wind," drifted across my mind. I knew all the words. I thought them very appropriate. If we are only dust in the wind, then we have nothing more to fear.

And then a line about how we are all stardust filtered through from another old song. It was from "Woodstock," an ageless Crosby, Stills, Nash, & Young tune my dad always said made him melancholy for something way before his time.

I ran my good hand into my pocket and pulled out the small rock of turquoise. I held it flat on my palm the way one would hold a carrot out to a skittish horse. I thought of all the destroyed veggies in the trunk of the car and even in the back floorboard, but then I pushed that thought aside. There were more important things in the wind just now.

The Taker poked the turquoise rock with the tip of its blunt finger. I noticed it had no nails. It was like a mannequin, or one of those unfinished wax figures just waiting for the human details to be added.

It looked down at its shirt, and then glanced back toward the cliff. Had it seen the turquoise light the way I had? The firestorm had dwindled. It was still a fire, but it was no longer a conflagration. The tornado was gone as well.

A hard wind whooshed up from the east, blowing dust and grit and char into our faces. To the west, the prairie still burned. The Taker looked at the sky, at all the scars that would flutter open at a moment's notice if the correct pheromones were released, or if the dimensional fabric gave way again, and then it pushed the turquoise rock back toward me and pointed toward the sky.

I didn't know what it meant, but it was such a human gesture, telling me something, showing me *something*, that I finally relaxed and returned the talisman to my pocket.

"Come on." I walked around the Chrysler and opened the passenger door. "We have to get medicine." Carlos lay back on the seat, eyes closed, breathing ragged. I wondered if his lungs were as singed as his face.

I got back behind the steering wheel and waited to see what the Taker would do.

It climbed into the passenger seat and pulled the door closed.

My heart pounded and my music thundered. If it hadn't been for the redemption words, I couldn't have done it. "Thank you," I said. "For saving my life."

If the thing understood, it didn't reply. But I saw the word *Grace* swim across its face. When we drove toward the remains of the Bitty Sloan house, it came to life and began to point with that same long, gray finger.

My gaze followed the finger. The old house was standing but partially stripped. I was glad it hadn't burned. In the backseat, Carlos moaned, and the Taker began to get agitated. It pointed toward the house again.

I decided there must be something important there, nevertheless, I almost turned and went the other way, across the prairie. I trusted this thing beside me, but what could it possibly want at the old house?

"Carry on," Kansas sang.

That was all I needed. I touched the accelerator and drove up into the side yard. The Taker opened the car door and stepped out as soon as I brought the car to a halt. It walked directly to the tumbledown porch, hefted a few boards, and threw them aside.

I couldn't believe my eyes. I shoved the gearshift into Park and stumbled out of the car as Snake dragged himself out from under the dark space beneath the remaining steps. One of his back legs hung at a broken angle, but he looked otherwise okay. He lurched toward me drunkenly. It reminded me of the night I first found him.

I fell to the ground, and my miraculous furry friend covered my face in doggy kisses. The rumble coming from his broad chest almost drowned out the last stanza of "Amazing Grace" that had swelled into my mind.

"I thought you were dead!" I didn't care if he could hear me or not. I knew he could feel my voice as surely as I could feel the wetness of his tongue.

Mom and Dad had been right. Grace did lead me home. Grace or forgiveness—maybe they were one and the same

I looked back at the Taker. He stood beside the porch, watching.

Snake didn't pay it any mind. Maybe the old dog had some sort of song playing in his head, too. Maybe we all did. Maybe grace had led us *all* home.

Carlos moaned from the backseat, and I remembered I was going to look for medicine. "Hang on," I called. "Let me see what it's like inside." I could see part of the roof was gone, but most of the walls appeared sturdy.

I went around to the back door and climbed the steps. The kitchen was intact except for blown-out window glass. I went through to the parlor, and there was Carlos' backpack full of medicine. *Thank you, God. Thank you.* I opened it up just as Snake appeared behind me on three legs. "I don't know if you can take these antibiotics," I said. "I'll have to find a veterinary clinic and some ACE bandages for you I think." But first, water. I hefted the backpack and headed down the hall toward the cellar door.

The Taker stood in front of it like a statue.

Trepidation filled my gut. Was the thing about to make a stand for some reason? Only one way to find out. I walked toward it confident Snake would let me know if I had anything to fear.

The Taker stood aside, and I opened the door and went down into the tunnels. If it wanted to hurt me now, there would be absolutely nothing I could do about it. I tapped the wall panel that opened the secret door to the cellar kitchen and the myriad storage rooms beyond. The Taker followed me inside.

The room still smelled of hops and barley. There were even a few ancient wooden kegs stacked in the corner of the room nearest the kitchen. I was so relieved to see nothing had changed down here. The well was toward the back of the kitchen; rope still attached to the pulley. I immediately drew up a bucket of cool, clear water and poured it over my head.

To my astonishment, the Taker did the same. Then I picked up the bowl we'd been using for Snake and filled it with water. He lapped until it was empty. I refilled it and splashed a bit on his head. I figured he had to be as hot as the rest of us.

And then I gathered as many of the empty plastic jugs as I could carry and began filling them with water. When it saw what I was doing, the Taker took over. Its many-faceted eyes still gave me the creeps; they reminded me of the eyes of a bee or a wasp. But it had done nothing to cause me any doubt. I wondered if it had saved Snake when I lost him in the monster forest. I thought it possible. Maybe even likely.

Carlos tried to sit up when I carried the first gallon jug of water back to the car. He drank as thirstily as Snake. "Did you see him?" I asked.

The burned man nodded. "A miracle, that's all. It saved you once, now you returned the favor by not running it down when you had the chance."

For a moment, I was completely confused. Then I understood what he meant. He thought I was referring to the Taker. "Oh, him. Of course. But did you see Snake? The Snake-man is alive. He was under the porch."

Carlos stopped drinking. "Seriously?"

I nodded and pointed toward the back door. "He has a hurt leg—probably broken—but he's alive. He's in the cellar kitchen with the Taker." I dug some Cipro tablets out of the backpack and gave them to Carlos.

He took the medicine without question. "Man. Saved you, saved Snake. What d'you think, he's somehow still human?"

I shrugged. "No clue. All I know is, he asked for forgiveness, so he's with us now. At least for the time being." A dark thought crossed my mind. *Had the Taker somehow acquired a soul along the way, a pure soul?* Nope, not gonna give voice to that thought. What good would it do? As some pundit once said, "It is what it is," and for now, that would have to be enough.

We had water and some food, and we had each other. Tomorrow, or the day after, or whenever our squashed-up vegetables gave out, we'd be forced to deal with the rest of it.

I still intended to go to Colorado, but after all the messages from Dad, I was certain I needed to go back to Eden first. Just to make sure he wasn't looking for me there. I no longer felt the need to rush. If the sky opened up again, downstairs in the tunnels would be the safest place for all of us. At least until we'd had a chance to heal.

I looked out over the rough black prairie. The silence and solitude had started to feel normal. Dealing with towns and closed-in places held no appeal for me. I liked the wide-open spaces where one could spot a Taker coming from a mile away.

"Do you think we killed them all?" I nodded toward the house. "Except that one, I mean."

"I doubt it," Carlos said. "I'm afraid this is just a lull." He began to cough and had to lie back again.

I held up my broken arm. "We both need to rest for a while. How bad are those burns?"

Carlos opened his good eye. "Could be a lot worse. I thought the Taker was going to pull my head off getting me out of the car." He lifted his chin to show me the necklace of bruises around his throat. "But then it got sucked up by the fire-nado." He grimaced and touched his swollen throat. "I think I'm okay, but it feels like my skin might crack open."

I leaned into the back seat to have a closer look at his throat. It didn't even surprise me when I saw the white shape of a tiny cross in the purplish hollow of his throat. "Did you lose your little gold cross?"

He nodded. "I guess I did."

"Your throat is bruised all around the tiny white shape of your old cross."

His expression was impossible to read. "Maybe it's permanent," he said. "Like one of their tattoos. I'll bet that's what protected me." He poured some more water over his face.

I was glad to see that a lot of what I thought was blackened skin was just char. "I wonder if I should purify that water somehow. Wouldn't want you to get an infection in those burns and those wounds."

Carlos poured some more over his face. "Maybe next time."

I shook my head. "I can't believe Thad is gone." I looked back at the house. "But Snake is alive."

Carlos poured more water over his arms. "And the Taker is in there with him."

"It's okay, I promise. It helped me fill up all these jugs." I indicated the one Carlos was holding in his hand.

He shrugged. "Got any of those pain pills left?"

I dug around in the backpack. "Yes, I do. But we have to get some crackers in you first. You don't want to take them on an empty stomach." I remembered my horrific trip with Thad when the Taker had broken my arm. "Can you walk?"

Carlos rose to a sitting position as the turquoise Taker approached the car. I hadn't heard it come out.

"We need to get him downstairs," I said. It didn't seem to understand me, so I walked around to the other side of the car and opened the door behind Carlos' head. When I slid my good hand under his armpit, the Taker understood and pushed past me to lift him out. Though the thing was none too gentle, it pulled Carlos out and carried him toward the house like a child. I was reminded of the crib in the farmhouse, but I pushed that image away and followed them inside.

When the wind changed, the smell of burning was strong. I liked it. It certainly beat the smell of putrefying body parts.

Snake lay just inside the front door licking his injured leg. I knelt beside him and hugged him again. "As soon as I get Carlos settled, I'm going to the farmhouse. They should have animal drugs in that underground barn. Ace bandages, too." I just hoped I had it in me to set his leg the way Carlos and Thad had set my arm.

A sudden wave of sadness poured over me. Thad had turned out to be a hero after all. Just like me, he had screwed up many times. If I hadn't overheard him telling Carlos about the fire at my house, I would never have known what really happened. But in the end, he had saved us all—well, him and the fire-nado—and we all knew where that came from.

Was it just coincidence that Thad had escaped the flames at my house only to wind up sacrificing himself in the inferno in the canyon? I'll probably never know.

I stood and glanced out the door at the road. I knew my dad was out there somewhere. As soon as we were all able to travel, I intended to go back to Eden to seek him out. Then it would be on to Abilene or Colorado, wherever the songs told me to go.

Snake whined, and I gave him another gentle hug before

heading to the kitchen to get Carlos some food so he could take the pain meds.

The soft refrain of "Take Me Home, Country Roads," an old song by John Denver, surfaced in my mind. I glanced through the blown-out kitchen window at the red dirt driveway leading to the highway. The song felt like a memory.

I dug inside my pocket. The small rock was there, still nestled between Dad's Mustang key and Mom's turquoise earrings.

"Soon," I murmured. "Going home, soon."

ABOUT THE AUTHOR

Ann Swann has been a writer since junior high, but to pay the bills she has waited tables, delivered newspapers, cleaned other people's houses, taught school, and had a stint as a secretary at a rock-n-roll radio station. She also worked as a 911 operator and as a police dispatcher.

Her fiction began to win awards during her college days. Since then she's published several short stories, novels, and novellas.

She's always reading and always writing, but even if no one ever bought another book, Ann would not stop writing. For her it's a necessity, like breathing. Most of the time, it even keeps her sane.

Connect with Ann online at:

http://annswann.blogspot.com

AUTHOR'S NOTE:

I hope you enjoyed *TAKERS: Book One of the Apacolypse in Eden* trilogy. It is chock full of beliefs, suspicions, and possibilities. Of course, I would never want to offend anyone on the basis of religion, but if you look at the world today, you might agree that for some folks, it *is* Heaven on Earth; for others, it's absolute Hell.

If you'd like to tell me your thoughts about this little allegory, feel free to contact me through my website, www.authorannswann.com. While you're there I'd love for you to join my reader's list for contests, news about upcoming releases, and more.

Can I ask you a favor? If you enjoyed *TAKERS*, please consider leaving a review on your favorite retail, social media, or book lovers' website. It makes a world of difference in getting the word out.

And now, here's a sneak peek at *SEEKERS: Book Two of the Apocalypse in Eden* trilogy.

Peace & Love,
Ann Swann

Foreword:

I'm writing this from the road. There are only three of us now—plus the Taker. Thad, the attorney, perished in the firestorm, but we picked up a monster, so some would say we made an even trade. I wish Thad were here to appreciate that little joke. He had a wicked sense of humor when he wasn't drinking.

It's still hard to believe we befriended one of the creatures that fell from the sky—fell *through* the sky—when the apocalypse began. He seems very loyal. I call it a *he* but the creatures have no gender. They are more like figures formed of moist unfinished clay with an overlay of translucent gray skin. Whatever the sex, there is no doubt about it; he is definitely part of us now.

The question remains—what *is* he? Does he represent a new race of beings that will coexist with humans? Or is he simply the last of his kind joining up with the last of our kind? We have no way of knowing—yet.

The sky could split open and rain monsters again tomorrow, and we wouldn't be able to do anything about it. That possibility hangs over our heads like a slayer's axe.

It's a hard way to live.

But we have our goals. We hope to find our families, or what is left of them. Nothing is set in stone.

First, we will go back to Eden and start from there, see where the journey takes us.

My name is Jack. I'm fourteen years old going on fifty. More than anything, I wish I could just go to sleep and wake up tomorrow back in my narrow bed in my old room. But that will never happen. For now, I am part of a small band of Seekers, cast out upon the land, searching for a better tomorrow.

ALSO AVAILABLE FROM

WordCrafts Press

Tears of Min Brock
  J.E. Lowder

The Awakening of Leeowyn Blake
  Mary Parker-Garner

Home
  Eleni McKnight

Furious
  Aaron Shaver

Summer on the Black Suwannee
  Jennifer Odom

Gretchen and the Bear
  Carrie Anne Noble

www.wordcrafts.net